Ca h her husband, daughters and assorted four-legged family members. She's been blessed to see the power of true love in her grandparents' seventy-year marriage and her parents' marriag over fifty years. She knows love isn't always sweet and perfect—it can be challenging, complicated and r er-afters are worth fig

D0537692

Also by Cari Lynn Webb

A Heartwarming Thanksgiving
Wedding of His Dreams
Make Me a Match
The Matchmaker Wore Skates
The Charm Offensive
The Doctor's Recovery

Discover more at millsandboon.co.uk

THE RANCHER'S RESCUE

CARI LYNN WEBB

MILLS & BOON

First Published in Great Britain 2018
by Mills & Boon, an imprint of HarperCollins*Publishers*
1 London Bridge Street, London, SE1 9GF

The Rancher's Rescue © 2018 Cari Lynn Webb

ISBN: 978-0-263-26546-0

1118

To my brothers: Scott, Dave and Mark. Your teasing honed my sense of humor and your love made me stronger. I'm so blessed to be able to call you my brothers and my friends. Love you!

Special thanks to Amy Vastine, Anna J. Stewart, Carol Ross and Melinda Curtis for your friendship and answering my endless texts and emails. And thanks to my husband and daughters for your support and making me laugh every day.

CHAPTER ONE

ETHAN BLACKWELL WAS surrounded by critically ill checking accounts.

Of course, up until two days ago, the only terminal one he'd been working with had been his own. He'd never expected his grandfather's finances to need resuscitation too.

He might've suspected Elias, or Big E as he was commonly known, to be up to one of his usual attempts at manipulation if his grandfather were still in town. But Big E and his thirty-foot motor home had departed four weeks ago, in early April, without a farewell to anyone, or a return date mentioned.

Ethan knew about departures. He had walked away to build his life, his own way, when Big E had accused Ethan of forsaking his family legacy and the land that had raised him to pursue a pretentious career in equestrian medicine. That day, Ethan had vowed to return to the Blackwell Ranch only for the reading of his grandfather's will. Though no funeral arrangements had been made, as far as Ethan and the rest of his brothers were aware, Big E was AWOL, not deceased.

Despite Ethan's promise to himself, he was back at the Blackwell Ranch, pacing around his grandfather's big office and scowling at the paperwork scattered across the oak desk. It was an accounting nightmare.

Jonathon, his older brother and the only reason that Ethan had come home, strode into their grandfather's office. Jon tossed his hat on one of the twin cigar-colored armchairs and dropped into the other. His dog, Trout, sat beside Jon's boots and regarded Ethan as if he were the deputy assistant his brother had brought in for backup. "Please tell me I heard you wrong on the phone."

"That depends. What did you hear?" Ethan leaned against the desk.

"I thought I heard you tell me that you planned to search Big E's bedroom." There was no question in Jon's tone. His brother had better hearing than a bat. Jon's gaze zeroed in on Ethan like a rifle scope, challenging him to change to his own mind.

Jon had developed this stare-down technique in their elementary school days, when he'd caught Ethan and his twin brother, Ben, shooting army men to the moon with bottle rockets. Jon had drilled Ethan with his relentless stare and waited. Ethan guessed he'd made the wrong choice when he'd explained that they'd already relocated once after successfully hitting the barn several times. Jon had immediately confiscated their entire supply of explosives.

"That's exactly what I plan to do. With your help," Ethan said. "The money's gotta be somewhere."

Jon's gaze fixed on Ethan. A frown fixed on his face. Trout stopped panting as if to better emphasize his own grimace.

It wasn't as if Ethan was asking his brother to hold the bottle rocket while he lit the fuse. Still, Ethan accepted that Jon always preferred explanations, and he picked up the worn notebook on Big E's desk. "This is the sum total of Big E's accounting system. So it seems likely he'd also stash hard cash between his mattresses, or in a hidden safe somewhere."

"We need to hire ranch hands, not tear apart the house like we're on a treasure hunt." Jon drummed his fingers on the armrest.

"We need Big E to return, but since that's not happening we have to find some money to pay people, including those ranch hands we need to hire." Ethan smacked the notebook against his leg. He'd earned a doctorate in veterinary medicine, was board certified in animal sports medicine rehabilitation and passed the national veterinary exam. He was desperate to get hired in the veterinary field to pay off his own debt, not waste time rescuing the Blackwell Ranch for his heartless grandfather.

He had come home to offer Jon relief from managing both the Blackwell Ranch and his own JB Bar Ranch. His older brother had never hesitated to help him in the past and Ethan owed him that same loyalty, even if his personal finances were about to flatline.

"He has to have money." Jon grabbed the notebook from Ethan.

The panic in Jon's voice focused Ethan. Ethan ignored his uneasiness and decided to take things one crisis at a time. With luck, he'd have the Blackwell Ranch stabilized with new staff before the end of the week.

"That notebook reads like a grocery list of numbers." Ethan moved toward the doorway, praying he was right about his grandfather's stash of money. But the recent purchase receipts he'd found in the bottom desk drawer made that unease inside him feel more like claws scratching against his bones. Not to mention the slip of paper he'd spotted on which Zoe had written in bold cursive confusing lines: *Pair of Llama Makers* and *Twin Sets of Long-Wool Providers*. "A budget would be helpful, so we'd know how much is coming in and how much is going out on a regular basis."

He'd learned as much during his undergrad when his academic advisor had urged him to take a business class as an elective. Unfortunately, the professor hadn't lectured about the pitfalls of cosigning a car loan for a good friend who turned out to be not so good, or two-timing roommates who left without a forwarding address and skipped out on paying their share of the rent and every bill. The professor had failed to explain how a very low credit score would later deter established veterinary offices from allowing highly credentialed and skilled graduates, like himself, to buy into their practices.

That unease hooked into him like two bull elks with locked antlers. Ethan had more debt now than when he'd left years ago. He hated being like Big E. Hated more that he was proving his grandfather right. Becoming a veterinarian might've been the biggest mistake of his life. Jon's muttered curse yanked Ethan back into the ranch crisis.

"I kept telling him to hire an accountant or a bookkeeper." Jon flipped through the crinkled papers. "He told me he'd been handling money since before I was in diapers and he'd keep on handling it his way."

"Did I mention there's a carbon receipt book mixed in with handwritten receipts on napkins in the top drawer of his desk? And don't get me started on the checkbook. Checks are numbered in sequential order for a reason." At least Ethan managed to get that right in his own, albeit empty, checkbook. He looked over his shoulder at his brother. "You coming to his room or not?"

Twenty minutes later, Ethan held up Big E's king-size mattress while Jon checked the box spring for a hidden pile of cash. His grandfather's underwear drawer remained open and neither brother had bothered to rehang the three large framed cowboy photos they'd taken from the wall. The only holes in the plaster were from picture nails and not a safe. The door to the gun safe stood ajar, empty of both rifles and any spare cash.

"If you've finished practicing your B&E skills, I could use a hand with some real work." A feminine voice mocked them from the doorway.

Ethan nodded at Katie Montgomery, the Blackwell Ranch's right and left hands. Katie's dad was getting up there in age and had basically left the foreman's job to her. He suspected his grandfather wouldn't have survived without Katie for all these years. Why did she stay when all of Big E's grandchildren had left the ranch? How long would she stay once Ethan confirmed the accounts were empty?

"As we've failed to find anything other than torn socks, it's probably best you look into a new ranch to manage."

"There's so much work to do here I don't have time to look outside the fences." Katie came into the bedroom and patted Ethan's shoulder.

"What's it today? Broken fence on the north pasture? Blocked fuel line in the ATV? Ruptured water pipe at the guesthouse?" Jon asked, passing Katie on his way out.

"It's the *south* pasture, the *battery* on the ATV and *a leaking faucet* in the bathroom attached to the ranch hands' bunk bed room." Katie rushed down the stairs after Jon, the thump of her boots on the stairs as firm and sure as his brother's, leaving Ethan no choice but to follow them.

The stairs creaked loudly, or perhaps that was his own uncertainty.

Katie glanced back at him. "Plus, Butterscotch needs your attention, Ethan."

"What was Big E thinking breeding her?" Ethan asked, entering the kitchen, where Katie already had her coffee refilled and a toasted bagel slathered with cream cheese. The new kitchen decor stopped Ethan in his tracks. It always did. Never mind the pink-feathered chandelier or bubble gum–colored paint, what he resented were the extravagant prices Zoe had paid for her superficial changes that had destroyed what used to be the heart of the house.

"I know. It's a bit scary. But you can blame Zoe for that one too." Katie tipped her coffee mug at Ethan. "She arranged the whole thing as a surprise for Big E. Something about bringing new life to the ranch."

"You aren't serious? She can't be that…" Ethan failed to find a suitable word, probably because his mind was overwhelmed with calculating the cost of the custom-made pink-trimmed cabinets and hand-cut sparkly backsplash.

"Insensitive?" Katie finished for him.

"Don't forget clueless about how a working ranch runs."

Jon swiped the bagel from Katie's hand and took a large bite before she could claim it back.

Katie was five years younger than Ethan and practically one of the family.

"Butterscotch is twenty-three." And a dependable, calm paint, Ethan thought, since the very first moment Big E had guided her off the trailer as a birthday present for Ethan's mother. Butterscotch hadn't spooked ever when one of Big E's new wives had wanted to ride her, despite each spouse being less suited for ranch life than the last. The white-and-chestnut-colored mare had earned her peace, not a risky pregnancy.

"Zoe wanted her mare and Butterscotch to birth at the same time because two foals in the pasture make for better pictures." Katie frowned at the empty cream cheese container as if searching for something to explain Zoe's reasoning. "For the guests."

If the older mare survived. If the foal survived. "Butterscotch needs to be under veterinary care." Ethan stepped out of Katie's way.

"And she'll have it now that you're home." Katie toasted Ethan with her second bagel.

Ethan wasn't home to stay though. He was as temporary on the ranch as his step-grandmothers. He was six days into the one-month visit he'd promised Jon. Surely that was long enough to straighten out the accounts, stabilize the ranch and, if Big E failed to return, sell the place. He'd pocket his share from the sale and move on with his life. "I'll check on Butterscotch and then take a look at the faucet." Because Jon had enough on his plate with his twin five-year-old girls and his own ranch to take care of. Never mind that Jon was also recently engaged to his former nanny, Lydia.

"First guests arrive at the end of the month. The faucet in the bunk house can wait." Katie pulled out her phone and swiped across the screen. "We need that fence fixed before I can release the cattle into the pasture."

"I have to be at Dr. Ross's office for the twins' appointments in an hour, but I can come back this afternoon and help with the fence." Jon put his hat on and strode to the back door. Trout followed, the click of his nails on the hardwood floor in rhythm with the thump of Jon's boots. "And I might have an extra ATV battery at my place."

Ethan appreciated the offer. "After I check on Butterscotch, I'll head over to Brewster Ranch Supply. The heifers need vaccines and the mares could do with supplements."

"When you're at Brewster's, ask Grace if she'll help with Big E's books," Jon said.

"Why would I do that?" Ethan rubbed his neck to remove the edge from his tone.

"Because you've been staring at the accounting stuff since you arrived." Jon waved toward the office and the stairs. "Because we weren't up in the bedroom looking for Christmas presents. And because we need a professional opinion on the financials."

"Grace and her family will also have leads on possible new ranch hand hires." Katie tossed the cream cheese container in the trash and the knife in the sink. "They always hear before I do."

Ethan massaged his chest as if the knife had lodged there instead of clattering in the sink. Certainly, his heart hadn't staled and stuttered at the mention of Grace Gardner. More like embarrassment kicked his pride, wedging regret between his ribs.

Grace and Ethan had spent one night together, but she had sneaked out the next morning without a goodbye. Whether too many champagne bubbles had blurred the signals and he'd misread the entire evening, or Grace's experience had been less than remarkable. Either way, he owed Grace an overdue apology. "But she can't be the only accountant in town," he insisted.

"Grace is certified with a real degree and she's quiet, so she won't be talking all over Falcon Creek about Blackwell business." Katie crossed her arms over her chest and studied him. "Don't tell me you still aren't over Sarah Ashley?"

Ethan blinked. Sarah Ashley was Grace's older sister and Ethan's long-ago, on-and-off-again girlfriend. The snag in his voice had nothing to do with his ex and everything to do with her younger sister. How was he supposed to apologize to Grace for crossing the friend barrier and then ask her for help as if nothing had ever happened?

"From what I've heard, Sarah Ashley married the man she rightly deserved." Katie shrugged. "What? Mabel keeps me up-to-date."

Mabel being the postmaster and beacon of all gossip in Falcon Creek.

"Well, some folks didn't get home until all hours from that wedding reception, so things must have started off okay," Jon said.

His brother was referring to Ethan not returning to Jon's house until the next morning, long after Sarah Ashley's reception. Ethan hadn't confessed to his brother where he'd spent the night or with whom he'd spent it.

Jon punched his brother's shoulder as he was leaving. "Talk to Grace."

"Listen to your brother." Katie let the back door slam shut behind her.

Ethan flattened his palms over his face and speared his fingers into his hair. He'd attended Sarah Ashley's Valentine's Day wedding after he'd received a series of manic texts from the bride saying she was having doubts. He'd tried to ignore her, but what if she was the one for him? When he'd arrived at the church, after another flurry of anxious texts from Sarah Ashley, Grace had blocked him from seeing the bride and told him it was past time to let Sarah Ashley go. That her sister was well and truly in love. That the match was perfect. Suddenly, Ethan had begun to think there was something perfect about Grace.

With one question, he interrupted Grace's extensive list of reasons that Sarah Ashley and her fiancé were meant to be together: Did Sarah Ashley's fiancé treat her well? Grace had blinked and answered: very well. And that had been enough. Ethan had sat in the back row for the ceremony. His gaze hadn't lingered on the bride and what he'd lost, but rather, it strayed too many times to a certain maid of honor, making him wonder what he'd missed.

It was only during the reception, when the champagne corks had popped, that Ethan approached Grace. And yes, maybe Grace had given a sweet, funny toast to her sister and new husband that won over the guests. And yes, maybe Grace had looked like a goddess in her sleek formal gown. And yes, he'd danced her into a dark corner and...

The next thing he knew it was the following morning and he was on his own. He'd been trying to forget that moment ever since.

WITH HER BABY's heartbeat echoing in her heart, a picture of her ultrasound resting in her pocket and her due date entered on her calendar, Grace Gardner drove toward her family's store, Brewster Ranch Supply, determined to get through the workday without vomiting. She was equally determined this would be the week she called Ethan Blackwell to tell him about the baby. One phone call couldn't be that hard, could it?

She rolled to a stop at the only light in town. It seemed the light spent more time on red than green, as if daring the locals to spot the seven differences between the downtown of today and that of a decade ago. Grace could find only one.

The morning after her night with Ethan she'd sat at this red light smiling and feeling slightly delirious.

The delirium had passed, along with the stutter in her heart, when the positive pink stripes had appeared on the pregnancy test. Somehow, she'd kept her smile in place, even though Grandma Brewster had warned her in high school that being pregnant was nothing to celebrate. But Grace wasn't a teenager with hormones and a crush. She was an adult with an accounting degree and soon she'd have her own business. More important, she had a baby plan.

Pushing her glasses up on her nose, Grace blurted out, "Ethan, I'm your baby." She tapped her forehead on the steering wheel and muttered, "*Having* your baby. Your kid. Child. Baby." Her sigh was loud and long and she shook out her arms, lifted her chin. "Ethan, I'm having your baby so—"

A horn blared behind her. And then another. Her practice conversation concluded, Grace accelerated through the light and parked in a stall behind her family's store. She weaved through the storage area to her makeshift office. Her father's burst of laughter from the front had her changing directions.

Perhaps a hug from her dad would bolster her confidence to finally contact Ethan.

Grace pushed through the swinging door that connected the storage area to the store proper and gripped the nearest shelf to keep her knees from buckling. She could forget the phone call. It hadn't been her father's laughter calling to her after all. It'd been Ethan Blackwell's.

A flush swept over her skin. She would've blamed it on morning sickness if not for the familiar blue eyes zeroing in on her over her mother's head.

The same blue eyes that had never wavered when she'd talked about herself and her dreams that night in the hotel bar while her sister's reception continued down the hall. The same blue eyes that had cataloged every detail about her while she'd been wrapped in his strong embrace. The same blue eyes she wished for her baby.

"Perfect timing, Gracie." Her father smacked the counter. "Look who wandered in and asked to see you."

Grace squeezed the shelf, the way her heart seemed to be squeezing inside her chest. Ethan might've asked to see her, but she wasn't starring in one of her sister's romantic fantasies. "Is there something you needed, Ethan?" *Like my heart.*

Grace chastised herself. Her heart wasn't going to be part of any conversation with Ethan. Ever. She hadn't earned the title of most levelheaded Gardner sister on a whim.

"Is there someplace we can talk in private?" Ethan asked.

"Take Ethan to your office." Her mother guided Ethan around the counter to the employees-only side. "When the two of you finish, Ethan, we can talk about the feed inventory and the reorder."

"Sarah Ashley handles the inventory now, Mom." Grace searched the storefront for her older sister.

"Your sister had a thing," her mother said evasively.

Sarah Ashley was just like her younger sister, Nicole Marie. The two always had a thing when work was to be done.

"I have a thing too," Grace said. "A call that starts in fifteen minutes."

"A call? Oh, Grace." Her mom waved her hand toward the front door. "We deal with our customers in person like we've always done. Whoever needs to call you can easily come on down to the store to talk to you and then buy some impulse merchandise." The hand wave shot toward a display of marked-down Easter chocolate.

Grace pulled out a peppermint candy from her pocket to keep her mouth from spilling secrets she wasn't ready to share. Her caller wasn't a Brewster customer, so there was no reason to encourage Isaac James Sr. to visit the store.

Mr. James owned IJ Farms on the way to Billings and needed tax advice. Grace intended for her advice to transition into Isaac hiring her as his new accountant. Grace crunched the candy into pieces and glanced at Ethan. "My office is over here."

Grace dropped her purse on the small desk in her makeshift office. She shared the crammed retail space with pig feed, goat kid milk replacer and alfalfa pellets. At least, she had a door that closed and locked. Not that she'd had a reason to lock herself in yet.

But having Ethan in here with her made the already minimal breathing space shrink until Grace swore they were both holding their breath to conserve oxygen. It wasn't long before she inhaled, deep and long, to prove to herself that she could handle the hurdles of the big wide world, including Ethan Blackwell.

Ethan shoved his hands in the back pockets of his jeans, rocked back on his boot heels and rushed to speak. "Grace, I know I shouldn't ask for your help, but I need it. Big E's motor home has hit the road, the heifers are going into heat, Helen and Pete Rivers retired and the books are total chaos."

Grace popped another peppermint in her mouth and tried to translate Ethan's fragments. Nothing she'd heard hinted that he was there to resume where they'd left off three months prior. Not that she wanted that. She just wanted him to know about the baby.

Now was her chance. Her turn to talk. Her turn to confess.

Grandma Brewster had always told Grace that the fork in the road had to stab her to get her to move. Or, in this case, speak. She'd swear the sharp twinge in her chest felt eerily close to the jab of a fork's tines. And she could swear she heard her late grandma Brewster's boisterous laugh. If only she could find her voice instead of her inner mouse. "How exactly can I help you?" *And how exactly do you want to learn about your child?*

"I can't figure out the ranch books." Ethan stepped forward. "I was hoping for your expertise."

Her expertise. Not her heart. "You want me to work on the Blackwell Ranch's accounting."

"We'll pay you for your time and discretion."

Discretion should be her middle name. No one, other than her doctor in the next town over, knew about her pregnancy. Grace took off her glasses and ran her fingers across her eyebrows.

"I can bring everything here if it's more convenient. Or drive you up to the ranch." Ethan moved to the edge of her desk within kissing distance. "I remember you mentioned preferring not to drive at night."

She could touch Ethan without any real effort now. Instead, she sank her hand into the peppermint candy bowl on her desk and wondered what else he remembered from their night together. Did he remember how they shared things no one else knew? Or recall how much they'd laughed about their childhoods? Did he treasure those moments? Or was she just as foolishly sentimental as Sarah Ashley? "That's fine."

"Then you'll help?" Surprise softened his voice and relief relaxed his mouth into a smile that made even the peppermint swirl churn through her insides.

Her phone chimed, alerting her of her upcoming call with Isaac and reminding her to focus.

Ethan twisted the door handle. "I'll get out of your way and let you work."

Grace looked at him and willed her mouth to open and the truth to come out. But it didn't happen.

"I'll bring the books by tomorrow morning and then we can put together a strategy to stabilize the ranch's finances?"

Grace nodded, clinging to her plan. A baby plan. One that did not include Ethan as more than an absentee parent. And one that definitely did not involve her heart.

CHAPTER TWO

ETHAN STOPPED HIS truck and stared at the white house with forest green shutters until his gaze blurred and all he saw was the land and home from his childhood. The house had so many good memories for him prior to his parents' fatal accident. The twin rocking chairs on the wide front porch and banging screen door. The lawn scattered with sticks from his brothers' sword fights, plastic army men and laughter.

He'd never wanted his home to change and wanted it back even more after he'd left his childhood at his parents' gravesite.

Too many potholes since, they littered memory lane and tripping in those craters now solved nothing. That home was gone and had been for quite a while. A two-winged, thirty-bedroom log cabin, more manor estate than quaint lodge, squatted nearby, surrounded by barns and outbuildings painted red as if cheerful about the massive guesthouse intrusion.

Like it or not, the Blackwell Ranch had expanded to also become a dude ranch and there was no turning back the clock. In Ethan's mind that left one option: sell the ranch that was no longer his home. No longer anything he wanted. What he wanted was the money from its sale to pay off his debts and buy his entry into a veterinarian clinic in Kentucky or Colorado, but definitely not in Falcon Creek.

First, he had to fix the accounts with Grace's help.

Ethan cut the truck engine, but not his guilt. That kept running like a high-speed train making up time for a late departure.

He shouldn't have asked for Grace's help in the first place. He should've apologized.

He shouldn't have searched for those familiar copper flecks in Grace's green eyes when she'd removed her glasses. It was futile to try to prove the vivid memory wasn't his imagination. Those same copper flecks had sparked under the chandelier lights on the dance floor at her sister's reception and continued to burn through him whenever he thought of her. He should've never agreed to Jon's suggestion to approach his accountant or stepped inside Brewster's.

Ethan shouldn't have come home.

He gripped the steering wheel, imprinting the leather into his palms. He should've called Grace the morning after their night together and every day after that until she'd answered. But instead he'd excused his behavior because she'd walked out on him first. How pathetic that he cared who'd left first, as if she'd dinged more than his pride. Yet Big E hadn't raised his grandsons to be weak-hearted fools.

And yet, his mother had raised him to be a gentleman, not callous and selfish. She would not be proud of him today.

That settled it. Tomorrow he'd say sorry to Grace and then find another accountant. Or straighten out the books himself.

What had Grace been thinking when she'd agreed to help him? And she had agreed. He hadn't missed that part. He might've missed hearing that she was glad to see him. Or that she'd thought about their night together. Or that she'd wanted to call him. But he really hadn't wanted to hear any of that, did he?

A fist rapped against the closed window of the truck cab. He glimpsed Katie's frown a second before she smacked a piece of paper against the glass.

Not just any piece of paper, but a delivery notice for one rabbit and four sheep. In bold print: *no returns or re-*

funds. The words mocked him. The notice also explained the invoice for twin sets of long-wool providers he'd found in Big E's desk. Zoe hadn't ordered wool bales, but purchased sheep for her new petting zoo. Clearly, he needed to look through the recent purchase invoices and translate Zoe's handwritten notes on those as well.

Before he could respond, Katie smacked a second piece of paper against the window. Thankfully, not another delivery notice. But, the title, "How to Set Up a Petting Zoo Business," drilled a hole in his stomach. As did the phrase *liability insurance required*, which she'd carefully highlighted in yellow.

Big E's checking account dipped further into the red. They were out of time. They needed professional advice and they needed it last week. There was no time to find a substitute. Help would have to come from Grace.

He climbed out of his truck, yanking the delivery notice from Katie. Curse words banged around inside his mouth like popcorn kernels chipping his teeth, but he located his inner gentleman before he spewed any into the air. "We don't have a place for these sheep." He needed to chase down spare cash, not sheep, across forty acres.

Katie checked her watch. "You have two hours to figure something out."

Ethan crumpled the delivery notice in his fist and lashed out. Each word pinged like a burned popcorn kernel. "What are you doing in the next two hours?"

"Locating a battery for the ATV and making sure all the linens are clean and accounted for." Katie shoved her hands in her jeans pockets and tipped her chin toward the stalls. "The horses still need to be ridden. Butterscotch could use another walk or even some more attention."

The mare had been a birthday present from the family to Ethan's mother. After his mom had passed, Ethan had become the mare's guardian, protecting the paint from

Big E's temperamental wives. Butterscotch hadn't judged Ethan when he'd curled up in her stall more than once to give in to his grief. But he'd left for college and abandoned Butterscotch to Zoe's whims. The mare deserved better. Ethan wouldn't fail her now.

He dug his boot into the dirt, grinding the last of his temper into dust. "Sorry. It's not you, it's me."

Katie punched him on the shoulder and grinned. "I didn't know we had a thing."

He laughed, but sobered quickly. "It just seems every day there's something else. Something we aren't aware of. Something we aren't prepared for."

"That's the nature of ranch life." She reached down and rubbed Hip behind her ears. Hippolyta was the Australian shepherd dog's full name and she was Katie's sidekick and one constant.

Lately, Ethan's one constant seemed to be bankruptcy-induced worry. "No, that's the nature of Big E's current wife." He frowned at the main house. Zoe's extreme over-spending had dismantled the past. The enormous guest lodge was the latest in a series of renovations to turn a working ranch into something from a movie set. There'd been nothing wrong with the Blackwell Ranch when his grandmother and parents had lived on the land. The origi-nal Blackwells had respected heritage. Bitterness replaced his frustration.

"We still have sheep arriving and nowhere to put them," Katie said.

"I'll figure it out."

"And the insurance," she prodded.

"That too." Ethan stuffed the delivery notice into his back pocket, stuffing the pain and memories from the past away too. "Grace agreed to help us. If we can get the books straightened out, we can get people hired."

"I hope she works fast." Katie whistled to her dog and strode off toward the supply shed.

He did too. But not for the same reasons.

Ethan didn't want to be around Grace for too long. What if he was tempted to have another thing with her? She was his ex-girlfriend's little sister. There were rules about that and he'd already broken them once. That was more than enough.

He strode toward the barn. He'd walk Butterscotch and then hammer together a pen for the arriving sheep.

He needed to find a full-time job that paid, unlike the Blackwell Ranch, and was preferably in the equestrian world. If he wanted to rebuild his credit, he couldn't default on his student loans too. He had yet to find a veterinarian that would look past his poor financial history and consider his skills. But he wasn't deterred. He'd prove to his grandfather he could make it on his own. And if selling the Blackwell Ranch aided Ethan, all the better.

An hour later, Ethan ran water from the hose over his head. He had to cool off. Jamming his baseball cap back on his head, he went to meet the delivery truck rattling to a stop in the driveway. All too soon, Ethan understood why the truck arrived ahead of schedule.

Ethan greeted the driver and peered inside at the sheep. Behind them, he saw the Angora rabbit huddling against the back of its wire cage. The lack of wool across the rabbit's back alarmed Ethan. There were many causes of alopecia, but until he knew the exact reason for the hair loss, he wasn't putting the rabbit with the other petting zoo animals.

Animals had been Ethan's companions since he'd been a toddler. He'd only required his mother's Maine coon cat curled up next to him to fall asleep as a kid. As he grew, he'd spend hours outside, searching the creek for frogs, catching fireflies and climbing trees to peer at the baby birds in the nests. After his parents had died, his bond only deepened. Animals, he discovered, were simple to figure out: they loved without conditions. Never had hidden agendas. Only ever seemed to want his love and attention. The wounded, the scared and the rejected always tugged at those invisible heartstrings he didn't want to admit to having. The pathetic rabbit tugged at those heartstrings now.

He sighed and signed off on the paperwork, bid the driver goodbye and frowned into the cage at the pure white rabbit. "Looks like we're going to be sharing a cabin for a while, Coconut."

Water bowl full, bath towels on the floor and an empty toilet paper roll stuffed with grass for Coconut's entertainment, Ethan returned to the petting zoo. He had to add a steel gate to the pen for the sheep. With the last nail drilled into place, Ethan gripped the new part of the enclosure and tested its strength to make sure there wouldn't be any escapees.

Katie approached, her boots kicking dirt and stones around her. "You can't spend all your time on these animal pens. There were calves born last month that still need vaccinations and branding."

"It's hardly a waste since this is the new petting zoo." Besides, he never considered protecting animals a waste of time. "We need a plumber and an electrician to finish. And last time I checked, I wasn't certified in either." The last time he'd tinkered with electricity had been in middle school and he'd blown more than the fuses that night. Big E had made him clean every stall three times a day all by himself for two months after that particular stunt. "The ranch is better off with me building things."

Katie seemed hesitant. "But a petting zoo implies, well, petting. These pens are shoulder height and hardly inviting."

"Letting guests traipse around the stalls is an unnecessary health risk." Ethan bent over and stuck his arm through the pen posts. If only everything was as simple and effective. Besides, he questioned how much the animals wanted to be petted. His pens offered enough room for the animals to watch the ranch guests from a distance. "See, the guests can reach through the fence posts like this."

"That's not on Zoe's sketch," Katie said.

"Neither are hand-washing stations, but we need two of those with running water and soap." Minimizing health risks to the humans and the animals was essential to ensure the ranch didn't spread disease. "Hand sanitizer isn't enough."

"It's supposed to be a petting zoo with a large pen where animals wander around and guests pet them." Katie unlatched the gate and swung the steel door open, her gaze trained on the hinges as if she didn't trust Ethan's craftsmanship. "Don't you ever remember visiting one at the fair when we were little?"

No, he didn't recall and Big E had had no time for fairs and frivolous games. And when Ethan was old enough to go to the fair alone, he'd been more interested in touching Sarah Ashley's silky shoulder-length curls than petting miniature donkeys in the zoo. Ethan set his hands on his hips and stared at Katie. "You're only getting a petting zoo if it's safe and done right."

"I don't know what I want anymore." Katie threw up her hands. "But we've got a website that promised the Zigler party of thirty arriving at the end of this month a real petting zoo."

Tension knotted through Ethan's shoulders as if he were carrying all the Zigler family's overstuffed suitcases himself. He stretched his muscles, but the reminder of the Zigler family's arrival in three weeks only made his shoulders spasm more. "They'll have a petting zoo. An actual one. But without the Angora rabbit."

"I never got a delivery cancellation notice for the rabbit." Katie let the gate shut and eyed him. "There's a picture of that rabbit on the guest ranch's website. Has it already arrived? Can I see it?"

"Update the website to put the rabbit on medical leave." Ethan carried his tools toward the work shed. "No, you can't see it."

"The website is locked down and I haven't found the password yet." Katie blocked him from opening the shed door. "Why can't I see the rabbit?"

"Website photo or not, no one is petting the rabbit." Ethan tried to nudge Katie out of his way.

She refused to budge, crossing her arms over her chest. "Because it carries a disease that can't be washed off with soap and water?"

"Because it's traumatized." Ethan stabbed the shovel into the ground and leaned against the handle. "And stressed out." Like him.

"That's why you won't let me see it?" Her twitching fingers stilled against her arms.

"Not you." Ethan pointed at her Australian shepherd sprawled in the middle of the dirt path like the main attraction of the petting zoo. "Your sidekick."

Noticing his regard, Hip wagged her tail, stirring the dirt into mini dust clouds.

"She's gentle with all animals." Katie tapped her leg, calling the dog to her, and placed her hand on Hip's neck as if she needed to protect her.

"I know that," Ethan said. "But Coconut doesn't."

"You've already named it?" Katie gaped at him as if he'd adopted a pet without the family's permission. "Can't we trade it in for another one that isn't a stress case?"

"This isn't like a pair of faulty pliers you return to Brewster's." These were live animals that needed proper shelters, beds and food. Ethan would ensure their safety before he left. "Coconut will settle in with time. Her stress should be temporary." Otherwise they'll have enough angora wool for new sweaters for the entire Blackwell family before Christmas.

"Speaking of stress, you've had six calls this afternoon from pet owners in town." Katie bent down to pet Hip as if to assure herself the dog was fine.

Ethan released the shovel and looked at Katie. "Who's calling here?"

Katie lifted her hands and began counting on her fingers. "Mrs. Hatfield. Her twelve-year-old cat, Sparky, is so lethargic he can't make it into the litter box. Mr. Jacobson. His one-year-old German shepherd puppy ate brownies and his granddaughter's socks, or so he thinks. The Kramer family says their chinchilla has strange spots on its—"

Ethan held up his hand and stopped her. "I meant why are they calling here?"

"They want your help." Katie scowled at him as if that should've been obvious.

"I'm not licensed in this state." He'd been trained in domestic animals and livestock and, later, specialized in equestrian rehabilitation.

"They don't seem to care." Hip rolled over onto her back, not seeming to care either. Katie rubbed the dog's stomach until Hip's leg scratched the air and her mouth opened in a toothy smile. "They want you over Dr. Terry, who, and I'm quoting here, 'if he worked any slower, he'd have to speed up to stop.'"

"I didn't tell anyone I was home," Ethan said.

"You're kidding, right?" Katie straightened and swiped a strand of hair off her face. The disbelief in her tone was as fiery as her red locks. "You walked into Brewster's this morning, didn't you?"

He rubbed the back of his hand over his mouth, wiping away the urge to curse. He didn't need the reminder.

His mind quickly recalled the image of Grace in her tissue box for an office, looking both sweet and tempting, capable and vulnerable. As if he could've opened his arms and she would've willingly stepped into his embrace. He scowled at that. In Grace's embrace, he'd discovered an overwhelming inner peace. For one night, the emptiness inside him had receded.

But he understood the danger of wanting to be with Grace. Understood the threat Grace posed to his equilibrium. Becoming used to Grace's embrace would only make him want more. Make him feel more. And feeling too much always led to heartache.

"This is the last time I'm passing along any messages for you." Katie slapped her hand on his chest, and trapped between her palm and his shirt were several notes. "Tell your patients to call your cell phone and stop clogging up the ranch phone line. We need that line to stay open for new bookings."

"I don't have patients," Ethan said.

"Looks like you do now." Katie smiled. "Just make sure those house pets don't interfere with the ranch. You're here to help save Blackwell, not the town."

As Katie turned away, Ethan scrambled to catch the scraps of paper floating to the dirt. He glanced over the notes, recognized the names, most he'd known all his life. He'd call them back because his mother had taught him manners and he'd suggest they consult with a licensed vet in the area.

But shortly after an exchange of greetings with Mrs. Hatfield, who invited him over for dinner and explained she only wanted advice from a trusted family friend, the conversation derailed. Four more calls later and four more "appeals for advice from a friend," Ethan had dinner, lunch meet-ups and one pie date arranged, along with one early-morning coffee meeting. The good news: he'd be too busy

visiting friends and neighbors, and could leave Grace alone
to untangle the ranch accounts.

GRACE UNWRAPPED ANOTHER mint to quiet her stomach.
Three hours past lunch and her buttered toast hadn't settled. She left her dad sorting a shipment of cat food in the
warehouse and walked to the storefront, passing her office. She wanted to sit down and prop her feet on her desk.
Five minutes. Ten at the most. She needed that much after
Ethan's unexpected arrival earlier.

His confident presence had filled the space even though
he'd remained near her door as if he'd been in a hurry
to leave. As if he believed sleeping with her had been a
mistake. Still, she'd forgotten how reliable his shoulders
looked. But would Ethan be a reliable dad? Maybe if she
just closed her eyes for a moment, she could find her balance. Surely, she'd be a reliable mother and that was all
that mattered.

Fortunately, Trina Matthews, one of their employees,
called out her name from the feed section with a question
about the difference between alfalfa varieties. En route to
Trina, Grace paused to assist Mrs. Timmerman with her
sheet selection in housewares. Grace pulled a set of jersey
sheets from a high shelf and explained she had the very
same ones on her own bed. She didn't mention it was her
twin bed from high school. Leaving Mrs. Timmerman to
decide between the heather-gray or navy sheet sets, Grace
decided she really needed to upgrade her bed to at least
a full. After all she was going to be a mom soon enough.

Finished sorting the Timothy-Alfalfa from the Orchard-
Alfalfa, Grace turned toward her office, but her mother's
shout redirected her to the cash register.

Her mom handed her the handheld register scanner. "It's
acting up and Todd has a rather large order."

Grace checked the scanner connections and handed it to her sister. "Should be fine now."

"There are several customers waiting." Their mother tugged the scanner from Sarah Ashley's grip and thrust it back at Grace. "You have more practice on the register."

Sarah Ashley wouldn't get practice if their mother wouldn't let her work. Grace gripped the scanner and greeted Todd Webster. "Let's get you checked out and on your way."

Grace was hoping for a speedy exit herself, but her mother had other ideas. "When you finish here, your dad needs you in the warehouse. The shipment for lawn and garden is arriving early and the plants need to be sorted and priced."

"I can handle that," Sarah Ashley offered. Her easygoing tone matched her relaxed smile, but her narrowed gaze challenged their mother to come up with a good reason to deny her.

But their mother had brought up three daughters without ever raising her voice and perfected the art of misdirection. "Grace can handle it. Did you know Ethan Blackwell was in the store this morning?"

Sarah Ashley flashed her three-carat, square-cut diamond ring at their mother. "I'm married now."

"Married, but living with your parents," said their father, who trundled past, looking over his glasses at them as he pushed a cart loaded with potting soil toward the garden section. "Without your husband."

Mom set her hand on Sarah Ashley's arm. "Your dad is frustrated. You know we'd do anything to make you happy."

"This needs more than an antiseptic wipe and bandage." Sarah Ashley carefully wrapped a ceramic pot in paper, bagged it and handed it to their last customer.

"If you'd talk to us, Sarah Ashley, we could help," their mom said.

"I know." Sarah Ashley straightened the pencils in the tin can holder until every tip faced down and then looked at them. "But this is something I have to do on my own."

Grace wasn't certain what her sister meant by *this*. She'd caught Sarah Ashley on the computer once, searching for online business classes. Every night she overheard her sister tell her husband that she wasn't ready to come home yet.

All seemed fine, but Sarah Ashley never did anything without someone to lean on, be it their parents, her best friends or ex-boyfriends. Sarah Ashley never used to spend more than five minutes in the store on any given day until now, and now Grace was always cleaning up after her sister's screwups.

"Just remember, you have family who are always here for you." Their mother nodded at Grace.

Grace's smile felt stiff and false. She tried harder, but her family didn't ever rely on Sarah Ashley. They only ever relied on Grace and she'd never minded. Until now. She wanted to step out on her own and start her business. But how would they get along at the store without her? How could she abandon her family and then expect them to help when the baby arrived? Her baby with her sister's ex-boyfriend. Her stomach dropped to her toes as if she'd been caught skimming from the cash register.

"Thanks, Mom." Sarah Ashley hugged their mother. Alice Gardner was a petite, farm-raised powerhouse while Sarah Ashley was tall, her movements fluid like a dancer's. Sarah Ashley looked like she should be twirling around a candle-lit ballroom in a waltz, not stacking bags of fertilizer. "I'm here now and happy to work."

Their mother searched the store as if seeking an intervention from the mannequins. The resident store cat, Whiskers, meowed and rubbed on the edge of the counter.

Their mother grabbed the large gray cat like he was the answer to her lifelong quest. "Your sister already inventoried the pet supplies and women's attire. We'll tackle the staff schedule and payroll next, after we place several reorders."

Sarah Ashley smiled and nodded. "I can help with that."

"Grace has always taken care of that with me." Their mom handed Whiskers to Sarah Ashley. "Why don't you check on your grandfather and his friends? Make sure they have enough sweet tea and water. Then you can wash off the stools on the porch."

Sarah Ashley eyed her mother and frowned as if she'd been asked to sit at the kids' table for Christmas dinner and sip sparkling cider. "You want me to wash the milk cans? No one ever does that, and shouldn't Pops and his friends get their own drinks? You're always saying that it isn't good for them to sit all day."

Their mother looked chagrined. "Well, uh…"

Grace was surprised their mother could suggest cleaning the milk can stools with a straight face. Sarah Ashley was right. That hadn't ever been done since Grace started working in the store as a teenager. It was also true that their mother reminded Pops daily that she wasn't running a restaurant. And if he or his friends wanted drinks or food, they needed to walk into the breakroom and get it like everyone else. It was their mother's way of ensuring her father exercised his hips, having had both replaced over the last five years.

Her mother touched Sarah Ashley's cheek. "You don't want to do anything that might make you dizzy or light-headed. You wouldn't want to fall again."

Grace bit down on the inside of her cheek. Sarah Ashley had fallen off a ladder in the warehouse as a child and hit her head. Their father had then forbidden the girls to climb on the ladders or shelves after that. Sarah Ashley had claimed she'd been trying to organize some stock, got dizzy and fell. Their parents had given Sarah Ashley a reprieve from all her chores and household duties. Grace had been more than happy to step in for her injured sister. She just hadn't expected to continue stepping in for her sister for the rest of their lives. Sarah Ashley had been hurt in the fall more than a decade earlier and hadn't suffered any similar incident since.

"I'll take care of it." Sarah Ashley hugged the cat, her voice low and quiet.

Resentment laced both her sister's tone and face. But that couldn't be right. Sarah Ashley had never been inclined to get involved with the store. What was Sarah Ashley's angle? After the warehouse incident, her sister had been more than willing to embrace her newly acquired princess status and she'd never relinquished it. Was her sister trying to impress Ethan? Grace doubted that, given her sister didn't seem interested in his visit earlier.

Their dad peered around the swinging door and called for Grace. She'd never been banned from the warehouse. Not once. Nausea washed over her, slowing her steps. She'd never resented her sister's princess status, but right now, she wanted to know how to get treated like that herself. Even if only for five minutes.

Sarah Ashley cuddled Whiskers, his welcome purr vibrated against her neck as she whispered, "Once you settle onto the pedestal, Whiskers, it's impossible to get off." Sure she'd been satisfied, more than content with her favored position among family and friends. But then she'd married.

The first month of being Mrs. Alec Landry had been as ideal as she'd expected. Her husband followed that by declaring his expectations for their marriage. For her specifically. Specifically, Alec had wanted to start their family now and expected Sarah Ashley to stay home to raise their children. But Sarah Ashley's pedestal had room enough for only one, or so she'd told Alec. She'd also added that she expected nannies and housekeepers to assist her. Alec's laughter and accusations that she couldn't do anything on her own still ricocheted through her.

She'd packed her bags and left their apartment to move back home all on her own that same night. But she'd been in Falcon Creek for three weeks and had yet to do anything else to prove herself.

Unlike Grace, her younger sister. Everyone trusted Grace. Never questioned Grace's abilities. Never put Grace on a pedestal. The answer was simple: Sarah Ashley needed to get off her pedestal and soon.

She watched Grace shove another mint in her mouth as if she'd binged on garlic sausage at the Clearwater Café for breakfast and was waging war against bad breath. Sarah Ashley thought it odd that she hadn't seen her little sister eat much more than crackers and mints in the last few weeks. Yet the caretaker role had always fit Sarah Ashley like last season's wool sweater shrunk in the dryer, itchy and too tight. Although she'd always welcomed concern and pampering for herself, even she recognized that wouldn't make her a good mother or a better person. Was it possible she lacked the skills to be a capable mother?

Stepping onto the wide front porch, she set Whiskers in Pops's lap and left her own doubts on her pedestal. "Who needs a refill?"

"Hello, Sarah-Snowberry-Ashley." Pops grinned, his usual lopsided quirk of his lips that had been there since she'd learned to climb into his lap as a toddler. He patted the milk stool beside him. "Come and sit with us for a spell."

Sarah Ashley sat because she loved her grandfather and had been raised not to question her elders. But she was tired of sitting and looking pretty, like the field of wild snowberry flowers her grandfather had always compared her to. Yet sitting around wouldn't prove Alec wrong.

"When's that successful husband of yours coming to visit?" Pops asked.

"Work has him traveling," Sarah Ashley hedged. "I'm sure he'll stop in when he's back in Billings for more than a day." Or when she agreed to do more than talk to Alec on the phone. Her husband wanted his princess home. But Sarah Ashley wasn't returning to him until she'd proven she was a queen, capable of much more than looking pretty on her throne.

To do that she needed to change how everyone viewed her. She rose and kissed Pops's cheek. "Time for me to get back to work."

CHAPTER THREE

"GOOD MORNING, GRACE."

Grace gaped and slowed on the porch steps of Brewster's. The other half of her child's DNA sat across from Pops. Ethan in his worn boots, faded flannel shirt and baseball cap smiled at her, stirring warmth through her. He returned his attention to the chessboard as if he'd been playing with her grandfather for years. As if this was their morning routine. As if he belonged here on this porch, waiting for her.

Waiting for her to confess.

Grace's hand drifted to her stomach, her slight bump concealed beneath her jacket. Why did the truth have to be so complicated?

Still she couldn't quite stall that swirl of warmth inside her from seeing Ethan.

She should be hot from irritation. She should be annoyed with Ethan for intruding on her usual morning routine. She always shared coffee and stories with her grandfather before the store opened. Before the other employees arrived. Before the customers took over the day.

Except this morning, they were a trio, rather than a duo. What was it with people inserting themselves where they didn't belong? First, there was Sarah Ashley trying to step into the family business for the first time ever, and now, Ethan.

Was it so wrong that Grace wanted one thing to remain the same? To remain normal? In six months, nothing about her life would be either. But she could at least have her usual mornings with Pops, couldn't she? Surely that wasn't too much to ask.

"Sit down, Gracie." Pops pointed at the empty rocking chair beside Ethan. The same one she sat in every morning while she listened to Pops reminisce about her grand-mother or his childhood. "Your Ethan here, he already took care of your morning chores for you." He eyed Ethan over the rims of his glasses and grinned. "Can't ever get this girl to sit. But I got her good this morning, thanks to you."

"I can make more coffee." Ethan's hand was on a stack of file folders. He glanced at her, and his guarded tone suggested he thought she needed several cups to tackle the Blackwell books.

"I've been making the effort to switch to tea." Grace reached inside her purse for her special ginger tea. She was going to need to steep more than one bag this morning. Sitting next to Ethan was unsettling. She cleared her throat to smooth the accusation out of her voice and looked at him. "You're up early."

"Trying to get some errands done before Katie notices I've left." Ethan placed a hand on his white knight and started to move the piece, but then paused to consider the chessboard as if everything hinged on this one particular move.

Whereas for Grace, everything hinged on her baby and keeping her stomach from objecting to the morning's excitement. Would Ethan expect her to say *checkmate* when she told him about the baby? As if she'd neatly trapped him into being a dad. And what about marriage? She didn't want Ethan to offer to marry her because she was carrying his child. But would he believe her?

"Keeping ahead of Katie Montgomery is almost as impossible as staying a step ahead of our Gracie." Pops stuck his elbows out and leaned on his knees, as if anticipating Ethan's move. As if Ethan proved a challenge to her grandfather. Ethan shifted his knight, taking Pops's bishop. Pops rubbed his chin. "Sometimes you get lucky."

Maybe Grace would get lucky and Ethan would confess he'd always wanted to be a father and couldn't think of another person he wanted to have a child with other than Grace. The tea bag crinkled in her fist. What a ridiculous thought.

Only fools relied on luck. Or her sisters. Especially Sarah Ashley, who had proclaimed her good fortune at meeting Alec in an elevator in Billings. Had she not been running late for a job interview—Sarah Ashley had been late for her own birth by five days and hadn't ever caught up—she'd have missed Alec's elevator completely. Sarah Ashley believed fate wanted her to be late. Grace believed in punctuality and relying on herself to ensure her own good fortune.

Ethan picked up Pops's bishop and used the chess piece to point down the street. "I'm just hoping the bank opens before the hedgehog arrives."

"Hedgehog?" Grace repeated, trying to latch onto something logical. Yet there was nothing logical about a hedgehog's arrival in Falcon Creek. Or sitting beside Ethan, while he played chess with Pops. She considered betting on luck.

"Zoe decided the ranch needed a petting zoo." Ethan's voice dipped low with disapproval.

Grace pretended Ethan censured her for thinking for one second she could believe in fate to right her world. "But I thought Zoe had left in the motor home with Big E."

"She ordered the animals before they drove off." Ethan slid back in his chair and waited for Pops to make his next move. "Animals have been arriving since last week."

Pops grimaced. "That woman is her own walking zoo with all the fur she wears. She certainly likes to live a pampered life."

Grace never wanted to be coddled. But she wouldn't object to an hour of pampering.

Ethan rubbed his hand over his mouth, but laughter escaped.

Grace, trying to rock a scold into her voice for her own

sake and her grandfather's, said, "Pops, you told me never to talk unkindly about our neighbors. They might need us someday or we might need them, right?"

"Zoe Petit would be the last person I'd be looking to if I needed help opening Brewster's front door." Pops removed his cowboy hat and scrubbed his fingers through his silver hair, his focus remained on the chessboard as if Ethan's move had really stumped him. "No offense, son."

"She isn't my grandmother. She's wife number six." Ethan's voice was detached and his tone flat as if he were rattling off the phone number for the dry cleaner two towns over.

Would he be just as detached when she told him about the baby? Would his sense of responsibility force him to offer to marry her in that same flat tone?

Grace shifted to study Ethan's profile without being too obvious. He seemed so sober. She wondered if Ethan would be like Big E, constantly searching for a better bride. Or would Ethan find one woman and stick with that one marriage like Grace's parents and grandparents? She gripped the chair arms and shook her head. Ethan Blackwell and his marrying preferences were the least of her concerns.

"That was five wives too many." Pops edged his knight toward the center of the board. "I bet Big E is looking for a place to hide from Zoe right this minute. He has to be worn-out from all the money she likes to spend on silly, expensive things."

Grace admonished her grandfather, drawing out Pops's name into a three-syllable word.

He shrugged and eyed Ethan. "A flea has more ranch in it than that woman."

Ethan made a counterattack and earned a grunt of approval from Pops.

"Your grandmother, Dorothy Blackwell, was just like my Sandy. Thoughtful, caring and loyal." Pops defended his king and focused on Ethan. His voice lowered, dipping into the serious as if he was about to impart the one secret to life. "Find a woman like them, son, and you keep 'em forever."

Pops tipped his chin toward Grace, but held Ethan's stare.

Surely her grandfather hadn't just suggested Ethan keep Grace. Pops grew up with seven brothers. He'd never been taught the sister code, didn't know the lesson about little sisters not dating their older sister's ex-boyfriend. Grace jumped up. "Since I have some time before we open here, I'm going to head over to South Corner Drug & Sundries."

"I'll join you." Ethan stood and stretched his arms over his head.

"That's not necessary." Grace reached down for her purse, but the leather strap hooked on her shoe.

"I need special supplements mixed for one of the mares." Ethan freed her purse, but the frenzy inside Grace failed to disappear. Ethan continued, his voice calm, as if he knew Grace needed a distraction, "Zoe decided both mares should have foals at the same time. Better photo opportunities for the guests at the ranch."

"Fleas have more sense." Pops's scowl was etched deep in his gruff voice.

And Grace had lost her sense too. Grace snatched her purse from Ethan, snatching her common sense back, and hurried to leave.

"Gracie, slow down and let your Ethan walk with you," Pops called out. "Everyone's in such a rush these days."

Grace was in a rush all right. A rush to get away from Ethan and her grandfather's innuendos. Why did Pops insist on referring to Ethan as *her* Ethan? He wasn't hers any more than the falcons belonged to Falcon Creek.

Ethan's long strides matched hers with ease. At least she'd escaped Pops's speculation. Ethan would prove harder to deter. She had one confession that might send him running. The words lodged in her throat again. "Sorry about Pops."

"There's no need." Ethan turned his baseball cap around and pulled the bill low on his forehead, as if he wanted to conceal his face from onlookers. As if he didn't want to be seen with Grace.

Ethan added, "I'd spend the day on the porch with Pops if I could."

Grace glanced at him. His voice lacked sarcasm and his expression was thoughtful. His sincerity touched her and she forgave him for not wanting to be seen with her. After all, she adored her grandfather and liked anyone who cared about Pops. "He requires a good dose of patience. Too much for most of the locals."

Ethan held open the door to South Corner Drug and motioned Grace inside. "I'm not most people."

She knew that all too well. He was the father of her child. Yet he hadn't brought up their night together. Not once. Clearly, he wanted to forget that night had ever happened. There'd be no forgetting once she found her courage, but blurting out the truth inside South Corner Drug was a surefire way to spark a Falcon Creek uproar.

Grace beelined for the feminine products aisle and found her first deep breath. As she'd suspected, Ethan had headed away from her. He was shaking hands with the pharmacist, Theo Watkins.

Grace turned left at the end of the aisle and spotted the candy.

Adeline Conrad called out to her from the checkout counter. "Grace, we have your ginger pops back in stock."

Grace smiled at her high school debate team partner and snatched the last three large bags of peppermint candy from the shelf. She wanted to have made her purchase before Ethan finished his conversation. But fate seemed to be in a nasty mood that morning and clearly had different intentions.

Ethan appeared at her side as if destiny had put him

there. That same warmth she'd felt on the porch earlier spiraled through her at Ethan's nearness. As if she welcomed his strong presence beside her. As if she counted on him being beside her. Good thing she never trusted destiny or she might believe what she felt was something other than her morning sickness making her cheeks flush and pulse race.

"The candy bowls at Brewster's looked quite full the other day, unless I missed one." He tapped the top bag of peppermint candy and eyed her. Laughter softened his blue gaze, pulling her in.

They both knew Ethan never missed a candy bowl. He'd had more than one sweet tooth just like her grandfather for as long as Grace could remember. She'd never understood why Sarah Ashley hadn't simply baked cookies or bought brownies for Ethan whenever she'd needed to apologize to him. Had Ethan been her boyfriend, Grace would've taken up baking and shared every dessert with him.

She didn't have time to get lost in blue eyes and charming smiles and decadent dessert recipes. "I like to be prepared."

"For the peppermint rush." Ethan walked beside her toward the cash register.

Adeline smiled at them like they'd won the Thursday night bingo challenge at the community center in Livingston, before she dropped four bags of ginger pops on the counter to add to Grace's peppermint candy. Ethan reached for one of the lollipop bags. Grace reached toward the row of coconut-flavored lip balm, extending her arm in front of Ethan and knocking his hand away from the ginger candy. Grace latched onto the oval containers and tossed several lip balms on her pile.

Ethan grabbed the packages of lip balm and juggled three to Adeline's delight. He asked, "Does the coconut lip balm enhance the peppermint flavor of the candy?"

Adeline watched the pair of them banter, her gaze jumping from one to the other, as if she were forming a response to land her the Montana State Debate title.

Grace shoved her items into a plastic bag, taking over Adeline's job duties and tossed her cash on the empty counter.

Adeline gathered the money without taking her attention away from Grace and Ethan. "You two come back soon."

Grace wasn't coming back anytime soon. The speculation in Adeline's gaze would only intensify to head-popping explosion once the town learned about Grace's pregnancy. Internet shopping was all the rage now, anyway. It was past time she joined in.

On the sidewalk, and far enough away from Sundries employees with eavesdropping habits, Grace blurted, "Was that the account paperwork and receipts from the Blackwell Ranch in those folders?"

Ethan shoved his hands into his jacket pockets and stared down Front Street. "Big E has an old-fashioned accounting method."

"At least he has a method." If Grace could translate Big E's system quickly and organize the books, she'd be done working for the Blackwells before the end of the week. That gave her three days to tell him about the baby.

"The books aren't really portable. Only the bank statements are in the folders I left those on the table beside Pops. If you need more, and you will to solve this accounting fiasco, it'll be best if you come up to the ranch." Ethan kicked a stone down the sidewalk. His voice sounded gravelly, as if he wasn't quite certain about his offer.

As if he wasn't glad about spending more time with Grace. On his family's land. In his family's house. Grace switched the bag to her right hand, holding it between Ethan and herself. Surely she'd find a moment to talk to him at the Blackwell Ranch. Three days offered plenty of opportunities. Like right now. Grace opened her mouth.

But Ethan misinterpreted her silence and filled the space between them with an uncomfortable truth. "Look, we really need your help. I really need you. We have a family of thirty checking in later this month. We can't cancel their reservation because we can't pay back their deposit. There's no money."

Grace closed her mouth. She'd already assumed that much about the Blackwell Ranch, given Jon's delay in paying their bill at Brewster's. She'd extended the due date on the Blackwell account twice already. But she'd never seen Ethan panic, not even when one of their bulls wandered onto the highway and Ethan had to rescue him. Yet Ethan looked panicked now. Would the baby put him into full-scale anxiety mode?

He stepped in front of her. "I can come into town and pick you up when you get off work, if you prefer not to drive those roads at night."

She would not be touched by his consideration. That looked like dread he was feeling. And any decent guy would've made the same offer. "I can drive myself."

Relief rushed through his words, reaching into his full smile. "Give me your phone?"

Confused, Grace handed him her cell.

"I'm adding myself to the top of your contact list. Call me when you get on the property and I'll come meet you." He typed quickly and handed the phone back to her. "I'm mostly there as there's so much to do and not enough ranch hands to help."

He scowled, and his voice sounded irritated, like he'd swallowed a handful of prickly burs.

They'd traded secrets during their night together. One secret for another. She'd confessed she'd once had a crush on him back in high school. Ethan had told her how he'd left the Blackwell Ranch, vowing he wouldn't ever need Big E's support or assistance again. From the conviction in his voice then, she doubted he'd take pay from the ranch now, even if the family wasn't facing a financial disaster.

At Brewster's, Ethan dropped into the rocking chair across from Pops. Grace frowned at Ethan. "With so much to do, I'd think you wouldn't have time to sit."

"I have eighteen minutes until the bank opens." Ethan settled into the rocker and grinned at her. "Besides, Pops and I have an important game to finish."

"Your mother was already asking about you, Gracie. Better get inside or she'll start hollering over that intercom. Seems Sarah Ashley got it into her head to update the inventory this morning." Pops rubbed his hands together and adjusted his chair closer to the chess table.

Inventory? Grace reeled. It had taken her ages to create a database that was a perfect fit for Brewster's. What had gotten into her sister?

Grace also had a conversation to rehearse.

One that was more overdue than last year's taxes.

CHAPTER FOUR

ETHAN CLOSED BUTTERSCOTCH'S stall and stretched. Between the chess game with Pops that morning and sitting by the mare for the past hour, his back had begun to protest. He'd spent longer with the pregnant horse than he'd expected, trying to coax her to eat. He should've been out in the south pasture, fixing the broken fence Katie discovered yesterday. The cattle had to graze there tomorrow, which meant Ethan had to fix the fence tonight.

He also had to apologize to Grace tonight. He decided to saddle up two of the horses, Faith Blue and Dewey, who were used for trail rides, and bring Grace with him. He'd mend the pasture fence and things between him and Grace at the same time.

A large black head shifted into his view. He strode over to Devil's Thunder and stroked the feisty stallion's neck. "Not today, Devil, I'm afraid. I need to concentrate on other things. But you and I are going out for a ride soon."

Being out in the pasture with Grace, he wouldn't worry about anyone walking in on their private conversation.

He smiled. His style contrasted with his grandfather's, who was always oversharing in line at the bank or South Corner Drug & Sundries as if he'd sought the approval of the teller or cashier that day. Big E had never even lied about his schemes, just doled out the truth, no matter the reaction from whoever listened to his latest ploy.

Should they be more worried about Big E's whereabouts?

Not even Pops had any insight to offer about Big E this morning when they'd played chess. Big E wouldn't have left town without telling someone where he was going, and why.

Ethan supposed there was a first time for everything.

Still, his grandfather hadn't changed in over seventy-five years. Ethan doubted he'd changed in the last month. Ethan just hadn't found the one person in town who Big E had confided in.

Ethan heard the rumble of a car coming down the road. He stepped out of the horse barn and crossed the yard toward the main house. He reached the curved driveway the same time Grace climbed out of her car. Her four-door sedan was economical and practical and suited her.

Yet there was nothing practical about his reaction to seeing Grace again. He liked that she looked relaxed and comfortable in her jeans and red flannel shirt with rolled sleeves. He liked her blond hair falling around her shoulders, instead of the confining ponytail, and her welcoming smile a little too much. And that didn't suit him at all. Suddenly, he was impatient to get on a horse and ride, preferably without Grace.

But they needed to talk. "I have to head out to the south pasture before nightfall."

Grace pointed at the main house. "I can get to work in Big E's office while you do that."

"I thought we could saddle Faith Blue and Dewey, and ride out together." Ethan tracked the sun in the sky and calculated how much daylight remained. "We can talk on the way."

"I'm not sure…"

"Katie doesn't know the exact financial distress the ranch is facing and I'd like to keep it like that. I don't want to worry her more. Between the new tractor, petting zoo arrivals and my own strained credit cards, it's looking rather bleak. Not to mention, Big E has another bank account that none of us have authority to use."

From the flurry of pricey renovations inside the main house, Ethan assumed Zoe had had full access to every penny. Too bad he couldn't get refunds on the bubble-gum paint and crystal chandeliers she'd hung in every bathroom inside his childhood home. He'd probably have enough cash to run the ranch for a month.

Grace asked, "But Katie knows I'm helping with the books, right?"

"Yes."

"Then she won't question my being in Big E's office." Grace straightened the cuffs on her flannel sleeves as if she needed to put herself back together. "Besides, I'd rather not ride."

It was easier to let her escape into the office. Easier to ride out to the south pasture alone. But then he'd spend the rest of the night questioning his own cowardice. The Blackwell men had been raised to be fearless and brave. He was already a coward for not having spoken frankly to Grace about their night together.

The solution was simple. He turned his baseball cap backward and concentrated on Grace like a starting pitcher with a no-hitter at the bottom of the ninth inning and the MVP batter at the plate. "You've been cooped up at a desk all day. What do you mean you don't want to ride? You were practically born in a saddle and barely left it as a kid."

"That was a long time ago." Grace stubbed the toe of her boot into the gravel and avoided looking at him.

"But you still ride." He clamped his teeth together, but too late.

Her head snapped up and her gaze centered on him. "How do you know that?"

He knew because he'd followed her posts on social media. He'd seen the picture of her at the horse show in Bozeman last month. Her wide smile couldn't contain all her joy in that one picture, and whenever he looked at it, he smiled too. He hadn't seen that kind of happiness in her since he'd returned home. Not that her happiness was actually due to him in any way.

He shifted his weight and shrugged. "Just guessing. You always had a passion for horses. You spent most of your weekends at shows in high school."

She eyed him suspiciously. "You were too busy with Sarah Ashley to know where I was in high school."

Sarah Ashley had spent her weekends with her girl-friends mostly. Ethan had definitely not been with her. When he'd needed a break from the ranch, he'd escaped to Brewster's. Frank and Pops usually had something they needed hauling or lifting. And Grace's mother most often had homemade cookies or a pie she'd insist he try. When Grandma Brewster had been alive, she'd fill him up on freshly squeezed lemonade.

The Gardners had always welcomed him, anytime, any day. Someone usually let slip Grace's success at the week-end's horse show or commented on her growing award shelf. He wondered if Grace knew how proud her parents and grandparents were of her. He wondered if she knew how lucky she'd been to have all their love for so many years. "As our high school years are firmly in the past, let's concentrate on the now and take a ride together."

"The sun is already setting and I'm not as familiar with the terrain out there as you are." Grace opened her passenger car door and pulled out a jacket. "The ATV would probably be faster. We can get to work in the of-fice sooner."

Ethan nodded, preferring even the ATV to the house. The ATV put her right beside him. She wouldn't have to strain to hear him, but he'd be stuck next to her. If he struggled to find the right words, he couldn't simply gal-lop ahead and collect himself. Still, he loaded the ATV and motioned for Grace to climb in.

Ethan guided the ATV around several potholes and waited until the trail evened out enough to not rattle his voice. He wanted to get this apology out the first time. Now seemed as good a time as any. But "sorry" never slipped past his lips; instead, he blurted out, "Why did you just leave a note that night?"

Ethan hit a bump. But not a large enough one to knock logic back into his thoughts.

Grace's shoulder tapped against his. "I didn't want it to be awkward."

But it was awkward. Perhaps more so because they hadn't said goodbye at the time. Worse, he'd never called her afterward.

She rushed on and filled the silence before awkwardness became a third passenger. "We're both adults. Both knew what that night was."

He thought he knew. Now he wasn't so sure. "What was that night?"

"You're going to make me say it?" Grace's voice pitched high despite the wind. "Certainly, you've had one-night stands before."

Maybe he had, but his past wasn't the topic of discussion. The only one-nighter that concerned him now was theirs. He'd doubted Grace had ever had a one-night fling. And if that was true, how could she be so cavalier about their evening together? Hadn't it meant anything to her?

He rubbed his chest, digging his knuckles into his ribs. He should be celebrating that Grace wasn't into messy emotions and long-term commitments. "That's all it was to you?" he asked.

"Was it something more to you?" Her tone was cautious as if she'd hesitated to voice the thought.

He slowed the ATV near the broken fence and twisted to look at her. Her gaze locked on to his, making him want to rub his chest again. She wanted his answer. Yet there was no right answer and he'd paused too long.

Grace zipped her jacket to her chin and yanked her hood over her head. "And now, it's awkward."

Ethan ran his hands over his face. "Not how I wanted this conversation to go."

"How did you want it to go?" She gripped the handrail and moved away from him.

"I wanted to apologize for not calling."

"I never called you either."

He touched her arm, pulling her gaze back to his. "Still, I don't make a habit of nights like those." Although, a quiet voice inside him whispered that Grace could become a habit. Good thing he was usually surrounded by so much noise, he could rarely hear said voice.

"That's good to know." Her chin dipped inside her collar. "I don't either."

"Okay." Ethan relaxed into the seat. Her thinking surprised him. And perhaps rankled a bit. As he'd never been one of those overly sensitive guys, he brushed off the discomfort as stiffness from climbing the ladder too many times to test the batteries in the fire alarms of every guest room in the lodge that afternoon. "What now?"

A pair of hawks screeched, circling above them. One hawk dived into the field and returned to the sky with a long snake thrashing inside its talons. Grace slapped a hand over her mouth and tracked the hawk's path over the ATV.

Ethan remembered their conversation at the bar when she'd shared her fear of snakes after he'd admitted elevators made him uneasy. "Don't worry. That hawk won't drop its dinner."

Grace kept her gaze on the sky and spoke through her fingers. "But it might drop pieces of the snake. Its talons are sharper than my knives at home. Is that blood dripping to the ground?"

"At least the snake will be dead when it lands on us," Ethan teased, and reached for the wire cutters inside the tool bag beside Grace's feet. "Snake can be good eating if it's breaded and fried."

"You didn't really just say that, did you?" Grace curled into her jacket.

He unlatched the safety on the wire cutters, and noticed her voice was unsteady. He paused to study her.

Her skin had paled to a strange gray color. She hadn't sounded uncomfortable with their conversation. They'd only just released the valve on their past. He was certain there'd be more for them to discuss, but she looked uncomfortable now.

Had the snake bothered her that much? She pressed her lips together, her bottom lip disappearing from the pressure. Bringing up the snake again probably wasn't the best approach.

He glanced at the setting sun. Dinnertime would be over before he finished his repairs, even if he was quick. Food had always been Big E's answer to everything. Maybe it would help here. "We've got chicken soup at the house. I'll make us something while you get your bearings in Big E's office."

"Soup would be perfect." She shifted her boots up onto the seat and set her cheek on her knees.

"We can head back now, if you'd rather."

"I'm fine," she said.

Nothing about the push she gave him on the shoulder was weak or frail. Still, he hesitated to leave her.

She pushed him again and said, "Go. You'll have one less thing to do tomorrow."

Ethan hurried to fix the fence and loaded up the ATV. He peeked at Grace, took in her pinched lips and the circles under her eyes. He hadn't meant to make her anxious when they'd talked about their night together, or sick, when he'd joked about them eating snake.

That he might've hurt her made him twitchy inside. For now, he'd table the conversation and come back to it later. Even better, he'd let her take the lead. If she wanted to dissect more about their evening together, then he'd listen and be there. Until then, he'd keep his mouth closed.

He gripped the steering wheel harder, but his first instinct was to grab her hand as if he wanted to comfort her. As if he had a right to hold her.

She'd asked if their night together had been something more than what it was. He wasn't sure. The only thing he wanted to do was hold her hand now.

But even if he'd wanted something more with Grace, it wasn't possible. It was impossible. He had nothing to offer but résumés, an uncertain future and an empty bank account. Grace deserved a lot more than that.

Silence rode between them on the drive back to the ranch. Less than five minutes was needed to introduce Grace to Big E's accounting system, leaving Ethan to prepare dinner in Zoe's extravagantly expensive pink wonderland.

Unfortunately, as a kid, he'd been more worried about shoveling food into his mouth before his brothers stole it from his plate than considering how it was made. He'd never wandered into the kitchen to help his mom. He'd only ever wandered into the kitchen to snatch a cookie or bag of chips.

After his parents had died, they all learned meals didn't just appear on the table. Big E had assigned a night for each one of the boys to prepare dinner for the family. That was when Ethan had figured out a handful of quick recipes that required one pot and little preparation. Chicken soup remained his go-to staple.

Soup reheated and ladled into bowls, Ethan carried dinner into Big E's office on a tray.

Grace looked up from a pile of receipts that covered every inch of Big E's oversize oak desk. "It might be easier to eat in the kitchen."

"In here is fine." He ate every night in the office, in the same leather chair. This was the only room that suited him. Even his childhood bedroom, which he'd shared with Ben and had once contained a bunk bed fort and countless army men, now resembled a giant box of glitter. He'd spent his first night in the room wondering how much the floor-to-ceiling silver curtains that shimmered like waterfalls had cost. He'd moved into Cabin Six after that and hadn't returned to his childhood room since.

He placed Grace's soup and crackers beside her. Setting his soup on top of the receipts, he pulled the leather chair closer to the desk and sat down.

"Is there something wrong with the kitchen?" Grace asked.

Ethan crushed crackers into his soup. "It's cold." Too pink. Too frivolous. Too dollhouse happy.

"It's updated and modern with every convenience sold on the market today." Her eyebrows pulled together behind her glasses. "A chef's dream."

But not his mother's dream. He couldn't find his mother in the house anymore and that put a chill inside the walls that couldn't be driven out with a roaring fire. He scooped up a pile of receipts from beneath his bowl and dropped them on the side table. "We can eat and work. It'll go faster with the two of us. What are you doing anyway?"

Grace pushed up her glasses and used her spoon to stir her soup. "Putting the receipts into piles by year."

Soup bowls scraped clean and receipts organized, Ethan eased back in the leather chair and watched Grace's fingers fly over a circa-1970s calculator complete with a roll of white paper. The pencil in her other hand scribbled across a legal notepad. "You're good at this."

"I should be. It's my profession." Grace tapped the pencil against her temple. "Certified public accountant with a master's degree in accounting."

"Impressive." Ethan steepled his hands and set them under his chin. He pictured her inside her cramped office with the equally compact metal desk. She'd seemed smaller inside that office. Now she seemed to own Big E's desk and the entire space. He decided she belonged in an office she could command. "You should have your own business."

"That's in the works." Her fingers paused on the calculator, a look of surprise in her wide eyes. "But that isn't public knowledge. I'd appreciate you not talking about it."

"But you're a staple at the store," he said. Grace had been working at Brewster's since they'd been kids. Everyone always knew she would be there. Everyone also knew if they needed something, they only had to find Grace. Always Grace.

Grace's entire face twisted into a grimace as if he'd called her the unwanted sweet potato hash on his plate. "I have more to offer than inventory spreadsheets and special orders."

"I agree." Grace was unexpected, like those over-easy eggs on his sweet potato hash.

Grace fumbled with her pencil and adjusted her glasses as if Ethan had messed with her paperwork.

Ethan let her fall back into her number crunching while he tried not to fall into the surprise of Grace Gardner. He listened to her fingers tapping on the calculator keys and the paper rolling out.

"Staring at her is not helping the ranch out." Katie stood in the doorway and peered around a stack of folded bedsheets in her arms. "But making beds in the lodge will."

"I don't want to make beds." He wanted to stay right where he was. With Grace.

Katie dumped the stack of linens on Ethan's lap. "I didn't want to iron and look how that turned out."

Ethan ran his hand over the smooth top sheet. "Nice job."

"They'll look even better on the beds." Katie smiled and turned to Grace. "Thanks for the help, Grace. If you need anything, I'll be in the barn. Ethan will be in the guest lodge."

"Looks like the team leader has spoken and I have more

work to do." Ethan stood and balanced the sheets so he wouldn't drop them. "Grace, text me before you leave."

Grace glanced at him, her gaze distracted, her smile distant. "Sure."

Katie rushed around Ethan. "Let me get the back door for you."

"Thanks," Ethan muttered as he left the study.

"Wouldn't want you sneaking back into the office for more one-on-one time with Grace," Katie joked.

"We were working."

"Grace was working." Katie swung open the back door, but caught Ethan's arm before he left. "I don't know what you were doing, Eth. Pining, maybe?"

"I've never pined in my life." He bumped his shoulder into hers as he stepped outside. "I was half asleep and you ruined my nap."

"Whatever." Katie kept pace beside him as he lengthened his stride down the back porch steps. "What's up with you and Grace? You can tell me. I'm practically your sister."

"Leave it alone, Katie." Ethan turned toward the guest lodge and smiled. Hip wasn't allowed at the lodge and he knew Katie wouldn't tag along without her dog. "Get back to work or I'll have to fire you for laziness."

"You wouldn't survive a day without me," she countered.

"An hour."

"What?"

He faced her and tried to look stern. "I wouldn't survive *an hour* out here without you, but don't let it go to your head."

"It's good to have you back, Ethan." Katie laughed and whistled for Hip to accompany her into the barn.

One king bed and a set of twin beds later, Ethan pounded his fist into a feather pillow. He'd spent the last hour tangled up in sheets and duvets and not in the good kind of way. Who put so many buttons on duvets when a simple zipper would work just fine?

Grace and Katie arrived at the second bedroom of the Big Sky wing and burst out laughing. "We came to see what has been taking you so long," Grace said.

"Fluffing a pillow." Ethan smashed the pillow again with his fist.

"That's a beating." Grace yanked the pillow away from Ethan and patted the stuffing back into place. Her hands gentle as if she did this every day.

"What does it matter?" Ethan fell face forward across the queen bed. "This is what beds are for. There's no pretty required." He could think of a few other things beds were good for, like holding Grace all night.

Fortunately, Grace and Katie chose that moment to pummel his back with pillows, pummeling his wayward thoughts away, and he grunted into the mattress.

Grace put her pillow back against the headboard. "How many more rooms do you have to do?"

"Too many. Who builds a lodge with so many rooms anyway?" Ethan turned his head and grinned at Katie. "Rooms four through seven are haunted and need to be closed indefinitely."

Katie smacked him with her pillow again. "Not happening."

"Come on," Grace said. "We'll teach you how to do pretty."

He thought Grace looked pretty with the moonlight streaming in from the window framing her from behind. "I don't want to learn."

"This won't leave a scar. I promise." She gripped his hand and pulled, trying to tug him off the bed.

Ethan rolled over, but kept his hand inside hers. "Tomorrow I'm doing all manly tasks. Nothing that requires pretty."

"Fine with me." Katie tossed her pillow on the bed. "Now get up, so we can get this done and finally call it a night."

With having called time on the pillow fights, the three of them finished the other guest rooms quickly. As he said good-night to Grace at her car, he thought she looked almost exhausted. Was he asking too much of her to try to make sense of Big E's accounts?

Ethan stretched out across the queen bed in Cabin Six after a midnight snack, and considered all the repairs that were needed in his cabin alone. The to-do list seemed to double every night. But Grace had offered a reprieve and made the evening less toilsome. Less lonely. And he'd learned to do pretty.

He'd learned more than that too. He now knew Grace's favorite color: purple, thanks to an argument between Katie and Grace about whether the shower curtain in one of the suites was lavender or lilac.

He'd learned Grace's favorite flower: sunflower. This came out after Katie and Grace agreed the large guest room in the Western Wing needed some decoration and that several different flowers should be painted as a border along the walls.

And her favorite time of the day: the witching hour, when magic happens. That, she'd let slip, when he'd walked her to her car. She'd pointed out a shooting star, smiled and closed her eyes as if making a wish.

Not that he intended to do anything with his new information about Grace. Or to even repeat the getting-to-know-Grace-better evening.

She worked for the Blackwells. Nothing more.

After all, he'd returned home to help his brother with the ranch, not discover if there was something more between him and Grace.

CHAPTER FIVE

GRACE SWISHED WATER around her mouth and spit it out into the bathroom sink in Brewster's warehouse. She'd avoided the newly renovated bathroom in the main store ever since her morning sickness had extended into days and evenings. Unfortunately, as her nausea didn't seem to be lessening, her stomach seemed to be expanding every hour. Thankfully she had a jacket with her yesterday to conceal her growing tummy from Ethan. Nothing managed to conceal her nausea though.

Ten minutes into the ATV ride at the Blackwell ranch last night, she'd decided the horse might've been the better option. Ethan had driven the four-wheeler like he was on an off-roading race course and trying to catch the leader. Grace had spent most of the ride trying to catch her breath and calm her stomach.

She'd thought her note at the hotel had ended any discussion of their one night together like an exclamation point ended a sentence. She'd lost that battle when Ethan had teased about eating the snake.

She touched her stomach.

Of course, their discussion was far from over. Far from complete.

But she'd never dare expect more from Ethan Blackwell than one night. One memorable night. She'd always been the friend. The confidante. But not the girlfriend. She'd been "like the sister" that a guy had never had so often that her family tree should've fallen over by the time she'd graduated from college. There wasn't a variation on the we-make-better-friends line that she hadn't heard.

Once she'd moved home from college, she'd shelved relationships and dating with her statistics books. Until

Ethan. She'd stepped into that hotel room with Ethan with her eyes open and her head clear. It was only ever supposed to be one night.

She touched her stomach.

Yet, Ethan had made her feel anything but plain last night when they'd been teasing each other and laughing for most of the night. She'd been anything but quiet around him ever since he'd come back to Falcon Creek. He also hadn't scoffed at her business ideas or suggested she rethink her goals. He'd even complimented her skills.

Nothing that made her heart trip over, of course.

Her heart had stopped tripping in middle school when Trevor Dixon chose her younger sister, Nicole Marie, over Grace for the holiday dance. Her sister had tried to persuade Trevor to take Grace. But he'd moved on to Dana Brantley by lunch. And Grace had moved into Brewster's, making herself a permanent and indispensable fixture in the store. She had her family, the store and her show horses. That had been enough.

Until recently. But now she had a baby to concentrate on. A baby to love.

Her name echoed over the store's loudspeaker. Grace splashed her cheeks with cold water and yanked open the door, but pulled back to keep from running into her sister.

Sarah Ashley handed her several paper towels, but remained in Grace's path, her gaze skimming over Grace's face.

"Thanks." Grace wiped the paper towel across her damp forehead. "Something I ate at breakfast didn't agree with me."

"That's been happening frequently." Sarah Ashley arched one perfectly groomed eyebrow.

"Maybe I need to make better breakfast choices." Her heart definitely needed to make better choices, like not to get involved in the first place. Otherwise she'd only have herself to blame if she let Ethan break it. She was even more ill this morning than she'd thought if she was considering hearts and Ethan in the same sentence.

"It's almost like you're pregnant, Grace." Sarah Ashley leaned against the doorway as if she was intent to wait out the long bathroom line.

Except this wasn't a concert venue in the city. And there wasn't an extended line at the women's restroom. Only Grace, stuck inside the tiny bathroom, adjusting her shirt to hide the truth from her sister's penetrating stare.

"Of course, that couldn't be possible." Sarah Ashley's mouth dipped into a pout. "You've always hated attention. Can you imagine the awful amount of attention you'd get if you were pregnant? Without a husband."

Grace didn't hate being noticed. It was just that her sisters demanded the spotlight and Grace had been content to let them battle for center stage. But Grace had always wanted to be like her sisters: beautiful, vivacious, all-encompassing. No one wanted to be Grace. There were more years than Grace cared to admit to when she didn't even want to be Grace. Not the practical, rule-following, ordinary Gardner sister bookended between two show-stealing siblings. Grace had always been the other sister. The afterthought Gardner. "Women have babies all the time without husbands, Sarah Ashley."

"Not in this family." Her sister's voice sounded solemn as if she was the newly elected head mistress of propriety and respectability.

But morals had nothing to do with Sarah Ashley's objections to a baby out of wedlock. In the Gardner family, any baby would steal the spotlight from Sarah Ashley. Any baby would threaten Sarah Ashley's princess status. "Did you want to discuss the reasons women have babies without being married?"

"No." Sarah Ashley waved her hand at Grace's stomach. "I want to know why you won't admit you're pregnant?"

"Why do you keep saying I'm pregnant?" Grace tugged on her shirt, wishing she'd put on the longer flannel even if she would've been too warm.

"You seem dependent on mints and ginger lollipops. You've stopped eating bacon and the night owl can't stay awake past sunset anymore." Sarah Ashley crossed her arms over her chest and tipped her head at Grace. "I might bleach my hair, but I don't bleach my brain."

Grace stopped fidgeting with her shirt and yanked her sister's arm, pulling Sarah Ashley the five steps down the hallway to her office. She pushed Sarah Ashley inside and shut the door, cramming them both inside. "Why are you here?"

"The shipment of dog food arrived. I added all twenty pallets into the inventory, but the prices were coded incorrectly from the vendor." Sarah Ashley brushed a curl behind her ear and shrugged as if everyone knew vendors weren't dependable. "Everything's ringing up wrong in the system. I need you to fix it."

Grace edged behind her desk as if the dented metal might shield her from confessing anything to her sister. "I meant, why did you move back home?"

Sarah Ashley sat in the metal folding chair that faced Grace's desk and crossed her ankles like royalty on a national stage. "Is this what we're going to do? Trade insider secrets. I tell you about my marriage woes and you fess up about the baby."

Grace jammed her hand in the candy bowl. Her sister had a man who had fallen in love with her, and yet, she'd moved back home after only three months of apparent bliss. No one knew the real reason.

"It's just that you've never liked the family business." Grace had spent every free hour after school and in the summers working at Brewster's. Sarah Ashley had spent those same days anyplace other than the family store. Sarah Ashley had majored in art and design, not business.

"I've never been given the chance to like it or dislike it." Sarah Ashley squeezed her wedding ring, and doubt filled her gaze just for a moment. "Everybody assumed I didn't. Besides, you were here first. You seemed to be all Mom and Dad needed."

All Grace remembered was their parents letting Sarah Ashley do whatever had pleased her. Whenever Grace had asked about her older sister, her mother would smile and say, "Sarah Ashley is off being Sarah Ashley."

"But you never showed any interest in Brewster's," Grace repeated. *Ever.* For her sister, it had always been about dates and trips with friends and finding the prettiest boots.

"I am now." Sarah Ashley's crisp voice matched her firm nod. "And you've never shown any interest in becoming a mother."

Grace smoothed her hand over her stomach. Would her sister understand the love she already had for her child? Would her sister understand that Grace had never imagined falling in love herself or finding someone to love her? Sarah Ashley believed in fairy tales, true love and pots of gold at the end of rainbows. Grace believed in the real world where people liked her because she was a Gardner. But she wasn't the Gardner sister a man fell in love with.

Grace fumbled with the wrapper on a mint. The plastic had melted to the candy like useless daydreams melted for her.

"Have you at least told the father about the baby?" Sarah Ashley rubbed her hands together, looking more like a prosecutor all too aware that the defendant's witness was about to confess, and she'd win the case. Her sister had wasted her interrogation skills on fashion design and art.

Grace crammed a ginger lollipop in her mouth along with the mint. "What are you talking about now?"

"You aren't as progressive as all that. We both know you didn't visit a sperm bank. So, there must be a father somewhere that you know about." Sarah Ashley's prosecutor-like gaze refused to release Grace from her focus.

Grace's teeth cracked down hard on the mint and lollipop, breaking the candy into pieces, releasing the peppermint and ginger flavors. But nothing stopped that slow flop of her stomach. Clearly, her sister wasn't ready to confess her motivation for being back in town. Likewise, Grace wasn't ready to spill the truth in her heart either. At least not until she knew her sister's game. "There will be a father when I decide to have a child."

"I've been running through potential daddies and I have a list." Sarah Ashley leaned forward. "Want to hear who I think it is?"

"Not unless you want to tell me why you won't go home, even as Alec begs you every night to come back."

Sarah Ashley scooted the chair closer to the desk as if she was prepared to offer Grace a perfect plea deal. "I bet I'll figure out who the father is before the father learns about his baby."

Grace searched her sister's face, looking for a warning or threat, and finding none. "How about we bet that you'll tire of the business before the end of the month and leave everyone to tidy up the mess you've created?"

"I'm not going anywhere." Sarah Ashley grabbed a peppermint from the candy dish on the desk and stood up. At the door, she turned and eyed Grace. "But it's May, not January, and you can't layer up to hide your baby bump for the next six months. You're going to need to trust someone if you intend to keep your secret."

Sarah Ashley walked out. Grace stared at her steel office door as if it were a magic mirror that would reveal everything. But all Grace knew was that a race had begun and she hadn't left the starting line. And time was about to run out.

Grace had to tell Ethan before Sarah Ashley figured out who the father was and took it upon herself to tell the daddy the good news.

CHAPTER SIX

"THIS IS THE first time I've sat down all morning," Grace said a few days later as she slid into a booth at the Clearwater Café across from Ethan and pressed her head into the stiff vinyl. It wasn't a plush recliner with a foot rest and comfy blanket, but it worked.

"It's past noon. I thought accountants spent their days behind their computers." Ethan handed her a laminated menu.

Grace never glanced at the offerings. She knew everything by heart. It was the same menu that had been in the Clearwater Café when her father had brought Grace to the diner for their first daddy-daughter breakfast. She'd been six and a morning with her dad all to herself had been the best treat. The tradition continued even now and they had a standing reservation for the corner booth on the first Saturday of every month at 9:00 a.m. They'd only missed one Saturday in all the years they'd been going there. "Cleaning up after Sarah Ashley requires a lot of time."

"Your sister doesn't seem too concerned." Ethan nodded toward the front entrance.

Sarah Ashley strolled into the diner like she'd just returned from a morning at the spa and seated herself at the counter. Her sister wasn't concerned. She was that prosecutor digging for the last piece of evidence. Then she'd snap shut her briefcase and shout, "Case closed!"

If Grace shifted just right, she could catch her sister's speculative gaze and grating smile in the reflection in the glass mirror behind the counter.

Grace leaned the other way, pretending to give their waitress, Delia Buck, room to set down their glasses of water.

Delia pulled a golf pencil from behind her ear and scribbled down their orders. She dropped her sleek bright pink glasses into place and looked Grace over as if checking for some rare skin disease. "You order soup so much, I'm beginning to think you've gone on one of those new age liquid diets. Sure you don't want a nice juicy burger?"

That was the problem with having a long-standing tradition in a small town. Delia served Grace and her dad breakfast each Saturday and served Grace any other day she stopped in for lunch. Delia knew Grace's eating habits better than she did. Sarah Ashley's grin in the mirror looked sharp enough to thin slice a steak. Grace pressed her fist into her stomach to ease the sudden cramping. "I'll stick to the soup."

"Ain't nothing wrong with good old-fashioned beef. Grew up eating it every day and the heart's still ticking." Delia wedged the golf pencil into her hair-sprayed updo. "I bet if you ask real sweet, your boyfriend here will share a few bites of his burger with you."

Ethan coughed and swallowed half of the water in his glass.

Delia winked and hustled on to her next customer.

Sarah Ashley swung around on the stool and arched one sleek eyebrow at Grace. Grace wanted to slide under the table and crawl out of the diner. But she was going to be a mother. Mothers needed backbones. Time to prove to herself and everyone else that she had one. She adjusted her glasses, returned her sister's smug grin with a smile and a challenge of her own, daring her sister to come to the booth. Daring her sister to tell what she thought she knew.

Sarah Ashley narrowed her gaze and dipped her chin before turning back to the counter.

Grace almost believed Sarah Ashley approved of Grace's bravado. But Sarah Ashley never liked to be challenged. Never liked to be questioned. Growing up, her sister had often told Grace that she liked Grace best because she always went along with whatever Sarah Ashley wanted. Sarah Ashley liked that it was easy to be around Grace.

Except Grace was about to be not-so-easy to be around. Who knew what kind of scene Sarah Ashley would cause when she learned Grace was pregnant with her ex-boyfriend's baby. Grace wrapped her hands around the glass of ice water, trying to freeze out her guilt.

Delia arrived with Ethan's iced tea and Grace's ginger ale and rushed off just as quickly. Grace tucked Sarah Ashley in the worry-about-that-later category and looked at Ethan.

"You do seem to have a penchant for soup," he said, as he tucked the laminated menu into its holder at the end of the table and reached for the sugar jar.

"Soup settles my stomach." She frowned at the bite in her tone. Ethan wasn't to blame. He was the father. Who had to be told.

"Are you sick?" His voice was mild as if he knew it was polite to ask, but didn't want to know the details.

"Nothing contagious." Grace tore at the ends of her paper napkin and decided to tear off the truth Band-Aid. There'd never be the perfect time to tell Ethan. Why not now? In the overcrowded café. With her sister watching. She'd always heard that breakups were best done in crowded places to keep the injured party from making a scene. This wasn't a breakup, she reminded herself. She ripped off the Band-Aid anyway. "It's only supposed to last for the first three months."

Ethan held the open sugar jar suspended above his iced tea glass. "That sounds like a trimester."

Thankfully, Ethan had never been slow. Grace stopped shredding her napkin. "It's exactly that."

Ethan lowered the sugar jar with a dull thud. "What aren't you telling me?"

Grace shifted and refocused on Ethan as if he were the only one in the diner. "I'm pregnant. It's yours. Mine. Ours."

Ethan downed his entire glass of iced tea and reached for her water glass to down it as well. He waved at a different waitress, asking for a refill. "But we used…"

His voice dropped off, the sound evaporated from his voice like water from desert sand. The waitress poured more water, and tea, ensured their orders would be up soon and backed away. Ethan downed another glass of water. "Doesn't matter now, I suppose."

"I wanted to tell you sooner." *I wanted you to tell me that you were excited. That while this hadn't been expected, everything would be okay. That they'd be okay.*

"Why didn't you?" His frown twisted into a scowl.

The accusation in his tone was as sharp as a scalpel. "First, I was in denial." Like now. Maybe he just needed more time to adjust to the situation. To the idea of a baby. She'd been in shock too, but that hadn't lasted long. "So I waited to take the test."

"And then?" he prodded, looking more like a caged tiger clawing the door to get out.

"Then I wanted the baby." Nothing wavered in her voice, her gaze remained locked on his. She wanted him to know that nothing would change her mind.

"I can't be a father now." His voice came out low and rough as if that cage closed in on him.

But his gaze. That bite in his cool blue eyes blamed her. It was there for only a blink. Only a second. But she'd seen it. They weren't going to be okay. She hadn't expected him to shout for joy. But she'd never expected this. "Then I'll be twice the mother."

"Didn't you hear me?" He leaned forward, his voice was bleak. "I can't be a dad right now."

But for one unforgettable night, he'd proven he could want Grace. Like she'd dreamed. Reality stared at her now and with cold blue eyes. "Maybe you didn't hear me. I'm having this baby. I can be a mother, and I want to be a mother. I want this child." And she would stop wanting more from Ethan. Right now. Right this minute.

He leaned back, ripped his baseball cap off and scrubbed his hands through his hair as if to make sure he was still the same. That nothing had changed on him. "I guess this explains the peppermint addiction and soup fetish."

Nothing explained the disappointment burrowing deep inside Grace's bones. She'd always known she was the Gardner sister the boys wanted for a friend only. It was her own fault she ached now. She'd let that small kernel of hope rest in her heart. The hope that Ethan Blackwell would be different. She sipped her ginger ale, washing the last bit of hope away. "Unfortunately, my morning sickness has lasted all day."

"And the baby's healthy?" He scanned her face, detached and clinical, as if she was one of his patients, not the mother of his child.

"I have an ultrasound scheduled the week after next." She wouldn't ask him to join her. He'd made his position more than clear.

Delia set their order on the table and asked if they needed anything else. Grace needed a to-go container for her lunch. Grace needed to go.

Ethan gaped at his hamburger as if he'd been a lifelong vegan and abhorred beef. Grace forced a smile at Delia.

"I need some air." Ethan slid to the edge of the booth. Grace grabbed her purse.

"Eat." Ethan set his hand on her arm, stalling her. His voice was gentle and calmer than it'd been in the last ten minutes. "You need to eat. I need five minutes. I'm not bolting. I just have to…"

The lost look on his face tugged at Grace. Tugged at places she'd only just vowed to ignore. "Go. I've had my five minutes to adjust."

"That's all you needed?" He squeezed her arm. The shadow of a tease passed through his gaze.

Grace grabbed her spoon, reminding her heart to be as hard as the steel in her hand. "That's all I'm admitting to right now."

Grace glanced over at the counter. Thankfully, the older couple beside Sarah Ashley seemed to have pulled her into a rather lively conversation. Outside, she watched Ethan pace up and down the sidewalk.

Well, she'd shared her secret. Ethan knew the truth. And now Grace knew the truth: she couldn't count on Ethan. Not that it mattered. She'd already been prepared to build her business and raise the baby herself.

If she'd wanted an involved father, she would've gotten married first. This wasn't the path others would choose, but it was her path. She was on it now and not about to step off.

She looked out the window. Ethan remained on the sidewalk, staring at the peaks of the Rockies. Grace tugged his plate toward her and reached for a slice of his bacon. Because she wanted to. Because she chose to.

NOTHING MOVED MOUNTAINS. That was a lie. Grace had just dropped one on him. He felt flattened right here, standing in his hometown, on the corner of Front Street and South Street.

If he'd outlined a timeline for his life, marriage and a family appeared in a much later section. After he'd secured a job and paid off his college debts. After he'd established himself in the equestrian world as a leading veterinarian in horse rehabilitation. After he'd built his own clinic. Once he could financially support a wife and children, then he'd consider dating, wedding vows and baby names.

At the moment, he had enough room on his credit card for two more tanks of gas. How was he supposed to buy diapers and baby formula? How was he supposed to be a good father? Grace deserved a good father for her baby. Their child deserved a good dad.

Grace would be an excellent mom. That he didn't question. He only questioned himself. And the answers weren't etched into the mountain peaks no matter how hard he stared. He could stand on the corner until sunset and be there for the sunrise, but nothing would change those facts.

Ready or not, panicked or scared, he was going to be a father. *A father.*

Ethan strode back to the café and pulled open the door. Sarah Ashley stood just inside. He could only handle one Gardner sister at a time. He lifted his hand to stop her from speaking, as if she'd ever respected his wishes. "Not now, please, Sarah Ashley."

"What's the matter, Ethan?" Sarah Ashley pursed her lips and regarded him. "Grace not telling you what you want to hear about the Blackwell Ranch accounts?"

He would've welcomed whatever Grace had to say about the Blackwell Ranch accounts instead of what Grace had already told him. Sarah Ashley eyed him as if she knew he'd been outside stomping his feet and ranting about the inconvenience and unfairness of life. Angry at himself, more like it. "Shouldn't you be at Brewster's creating another mess for Grace to clean up?"

Sarah Ashley winced and stepped back as if he'd jabbed at her pride. Generations of Blackwell fathers would be so proud of him right now. He was supposed to be a man, not a spoiled brat. Time to act like one. Time to take responsibility. "Sorry, Sarah Ashley. I need to get back to Grace."

Thankfully Sarah Ashley let him pass without another

word. For as long as he'd known her, Sarah Ashley had always had the last word. He'd have to wonder later why she'd kept silent now. And when she'd offer a comeback. Knowing Sarah Ashley, he wouldn't have to wait long.

Ethan slid into the booth, noticed the absence of most of his french fries and looked at Grace. Her soup bowl was scraped clean. The color was back in her cheeks. The calmness that usually settled around her had returned. At least, one of them wasn't consumed by stress. That must be the reason he lost his cool and blurted, "Let's get married."

"It isn't the 1800s anymore." Grace dipped another one of his french fries into a small dish of ranch dressing and frowned at him. Her voice matter-of-fact and reserved. "No, we're not getting married."

Was it wrong that relief splashed through him like a hot shower after snowplowing in ten-below weather? Between Big E's string of ex-wives and Jon's disaster of a first marriage, Ethan wanted nothing to do with loveless unions. "Okay, but what are we supposed to do now?"

"I'm going to have a child and start my own business." Grace pointed the french fry at him as if she was making a point about her favorite TV show, not discussing their future as parents.

Ethan eyed her. How could she be so casual? He hadn't told her anything she'd wanted to hear. Even he'd cringed listening to himself tell her that he didn't want to be a father. Certainly that wasn't something a pregnant woman wanted to hear. Even if it was the truth. He had to have hurt her. That hadn't been his intention. His thoughts were more twisted up than a tangle of barbed wire fencing.

But Grace only bit into the french fry and chewed slowly as if her world hadn't changed. Wouldn't change with or without him. Finally, she swallowed and added, "You're going to rescue the Blackwell Ranch and... Do you have plans for the future?"

Not baby plans. The paper embossed with his veterinary degree and his free work at the ranch wouldn't support a child. But fathers supported their families. "A baby wasn't a part of my current goals."

"I have the finances already worked out." Grace polished off another french fry and wiped a napkin across her mouth. "If money is your concern, you can let that go."

She maintained a cool, cavalier tone. But the Grace he thought he knew had passion, heart and compassion. Yet she had everything all prepared, even the finances. She acted like he was nothing more than a sperm donor, which he technically was. A sperm donor still signed a consent form to become a sperm donor. He'd never signed anything to become a father. To have a child. With Grace Gardner. "Why did you tell me?"

He winced at the resentment in his voice. Everything coming out of his mouth today seemed to be wrong. Maybe he should've taken a longer moment earlier. Perhaps walked up and down both Front and Back Streets, not just to the corner.

Grace's gaze narrowed. The first crack in her reserve. "Every child should know their father."

And every father should be present in his child's life. Ethan regretted every day that he'd missed with his own dad. Still felt fate had cheated him, even though he'd had more time with his dad than some of the other kids he knew. Ethan scrubbed his hands over his face. "A child should have both parents in his or her life."

"I agree." She'd wrapped her reserve back around her like a shield, giving away nothing about her true feelings.

She didn't offer suggestions or solutions. She left him to flounder across from her in the booth. She'd also refused his marriage request without hesitation. That had to mean she wasn't interested in a loveless union either.

But how was their child going to have both parents in

his or her life when he moved to Kentucky or back to Colorado to join an equestrian practice? Falcon Creek lacked the opportunities he needed.

No matter what Grace claimed about the finances being settled, Ethan intended to provide for both his child and Grace. He had to send out more résumés. That afternoon. Forget saving the ranch, he had to save his bank account. "Who else knows?" he asked.

"Sarah Ashley suspects that I'm pregnant." Grace glanced at the counter, where her sister was sipping from a coffee mug. "She's made it her personal mission to figure out who the father is."

No wonder Sarah Ashley had been waiting for him when he came back inside. Sarah Ashley had many faults, as did he, which had made them the not-so-perfect couple, but even that hadn't granted him permission to make love with her younger sister. Or have a baby with her younger sister.

Grace should've been off-limits. But he hadn't wanted to respect the rules. He'd wanted Grace. And if he was honest, he was still drawn to her.

Ethan chewed on what was left of his hamburger, trying to sort through his irrational thoughts. He slid his plate with the last of his french fries closer to Grace. "We need to tell Sarah Ashley."

"My parents need to be told too." Grace accepted his offering and preempted his next thought.

Ethan both liked and respected the Gardners; he had since grade school, and Pops as well. What was he supposed to tell Frank Gardner? Surely Frank would expect Ethan to step up and be a man, which Ethan had done. Yet, Frank's middle daughter had turned Ethan down faster than an eight-second champion bull rider. Ethan hadn't argued. "Your parents are going to notice soon."

He noticed a rosy shine to her cheeks now that he looked

at Grace in a new light. Or, not exactly a new light. He'd been aware of her since the moment he'd walked into that closet of an office of hers less than a week ago.

He'd been aware of Grace Gardner, the woman, the moment he'd stepped into the crowded reception hall three months ago to wish Sarah Ashley a happy future, but couldn't keep his gaze from tracking over to Grace again and again.

"I'll tell my parents." She finished her ginger ale and stacked all the dishes into an organized pile as if that likewise straightened up their situation. "You don't need to be there."

"It's my baby too. I should be there." Once he left town, possibly the state, for a new job, he wouldn't be there for her. But he was here now. He could be with her to talk to her parents at least.

Her green gaze was steady and direct, even behind her glasses. "I'm not marrying you."

Such an automatic, unapologetic refusal. He blamed that quick stab in his core on his burger. He should've had soup like Grace. "I heard you the first time. You don't need to keep repeating it." Besides, he wasn't asking again.

Sarah Ashley strolled up to the booth, carrying the diner's boxy cordless phone, an old-fashioned kind, like the diner's milkshakes and jukebox. She handed the phone to Grace and grimaced at Ethan. "Grace isn't answering her cell phone fast enough for Mom and Dad."

Grace spoke quickly, ended the call and looked at Ethan. "There's an emergency. I need to get back to the store."

Ethan checked the time on his phone. They'd sat down in the booth less than forty-five minutes ago. His world had imploded in less than an hour, and he hadn't quite found his balance. Heaven knew he hadn't said anything right to Grace since her news. "Don't you get a full hour for lunch?"

Sarah Ashley shook her head before handing the phone to Delia as the busy waitress passed by. "Grace prefers to work through lunch. Actually, Grace prefers work over everything else."

Grace glared at her sister, but Sarah Ashley just lifted one shoulder as if goading her to argue.

"I'll come with you." Ethan dropped cash on the table and stood.

Grace glowered at him. "An escort isn't necessary."

He'd never known Grace to be dependent on anyone. She'd made it more than clear that she didn't need him to raise their baby either. What with her financial and professional agendas already in place. She had everything figured out. Everything, except Ethan.

Tucking his wallet and his frustration in his pocket, he said, "I want to talk to your father about any available ranch hands in the area."

She looked at him suspiciously. "I haven't finished the budget for the ranch yet."

Or their conversation. He motioned for both Sarah Ashley and Grace to walk ahead of him. "Staffing is getting rather desperate up at the Blackwell Ranch."

"Whenever it's desperate at Brewster's, everyone knows to call Grace." Sarah Ashley glanced at him over her shoulder; her smile lacked her usual sparkle. A tartness, not sweetness, laced her voice. "Grace likes to rescue everyone. All the time."

"If people followed my instructions, I wouldn't need to keep saving them." Grace shoved open the doors to the café and started down the sidewalk toward Brewster's.

"If you let people make changes, you might find their ideas have merit." Sarah Ashley matched Grace's sure stride even in her high-heeled boots.

"Or I might find the entire inventory database has

crashed and taken down the point-of-sale system," Grace countered.

Sarah Ashley shook her head, her long curls swinging across her shoulders. "Computers are so unreliable."

"I find people are even more unreliable." Grace stomped up the stairs to Brewster's, never sparing a glimpse at Ethan.

Had she already decided he'd be an unreliable father? She'd only just announced she was pregnant with his child. *His child.* She'd had the past three months to prepare. He'd had thirty minutes. Ethan hurried after Grace and stopped her before she disappeared inside the store. "We need to talk more."

"Fine, but not now." She edged inside the entryway. "Mom needs me and I have a three o'clock with a potential client."

"I'm your client." *And the father of your child.* Wasn't there a priority ranking or something?

"I can come up to the ranch tonight." She took off her glasses and rubbed her eyes as if that was all she needed to refresh herself. "We can look at the books then."

But not discuss the baby. Had Sarah Ashley been right? Did Grace put work before everything else? She was coming up to the ranch, but not to do more accounting.

Didn't anyone notice the dark circles under her eyes but him? She needed to rest. To eat. His child would arrive exhausted from his or her mother's nonstop pace. "You'll be there by six, or I'll drive down here to get you myself."

"My parents—"

"Six o'clock, Grace."

She nodded before sprinting into the store at her mother's shout.

CHAPTER SEVEN

ETHAN LET THE door to Brewster's close and shook his head. He was having a baby with Grace. *Grace Gardner.* If the fates had showed him this part of his future in a crystal ball, he'd have consoled the trio and explained that everyone made a mistake at some point. His world had shifted off-kilter even more now that the frustration inside him was for Grace, not himself.

Everyone demanded too much from Grace. That irritated him. She was only one person after all. He didn't want to curse at the inconvenience of becoming a father now. He wanted to shout at everyone inside the store to leave Grace alone.

He suddenly wanted to protect her.

He'd once gotten caught in a tailspin on the mountain bypass courtesy of black ice and had to steer into the turn to keep from slamming through the guardrails and into the trees. A simple overcorrection was all that had been needed. Now the only overcorrection he could come up with: ignore his inclination to protect Grace.

After all, Grace hadn't asked for his help. Would most likely resent him if he tried. And he had no claim like that on her. Wanted no claim like that. Love and all those wild emotions required too much of himself. And later made him hurt too much.

His mind made up to let Grace defend herself, he wondered why his legs wobbled like he was still in that tailspin. Time to leave. Certainly, distance from Grace and hammering some loose fence up at the ranch would center him.

At the porch stairs, Pops's gravelly voice stopped him.

"You'll be hearing from my granddaughter later about your high-handedness." Pops tipped back in his rocking chair and eyed Ethan from beneath the rim of his faded cowboy hat.

Frank Gardner came around the side of the building, stepped onto the porch and dropped onto one of the milk can stools. He wiped his forehead and looked between Ethan and Pops. "What did I miss?"

"Grace's Ethan tried to order Gracie around." Pops grinned.

He wasn't Grace's Ethan. He didn't want to be hers. "We're in a mess financially at the ranch," Ethan admitted and walked closer to Pops's chessboard. "We really need her help."

And Ethan really needed to figure out what to tell Frank about the baby. When to tell Frank. Now hardly seemed appropriate when he couldn't even figure out his own thoughts about being a father.

"Everybody needs Gracie," Pops said. "That girl is indispensable."

Pops made Grace sound like a reliable pocketknife. But she was way more than that. Pocketknives got tossed in glove boxes, toolboxes and junk drawers and were only discovered later by accident during a search for something else. Grace was more precious, deserving kindness and care.

Ethan picked up the black knight and moved it toward the center of the board.

Pops sat forward, set his hands on his knees. There was both censure and excitement in his tone. "That was an unexpected move."

So was learning he was going to be a father. Ethan crossed his arms over his chest and smiled at the board, satisfied he could still make at least one good decision. "Can't argue with it."

Frank laughed. "But he wants to."

To his delight, Ethan realized he could see into the store

and watch Grace. She might have something to say about his so-called high-handedness, but he was starting to have plenty to say about her sprinting around the store like a blackbuck antelope. He decided right there that the stubborn woman would rest that evening, even if he had to rope tie her to the chair in Big E's office.

Brewster's front door swung open and Randy Frye, Falcon Creek's lumberjack of a postman, stepped onto the porch, several cookies staked on his open palm. He brushed cookie crumbs off his US Postal uniform shirt and grinned at Ethan. "Sorry, Ethan, you'll have to go inside if you want one of Mrs. Gardner's warm double chocolate chip cookies."

Pops rubbed his hands together and accepted a cookie from Randy.

"Although I do have something for you, Ethan." Randy rummaged through the mail bag hanging from his shoulder. "It's a certified letter. If you sign now, it'll save me a trip to the ranch later."

Ethan signed for the letter and opened it. His gaze stuck on the words: *Notice of Default* in bold red on the top of the page. He dropped onto the milk can stool next to the chessboard and scanned the letter from Billings Bank and Trust.

"Big E must be having a grand adventure," Randy said. "Never known him to leave the ranch for longer than a week or two."

More like a grand escape. Payments on a credit line in Elias's and Zoe's names were three months behind. The bank granted them thirty days to correct the delinquent account or they'd collect the agreed upon collateral. Ethan thought Zoe's renovations had been extravagant; he hadn't expected quite how much. Had Big E left to avoid the cash crisis at the Blackwell Ranch? But his grandfather had never been a quitter. *Never.* Ethan folded the letter and stuffed it into his back pocket. One crisis at a time. "How old are your boys now, Randy?"

"Just turned twelve last month and almost as tall as me." Randy scratched his thick beard, as if he couldn't quite accept the changes in his world.

"Then they aren't quite ready for ranch work yet." Ethan picked up a pawn and smoothed the disappointment out of his voice. "Too bad. We could really use the extra hands."

"Give them a few years to stop tripping over their own feet and they're all yours." Randy adjusted his mail bag. "I can't be much help with ranch hands, Ethan. But the Pierces could sure use a second opinion on their pregnant mare."

"I'm not licensed to practice in Falcon Creek," Ethan said.

Randy blinked, slow and steady, seeming unmoved by Ethan's curt tone. "The Pierce family have been my neighbors for more than two decades."

As if that explained everything. And Ethan's lack of a license wasn't an issue.

"The Pierce family are real good folks." Pops studied the chessboard.

As if that was all that mattered in Falcon Creek. As if Ethan didn't fully understand the neighbor protocol in Falcon Creek. But Ethan had left home years ago and not looked back. He hadn't returned to reconnect with Falcon Creek and its residents, apart from Sarah Ashley's wedding. He'd promised his brother one month. The town had to understand that too.

"Time for me to finish my route." Randy walked down the steps and called over his shoulder. "I'll tell Mr. Pierce to call you, Ethan."

Why didn't anyone seem to care that he wasn't licensed to practice in Montana? Ethan clenched his teeth together. The Pierce family could call. Didn't mean he had to answer. He vowed not to accept another call from a Falcon Creek resident about their pets or livestock.

Right now, he'd stick to the safest and easiest discussion he could have with Frank Gardner. "Frank, do you have any other leads on ranch hands?"

Frank rubbed his chin. "Art Mason has a cousin."

Pops grunted. "That boy couldn't plow through an open field. What about Len Landry's stepbrother?"

Frank shook his head. "Heard that boy spent too much time with his girlfriend in the loft at the Double T, rather than herding the cattle."

Pops slapped his knee. "From Mary-Sue's growing belly, I'd think the boy would be working any job he could get. Gotta have money to support a baby."

"He doesn't seem all that inclined to find a job." Frank frowned.

Ethan ran his hands over his legs, pushing the dread out of his muscles. He lacked the money but not the inclination to work. He wanted to support his child. Yet he'd tumbled into a money pit and would need everything he had to crawl out. And the problem was: he wasn't sure if he'd landed at the bottom yet.

A failed credit check and mounting debt kept blocking his entrance into established veterinary practices. He couldn't accept that. Couldn't give up. Surely, he could convince someone to let him into their practice. He had to succeed, for more than himself now. "I'm not sure how long we can keep the ranch running without help."

Yet, putting the Blackwell Ranch on the fast track to sell required money they didn't have and suitable ranch hands, which weren't available. And now Billings Bank and Trust threatened to collect and auction off the livestock Big E had put up for collateral if they didn't right their account in thirty days. He had to tell Grace, yet now wasn't the right time. Ethan stretched his legs as if warming up his muscles to join some phantom game.

"There are more apples in this town than rotten cores."

Frank gripped Ethan's shoulder like a football coach encouraging his star running back after a fumble. "I'll put out some feelers for responsible kids who want to work. Do you have an age requirement?"

Ethan relaxed, appreciating the older men's support. He only hoped he could keep it when the truth about Grace came out. "At this point, if they're capable and want to learn, we'll take them. Katie can train anyone."

Pops rattled off several family names with high schoolers. The last name got cut off by the rumble of a large truck skidding to a halt in the gravel parking lot. A shout for Ethan Blackwell echoed over the idling engine.

Ethan rose and squinted at the red truck with deep tinted windows. The driver scrambled down and raced around the oversize truck, shouting Ethan's name again.

"What's gotten into Gordon Combs?" Pops stopped his rocking chair. Concern framed the downturn of his mouth and the slow shake of his head. "Never seen that kid move faster than a rock."

Ethan jumped down the stairs. He hadn't seen Gordon since they'd played their final football game senior year. "Gordy?"

"Luck is with me today. Can't believe I saw you up there." The relief in Gordy's wide gaze faded. Terror made him miss the truck handle before he yanked open the back door. "You gotta save them, Ethan. Tell me you can save them."

Ethan stepped aside, trying not to look at the furry dogs in the back seat. Trying not to think about their possible injuries. Trying to sink his impulse to help deep inside the money pit. His patients were supposed to be one thousand pounds and fifteen hands tall, not seventy pounds and barely over knee height.

Not to mention the fines he could face for practicing without a license. The veterinary board would consider his neighborly house calls earlier in the week much more than friendly advice over coffee. There was so much risk. "I'm not practicing as a..."

Gordy cut him off. "You graduated. Passed the tests. Mom calls you Dr. Blackwell now."

"Dr. Terry is around the corner." Ethan turned his baseball cap backward to look into his friend's eyes. To convince Gordy and himself that he couldn't get involved. He'd only just vowed not to help a Falcon Creek resident with a pet problem. The best he could offer Gordy was Dr. Terry one block away.

Norman Terry had been the local vet since before Ethan's birth. Ethan had brought him a sick turtle he'd found on the side of the road in fourth grade. Dr. Terry had told him to stop stealing wild animals and return it to the creek to die in peace. Ethan didn't want to be accused of poaching on Norman's clients. Not to mention, Ethan wasn't looking for patients in Falcon Creek.

"Terry is closed for extended lunches now." Gordy grabbed Ethan's shoulders and hung on as if Ethan was his last thread. "I'm still waiting on a callback. You're my boy, Ethan. I need this."

So many reasons, valid reasons, to say no. To walk away. No one could blame him for protecting his career. Protecting his future. Gordy would understand. This wasn't the kickball field with bases loaded. This was his professional life.

Gordy released Ethan and shifted, giving Ethan a direct view into the cab of the truck. Ethan cursed softly. This might be his life. But there were two other lives at stake. Two other lives in need. He'd been trained not to walk away. Trained to save.

He stepped around Gordy and assessed, not as a detached onlooker, not as Gordy's longtime friend, but as the veterinarian eight years of schooling had taught him to be and a lifetime of rescuing animals had instilled in him.

An adult golden retriever dog and cream-colored puppy lay stretched out across a blanket. Puncture marks bled from the puppy's swollen muzzle. More puncture marks on the adult's paw and muzzle oozed. Too much swelling on both animals. Their breaths too rapid.

Ethan mentally listed the items he'd been adding to his medical bag for the animals at the ranch. He'd just added antivenom shots, having only limited antibiotics.

He leaned slightly into the cab, noticed the drool on the blanket covering the bench seat. He reached out, palm first. A deep growl proceeded the snap from the adult. Even in pain, the dog protected the young.

"None of the other puppies survived their birth. She won't let me touch this one. Pit viper attacked the puppy, momma tried to help. Both got bit more than once." Gordy paced, yanked on his red hair. "Ethan, I got three girls now. They can't lose their dogs. My youngest, Rosie, she named…"

Gordy's voice dropped away. Ethan held his breath. He had a niece named Rosie—his youngest brother Chance's daughter. And Jon had twin girls. What if these were his nieces' dogs? How could he break a little girl's heart?

Frank stepped up to Gordon. "Come on, son, let Ethan treat the dogs."

Gordy stepped away with Frank and Grace moved in beside Ethan. "What can I do?"

She could go sit down. Later. Right now, he needed help and he needed it fast. "We have to get the puppy out of there." Ethan glanced over Grace's head and called out to his friend, his voice stern and commanding to break through Gordy's panic. "Gordon, what are their names?"

"Lucky." Gordy's voice shook along with the hand he

used to wipe across his mouth. "The momma is Sunshine. Rosie named 'em."

"Frank, I've got a supply bag in the back of my truck." Ethan tossed his keys at Grace's father and looked at Grace. Would she forgive him for putting his career in jeopardy? He'd apologize another time. "You have a quiet place inside where I can treat them?"

"My office." Grace never hesitated, never second-guessed her decision.

Ethan nodded, finding even more strength in her composure. "Lucky first. But we have to convince Sunshine to give her to us." Sunshine bared her teeth at Ethan's approach, her growl deep and guttural and pain induced. Had he not already decided to help, Sunshine's suffering would've moved him into swift action. He'd always ached for an injured animal, no matter the size or the kind. Now the dog's distress squeezed the breath inside him.

Grace edged in front of Ethan before he could stop her and cooed at the sick, scared dog. Sunshine's teeth slowly disappeared with each gentle sound. Grace extended her hand, let Sunshine sniff her palm, all the while talking to the dog about needing to treat Lucky and convincing the mother she wouldn't be far from her baby.

Grace moved in front of Ethan, blocking him from Sunshine's view completely. Finally, she turned, her eyes round with surprise and triumph, Lucky cradled in her embrace.

Ethan's breath released. Apparently, mothers understood each other. "Let me get Sunshine. We'll walk inside together. Don't move out of Sunshine's eyesight."

Grace waited while Ethan embraced the dog, keeping her within view of her puppy, and tried to mimic Grace's earlier cooing.

Pops held open the door and Sarah Ashley raced to clear Grace's desk for their unscheduled patients. Frank followed and set Ethan's medical kit, which was more toolbox style than black bag, on the metal folding chair. Alice brought blankets and clean cloths.

Antivenom shots located and pain medication given, Ethan treated the dogs' wounds with Grace's assistance.

Irritation once again climbed through Ethan. Grace was pregnant and needed to relax. To rest. Not tote around and help care for injured puppies. Ethan stroked his hand down Sunshine's neck and said, "Looks like I'm having one of these too. I won't hurt your little one, I promise."

Sunshine licked his palm as if to tell him everything was going to be all right. "I appreciate the vote of confidence. Your puppy, I can definitely help." As for his own child, what did he know about being a father? Being a dad? Big E wasn't exactly the example he wanted to mimic. The my-way-or-the-highway approach Big E preferred had never sat well with Ethan. Animals, he understood. Little, tiny babies. Not so much. And what if he had a girl? He knew nothing about bows and braids and butterfly kisses.

He did know veterinary medicine. Knew how to heal sick animals. Ethan focused on the puppy and what he was good at. Everything else he'd deal with later.

Gordy peeked into the office with Alice beside him. Gordy looked anywhere but at the dogs. "Tell me they're good, Ethan, please. I haven't been able to answer the calls from home."

"They're going to be good." Ethan adjusted Lucky's IV line. "But, Gordy, they need twenty-four-hour care with IV antibiotics."

Alice grinned and patted Gordy's arm. "We set up a kennel area for the dogs at Pops's place for the night. I already had everything from the fosters I've taken in over the past few years."

Ethan massaged the back of his neck, relieved the dogs wouldn't need to be moved up to the Blackwell Ranch. He'd worried about the bumpy drive. Though he'd imposed on the Gardner family too much already. If he stayed around the Gardners much longer, he was bound to blurt out that Grace was pregnant. If only in an effort to ensure Grace got some well-deserved rest. Yet Grace and he hadn't even decided how or when they'd tell Alice and Frank.

"You aren't going to change my mind." Pops pointed at Ethan. "I don't sleep well these days. The dogs will give me something to do tonight."

The dogs would give Ethan something to do tonight as well besides running through more possible places where Big E might've stashed extra money. Or corralling his panic over his bleak list of job prospects. Or dissecting all the ways he might fail as a father. Sunset was still hours away and yet Ethan's evening already seemed endless.

"I'm making beef Stroganoff for dinner." Alice adjusted the blanket around Sunshine, gathered the soiled towels and emptied the trash can into a garbage bag she'd pulled from the shelf all within the short pause between sentences. "Ethan, you can stay for dinner and watch over the dogs until you need to head home."

Grace obviously grew from the same family tree branch as her mother. Neither one seemed capable of shifting into a slow gear.

Frank's voice drifted from the hallway, although Ethan couldn't see him. "Pops has a couch Ethan could sleep on, if he doesn't want to leave the dogs."

"I'm capable of caring for two dogs." The surly catch in Pops's voice matched his deep frown. "I've seen the births of more calves and foals than all of you combined."

Grace took the garbage bag from her mom, tied it and thrust it at Gordy, who shrugged and wormed his way out into the hall. Grace said, "Mom, I'm supposed to do the books up at the Blackwell Ranch tonight."

"That's fine, dear." Alice produced a cloth from her

apron pocket and wiped down the desk. "You two eat with us, then head to the ranch. Ethan can drive you back here, and check on the dogs one more time before Pops takes over as the night nurse."

Grace set her hand on her forehead. "What did you say we were having for dinner?"

"Beef Stroganoff." Alice swung around with a wide smile for Grace. "Your favorite."

Ethan saw Grace's cheeks pale and pull in like an over-juiced lemon. "Can we take it to go, Alice? We can have a working dinner at the Blackwell Ranch and I can get Grace home faster."

"I'll get everything ready." Alice tugged on Gordy's arm. "Come along, Gordon, you need to call your family. I have some butterscotch cookies you can bring to the girls."

The office and hallway cleared out, leaving him free of further distractions and diversions. Even the dogs rested quietly on their beds that Ethan had put together, content to let him wade through the sudden awkwardness alone.

He hadn't been this unsure since the time his teenage brothers had encouraged, or rather dared, him to ride the thousand-pound bull, Buckeye, at the Falcon County rodeo. Did he press Grace to sit down and rest? It was her office. An invitation from him to sit wasn't necessary.

Did he ask how she felt? Did he ask her if she needed anything, like water? More mints? He needed several peppermints to calm his own restless stomach. He'd been around pregnant animals of every breed. Delivered numerous foals, calves and a dozen piglets from a sow more than once. But a pregnant woman?

He watched her gather a stack of papers that had been knocked to the floor in the rush to make an exam table for the dogs. She avoided approaching the desk. Thinking the self-reliant Grace Gardner might be struggling too made him smile. He waited.

Every stray paper picked up, Grace stood, her gaze skipping off the floor-to-ceiling shelves. "Thanks for the save with dinner."

"Figured you might want more soup instead up at the ranch." Ethan bent down, spread his fingers into Sunshine's fur, feeling the dog's steady, even breaths. And steadied his own breathing. She was the steady Grace he'd known since grade school. The reliable middle Gardner sister. The mother of his child. He cleared his throat. "Sorry about your office."

"I'm just glad you were here to treat the dogs." Grace waved the papers she held, but seemed confused about where to put them. Even more confused about what she was saying. "By the time Dr. Terry finished his third apple turnover from Maple Bear Bakery, the dogs would've been in critical condition."

Ethan's eyebrows lifted. When he had a chance to be alone with Grace, the last thing he wanted to talk about was the elderly vet. Of course, he hadn't figured out what to say about the baby. Perhaps he'd stick with the safe topic too. "Dr. Terry has always been a good vet." If not the most amicable person.

"That's been an ongoing debate the past few years." Grace waved her hand about her as if she needed more air in the cramped office. "I believe there's a pool over at Misty Whistle Coffee House for the month and year of Dr. Terry's retirement. Winner gets free coffee and dessert for a year."

That wasn't a bet Ethan would be placing. He didn't want to risk becoming connected to Dr. Terry's retirement debate. He certainly didn't want to look like he might be interested in replacing a town staple like Dr. Norman Terry. That was the very last thing he wanted anyone to think, especially Grace.

He'd treated Sunshine and Lucky for his longtime friend

and football teammate. Nothing more. Setting up shop in
Falcon Creek meant breaking a promise to himself. And
like that, their conversation no longer seemed safe. "Can
you help me carry the dogs over to Pops's place? I need to
get more antibiotics in Livingston."

"Sure." Grace stuffed the papers she held between two
bags of feed on the middle shelf as if she'd always filed
financial reports among the inventory. "I'll just drive up
to the ranch later."

Ethan stroked Sunshine's neck and whispered an apology for disturbing her. "That might be good. I'm not sure
how long it'll take me to get back from Livingston." Or
to think of what he wanted to say to her about the baby.

"What about South Corner?" Grace adjusted the blanket around Lucky.

"They can't get the medicine until later tomorrow afternoon. I missed their deadline for deliveries by an hour."
As if he needed another con for living in a small town:
the lack of readily available supplies. Life moved slowly
and access to the latest of anything was always delayed.
Sometimes the delay extended until the latest version had
already been replaced by something newer, faster, sleeker.
Had he been in the city, he'd have had the medicine he required within the hour, if not sooner.

Grace cradled Lucky in her arms like an infant. She'd
even secured the IV bag in her grip as if she'd transported
ill little ones all the time. He lifted Sunshine into his arms
and rose, leaving the small office and his indecisions behind.

CHAPTER EIGHT

GRACE SORTED THROUGH the paperwork that had been scattered on the floor during the rush to get Sunshine and Lucky treated. Ethan had been calm and composed. Grace, at first, had felt frantic for the dogs, unable to stop wanting to order Ethan to take away their pain faster.

He'd worked around Grace when she'd refused to move from Sunshine's side, never complaining or insisting she leave. Her family had called her away enough. Once Grace had wrangled her distress, she'd managed to help Ethan, handing him the correct things from his bag as he called out for them. They'd made a good team. Same as they had when preparing the rooms in the guest lodge.

Grace slammed her file drawer closed. She already had a team: her and the baby. She'd never considered Ethan a part of it because if she did, she'd want other things. Impossible things like the kind of love fairy tales promised. Things that Grace knew better than to wish for.

Sarah Ashley strolled into Grace's office and shut the door. "I tried to keep the parents away while you helped Ethan. But, as usual, they only wanted your assistance."

Seriously? Sarah Ashley couldn't decide that she wanted to be involved in the store less than two weeks ago and expect everyone to believe her. Even if she did wear a Brewster's polo shirt and matching name tag. "Is there another problem with the inventory you entered today?"

Sarah Ashley perched on the edge of the folding metal chair and surveyed the tiny space. "You wouldn't know two dogs had bled on these floors and all over the desk."

"That is the wonder of bleach and quality paper towels." Grace shuffled papers from one side of her desk to the other, waiting for her sister to get to the reason for her impromptu drop-in.

"Your abilities really don't know any limits, do they?" Sarah Ashley sat back and studied Grace. "You are Mom and Dad's left and right hands, a wizard with all things accounting, a competent vet tech and my ex-boyfriend's confidante."

Her sister forgot the mother of her ex's unborn child. Grace rolled her chair away from the desk, looking anywhere but at her sister as if she was back in elementary school and praying her teacher wouldn't call on her to show the class how to solve the math equation again.

"He won't love you," Sarah Ashley said.

"Who?" Grace already knew because wishes on shooting stars didn't come true. Leprechauns and pots of gold weren't waiting at the end of rainbows. Men fell in love with Sarah Ashley, not Grace. She shoved more papers into the drawer.

She locked her gaze on Grace. "Ethan Blackwell."

Grace took off her glasses and rubbed her eyes. "You're telling me this why?"

"You need to know." Sarah Ashley grabbed Grace's glasses and cleaned the lenses as if she intended to help her sister see more clearly. "Marriage won't be possible with him either."

Grace snatched back her glasses. She saw things just fine, especially when it came to Ethan. Still, her voice snapped as if they were grade-school age and arguing about who got to choose what they played for Family Game Night. "This is all very informative. But if it's all the same to you, I'll leave marriages and husbands in your hands."

"Like I need another husband." Her sister grimaced as if Grace had suggested white after Labor Day was no longer a thing. "One is proving more than enough."

Grace tipped her chin up and pushed her glasses into place. "I don't need a husband either."

Sarah Ashley's expression seemed confused. "You don't want to get married?"

"You always wanted to be the bride, not me." Since they'd been kids Sarah Ashley had fantasized about her wedding. She'd spent her allowance on bridal magazines in high school and changed her mind about bridesmaids weekly. Grace had gotten her sister's vision: the fairy-tale setting, the princess wedding gown, the flower crown, she'd just never envisioned it for herself. If she did, then she'd have to believe in love. She'd have to believe someone could love her with all his heart. Life had proven otherwise. And Grace would rather be alone than be second choice.

"If you don't want all that, then what do you want?" her sister asked.

She wanted to stop talking about love and marriage and impossible dreams. She wanted to stop talking about falling for Ethan. Not that they'd started that conversation, but she was certain her sister would have multiple reasons Grace couldn't be in love with Ethan. "I want my own business."

Grace cringed. She'd traded one secret to keep another safe for a little while longer. No one except Ethan knew about her work goals.

Sarah Ashley lifted her hand to keep Grace from pulling back her confession.

Her sister's pageant-wide smile, the one she used when she knew she'd gained the upper hand and further secured princess status, told her everything.

"I cannot believe you're going to abandon Mom and Dad." Sarah Ashley shook her head. "And leave the store to start your own firm as if the family business wasn't good enough for you."

"I'm not abandoning Mom or Dad, or the store," Grace clarified. "I intend to do both."

"Even you, with your cape and superpowers, cannot work two full-time jobs. And let's not forget the baby you won't admit to. Being a mother is a full-time job by itself."

"And you know that because you've had... Oh, that's right. You don't have children." Grace lashed out, tired of her sister's continuous list of noes: no, Ethan won't love you. No, you can't handle your own business.

Sarah Ashley lowered her shoulders and lifted her chin. "I have a husband and can start a family anytime I choose."

"No, you can't, Sarah Ashley." Grace relished the chance to say no to her sister. "You can't have a child, Sarah Ashley, because you can't put anyone else first. You're too selfish."

Her sister drew back and winced. Just the smallest flinch around her eyes as if someone had blown dust into them. Grace knew she'd hit her mark.

And just like that, the satisfaction dissolved. "Sarah Ashley, I'm so..."

Her sister jumped up and smoothed her hands down her Brewster polo shirt as if she were checking for open wounds. "I told you what I did to protect you. To keep you from getting hurt. I may not always have the perfect words, but I come from a place of love. Sisters help each other."

Or in Grace's case: betray her sister. By sleeping with her sister's ex and then having his child. Worse, Grace was the selfish one. She'd didn't regret her night with Ethan. And if given the chance, she'd repeat it. Guilt washed through her like a rainstorm on a parched pasture. "Sarah Ashley, you'll make a good mother."

Her sister walked to the door and left without another word. Grace dropped her head on her desk and wanted to blame Sarah Ashley for goading her. But her sister had only told Grace what she'd already known. Only Grace hadn't wanted to hear any of it. Perhaps she'd needed to hear it. Was better for her sister's bluntness.

She just couldn't say the same for herself. Was Sarah Ashley better off for Grace's cruelty? And how was Grace supposed to make it up to her?

SARAH ASHLEY SHUT her sister's office door and straightened her shoulders. Into the empty hallway, she vowed, "One day, I'll be a great mother."

But until then, Sarah Ashley would just be true to herself. That meant she'd always make sure she had the upper hand and the control. Her sister had given her both with her slipup about wanting her own business.

Sarah Ashley decided to give Grace a break. She'd meant what she had told Grace. Sisters helped each other.

For all her sister's smarts, Grace lacked a backbone. She lacked fight. Sarah Ashley had too much. After all, she hadn't moved home to sit in her bedroom window like some neglected princess, waiting for her Prince Charming to rescue her. No, she'd come home to prove to her husband she was a queen.

Now she'd get Grace to realize whatever she wanted was worth fighting for. That Grace herself was worth fighting for. She'd force Grace's inner queen out and teach her what it meant to conquer her world. That's what a good fellow queen would do.

Sarah Ashley strode toward Brewster's storefront, working on her new strategy in her mind. It was unfortunate that building a kingdom happened one small magisterial step at a time. She'd have liked to already have been crowned.

CHAPTER NINE

GRACE HEADED FOR the storage room turned temporary recovery area for Sunshine and Lucky, since Pops was in session on the porch. She tried to stall another yawn and find a reason, beyond her pregnancy, for the tiredness. But the day held none of the taxing highs and lows like yesterday. Yesterday, she'd shared her secret with Ethan (a relief), rewrote the inventory database (frustrating), lent a hand to save two dogs (rewarding) and hurt her sister's feelings (deflating).

Today, Sarah Ashley managed the cash register without assistance and caused only one minor hiccup over a return. That left Grace time to finish paperwork and answer questions from the steady flow of customers. Working on the floor gave her the chance to catch up on the residents' lives. Connecting with the people of Falcon Creek was one of her favorite parts about the store. She worried about losing that connection when she moved and opened her own business.

She swallowed around the snag in her throat. Building her business was the right thing to do. She'd have to find other ways to keep connected with the town's residents.

She should be happy. This afternoon she'd secured her second new client, bringing her total to four, including the Blackwell Ranch. Grandma Brewster's reminder that slow and steady won the race whispered through her. Every client brought her an inch closer to a firm that could thrive like Brewster's—the business her grandmother had built with passion and hard work, and with Pops always by her side. Grace might not have a partner beside her, but she had the passion and drive. That would be enough.

Grace stopped in the entryway to the storage room, her

breath lodged against a snag in her throat. Ethan sat on the floor, Lucky stretched across his lap and Sunshine's head propped against his leg. He stroked the dogs, gentle and easy, as if he had all the time in the world and no place he'd rather be.

There was something about him too. Something she couldn't quite define, but that pulled her to him and made her wish... Grace grabbed a mint from the package in her tote bag and reminded herself she wasn't tossing a quarter into a wishing well. And giving voice to any impossible wishes. To do so would be dangerous. "The dogs look like they're going to make a full recovery."

"They'll be fine." Ethan fluffed the blankets beside him, shifted Lucky onto the soft pile and adjusted the bedding around the sleeping puppy.

Would he do the same for a restless newborn? Rock the baby to sleep and tuck him or her back into bed. Or would he be content to hold a baby for the whole night? Grace squeezed the candy in her hand. She really needed to learn Ethan's intentions when it came to their child, in case she had to make adjustments, like for him not being here and locking down her heart permanently.

One last rub across Sunshine's back and he stood up. "Ready to head to the ranch? I'm starving. Your mom already stashed a Crock-Pot of beef burgundy in my truck. It smells like our kitchen used to when my mom cooked. Inviting and delicious."

Grace wrinkled her nose and unwrapped her mint. "It's all yours."

Ethan joined her in the hallway and grinned. "You're addicted to that chicken noodle soup we have at the house, aren't you?"

"Not quite." If she wasn't careful, she'd become addicted to him and the glint in his gaze. Grace tossed the mint into her mouth, interrupting the misstep in her thoughts. She wasn't addicted to Ethan, only his soup. She considered driving straight home. Better to call it a night before her sleep-deprived mind completely derailed her.

Ethan pressed his hand against her lower back and guided her out to the parking lot. One small move toward him and she'd be tucked fully into his side. There was something reassuring and capable about Ethan. If she rested her head on his shoulder, would he watch over her? Not that she wanted that kind of undivided attention. She just wanted to take a quick power nap. Or maybe an extended nap that lasted until morning. But not in his bed. In her own bed, in her own room.

Grace inhaled the brisk evening air desperate to find her focus. Settling on something that wouldn't encourage her to edge closer to Ethan, she said, "Dr. Lancaster was in the store earlier. He put the stitches in your head after you collided with Gordy during a touch football game in high school. I remember Sarah Ashley coming home and crying about the mess your face was when she dropped you off at Dr. Lancaster's office. Well, I promised him I'd ask you to check his macaw, Peabody."

"No." His voice was rigid, uncompromising. So very different from the gentle, compassionate man in the storage room only moments ago.

Surprised at his swift denial, Grace stopped beside Ethan's truck and rounded on him. His hand no longer lingered on her back, but the warmth of his touch remained. She searched his gaze for that same warmth. Only a cool hardness stared back at her. "But you have to."

"Why?" He stood, feet braced apart, arms crossed over his chest. The rays of the setting sun framed him in shadows that lengthened the distance between them.

How could he be so unkind to the people he'd known all his life? The same people who were her friends and customers. The same people she looked after and who looked after her. That was what made Falcon Creek so special. Couldn't he see that? "It's important to take care of the people in your community. That's your job."

His eyes narrowed, his expression never softened, even his shoulders looked rigid. Inflexible.

Grace searched his face for any ounce of weakness. Any way past his resolve. There hadn't been any defenses up, during their one night together. That night, Ethan had confessed he'd had a falling-out with his grandfather during his senior year in high school. Big E had tried to tie his grandson to the Blackwell Ranch and Ethan had resented his grandfather's control. Ethan had accepted his diploma from Principal Hatcher and left Falcon Creek two days later. He hadn't just walked away from his grandfather though, he'd left his childhood home and everyone associated with it. He'd come back now only at his brother's emotional request.

The mint dissolved in her mouth, yet its refreshing sensation never overcame her. Rather, her throat scratched as if she'd swallowed dry sand. Sarah Ashley had been wrong. It didn't matter if Ethan could love her, he was never moving back to Falcon Creek. And she was never leaving. That truth scraped through her and cut her voice into a rasp. "You don't like being home."

"I like being with my brother and nieces." He allowed nothing more. Simply pressed his lips together and waited.

What about her? Did he like being with Grace? She rubbed her arms, smoothing away the chill that had nothing to do with the night's approach. He was having a baby he never wanted. Surely, that was one more con on that side of his Falcon Creek list.

His voice broke through the silence. "I saw a potential office space for your business. You should look at it."

"No." The word burst out as if she'd launched it between them. He'd moved on years ago. She wouldn't be pushed.

"But it's important." His voice was mild. Too chiding. "You have to have the right office to take care of your customers. What about the community and their financial needs?"

Now Grace's focus tightened on Ethan. He was stubborn, but Grace was more than determined. "Ha. You're the only one who can treat Peabody."

"I don't have a license to practice in this state." He eyed her. "About that office space."

Grace tipped her chin up and met his challenge. "I don't have my own business yet."

"You seriously won't go see the place?" he asked. "What if it's the perfect building?"

"What if Dr. Lancaster loses his favorite pet ever?" She pushed. Couldn't stop herself. Had to know that his helping Gordy's dogs wasn't the exception. Had to know if he had any compassion for the town that meant so much to her. Had to know that the people of Falcon Creek weren't so easily forgotten. That she wasn't forgettable.

She persevered. "His wife died last year, so it's just him and Peabody in that big house together. I think people in town make up illnesses just to see Dr. Lancaster to check on him. Every week, my mom cooks dinner for him and I drop it off."

He watched her. Stoic and silent as if unmoved by her rush of words.

Frustration surged. "Dr. Lancaster is Big E's doctor."

"Why is that important?" Surprise and confusion tinged his voice.

"Because he's practically family." Grace always put family first. Always.

But the Blackwell boys had lost so much of theirs. First, their grandmother Dorothy had left their grandfather after a dispute with their daughter. Then the boys' parents had died in a freak accident.

From what she'd heard over the years since, it had been those two events that had started a series of chaotic marriages for Big E. To the man's credit he had taken on the task of raising five young boys. Adults now, almost all of the Blackwell brothers purposely lived thousands of miles apart from each other and their childhood home.

She reached out. Her apology ready. Her fingers brushed against the cold air as Ethan turned away.

"You're probably cold." He opened the truck door and pointed at the passenger seat. "Hop in."

Grace studied him; tension still pulsed around him, but his frown had eased, his gaze had tempered. Seeking the warmth, Grace climbed inside and tracked Ethan's path around the front of the truck. He paused, only a momentary midstep, to lift his gaze toward the mountains. He shook his head. Once. Twice, as if he'd come to a decision.

"Okay, Grace." He slid into the driver's seat and started the engine. "But this is the last house call I make for a pet in town. The last one."

Grace settled back and buckled her seat belt.

"We're driving by that potential office on the way. If you like it, you just have to call Dana Brantley. She's the listing agent."

And one of Grace's friends. She'd had lunch with Dana last week—they'd discussed upcoming horse shows, not rental property. Grace kept silent. She'd already argued for Peabody. That was enough for now.

Five minutes later, Ethan stopped at the curb in front of a single-story house with a For Lease sign staked in the front yard.

"It's a house." Her voice held no more force than a whisper.

"It's a space to live and work in." Eagerness streamed into his tone. "Office in front, home in back. I figure you'll want the baby close while you work."

But it was a *house*. For a family: a couple, two kids and their dog. "It's…"

"You don't like it?" He leaned closer to her and looked out her window as if trying to see the house like she did.

"I was thinking more of a traditional office." And less of a traditional home. This was happening. She was having a baby without a husband. She thought she was ready. Prepared.

But staring at the house with the shutters, perfect porch and a tree tall enough for a swing, doubts surrounded her. Uncertainty suffocated her until all she wanted was for him to press on the gas and speed away. "I'll consider it."

"That's all I ask." Ethan drove on.

Grace pressed her fingertips into her temples, but the pressure refused to push the image of the charming family home out of her mind. Irritation rolled through her. For that she blamed Ethan and his insistence that she see the property. She hadn't hired him to build her business, or find her an office location. He'd only hired her to fix the Blackwell Ranch's accounting books. She tugged on the zipper of her tote bag. "I'll stay in the truck while you examine Peabody. I want to look into these statements for that second bank account of Big E's."

"I'd like you to come inside." Ethan directed the truck toward Falcon's Nest: a small community of houses that overlooked the river.

"I want to work." Centering her attention on numbers and spreadsheets lessened her panic and made her more certain of herself.

"None of us can get access to that second account." Ethan slowed and turned onto a private, wooded driveway. He hadn't totally forgotten his way around Falcon Creek. There'd been no need for him to ask for directions to Dr. Lancaster's house.

"We need to get access to that account."

"Jon is smart." He navigated a sharp bend in the road. "My brother would've done that already, if it was possible."

She didn't doubt Jon's smarts or his effectiveness. But Jon had been stretched thin running his place and the Blackwell Ranch, along with caring for twins, so maybe an option had slipped by him. Fortunately, Jon had Lydia now. A partner like Pops had had with Grandma Brewster.

Not that Grace needed a partner. She was perfectly fine without one. "If we can't figure out a way to get access to this account, what's your idea to bring in money?"

"Continue searching the ranch for Big E's hidden cash."

"That's ridiculous." Looking like she had more to argue about with him, she waved the bank statement over the console between them. "You're going to waste time tearing up the ranch for some make-believe treasure and you don't even have a map, when this account contains real money?"

"What's ridiculous is Big E going AWOL and abandoning the ranch and his family." Ethan parked and shoved open the old truck door. "What's ridiculous is making a house call for a patient I don't have in a state I'm not licensed in."

Grace scrambled out after him and hurried around the truck to confront him. "Maybe you'll learn something about Big E from Dr. Lancaster."

"Like what?" Ethan grabbed his medical kit from the back of the truck.

Grace followed Ethan to Dr. Lancaster's house with the wide arching double doors. "Like what if Big E switched medication and that is the cause of his erratic behavior."

Ethan was being illogical with his insistence on searching for money on the ranch. Was that a Blackwell family trait? She hoped the baby didn't inherit that particular strand of Blackwell DNA.

Dr. Lancaster opened the door before Ethan could knock. Too late, Grace realized she'd said she'd stay in the truck and work.

Ethan smirked and motioned her inside. She wanted to kick him in his illogical backside. Fine, she'd let him continue his childish treasure hunt and she'd be the adult. She'd figure out how to access the account herself. Stubborn man. That was another Blackwell trait that could stay on his side of the family tree.

"I knew you'd get Ethan to come by." Dr. Lancaster hugged Grace and then shook Ethan's hand. "Everyone in town says if you want something done, you just ask Grace Gardner. She's the most reliable person in Falcon Creek, not just at Brewster's."

Grace smiled at Dr. Lancaster's praise. She hadn't lied to Ethan earlier. The people of Falcon Creek were a part of her extended family. She liked helping each one. She stepped into the foyer that granted a peek at the river view from the family room in front of her. "Dr. Lancaster, every time I come here, I find something about your remodel that I didn't see before. The wrought iron railing leading upstairs is lovely. Did you get design tips from Zoe Petit? She did quite a bit of remodeling herself."

Ethan frowned, looking like he wished she'd remained in the truck. She knew the feeling. But she was going to do what he refused. One of them had to ask about Big E.

"Of course, you used a much more subtle color palette." She widened her smile. "I'm sure if you've made any house calls out to the Blackwell Ranch you saw Zoe's bolder choices."

"Elias always prefers to meet with me at my office." Dr. Lancaster led them through a comfortable family room—the kind that encouraged a guest to have a seat and put their feet up. "Fortunately, we finished the remodel before my wife became ill. She got to enjoy the view for a little while."

"It's quaint and peaceful." And despite Dr. Lancaster's continued pain, his home was inviting and welcoming. Grace ached for him and his late wife. The Lancasters had been married for over forty years. Would she avoid falling in love and possibly suffering like Dr. Lancaster?

Dr. Lancaster led them toward a pair of closed French doors. "Zoe did show me pictures of their home renovations on her phone when they argued about Elias's need for tinted designer indoor glasses."

Ethan coughed and switched his medical kit into his other hand. Grace heard his laughter though, and struggled to conceal her own.

"Those May-December romances can be challenging. It's good Elias and Zoe have found the means to weather their challenges." Dr. Lancaster reached for the door handle. "Elias would most likely forget his medicine without Zoe there."

Grace stared at Ethan, trying to tell him with her wide eyes that she'd created the perfect opening. All he had to do was ask about Big E and his medications. He was Big E's grandson—surely he had a right to inquire.

Ethan scowled at her.

This was important. Every avenue had to be followed. Didn't he understand how much trouble the ranch was in? "Has Elias recently changed medicines?"

Dr. Lancaster smiled fondly. "You know I can't talk about my patients' records."

"We're just worried about Elias. We're searching for any clue about his latest road trip. He's been gone longer than usual."

"I'm afraid I can't be of much help." Dr. Lancaster opened the French doors and glanced over his shoulder. "But when you talk to the pair, they both have medications coming up for refill. Important medications."

"We'll pass that along when we speak to them. Eventually." Ethan ushered Grace forward.

Dr. Lancaster looked between them, his smile softening into the wrinkles around his eyes. "You two have a nice sensible age difference. You won't face the continuous challenges of a May-December romance like Elias and Zoe."

Ethan coughed.

Grace opened her mouth to correct the doctor's impression, but Ethan spoke first. "We're here to treat Peabody, not bother you about Zoe and Big E, who've been defying the odds for a while now."

Grace stiffened. She wasn't bothering Dr. Lancaster. She was trying to get information from the kind doctor. About Big E, who wasn't even her grandfather. For a stubborn man who wasn't...hers. "I'll step outside."

Ethan tugged Grace farther into the room. "I might need your assistance."

"It's wonderful to have an assistant you can trust." Dr. Lancaster grinned. "My two nurses keep my practice running."

Grace stepped back, but Ethan's hand at the small of her back prevented a full retreat. Something about Ethan needing her did stick with her, but she wasn't analyzing that now, or perhaps ever. She shook her head. Ethan didn't need her help with animals any more than she required his assistance with a balance sheet. He had to be up to something. "I'm not trained in animal care."

"But Grace has such a wonderful manner with pets. You just need to ask Gordy Combs. Grace helped me with his injured dogs yesterday." Ethan's tone was pleasant. Too pleasant. Too friendly. "And this is simply a courtesy house call to a longtime friend and our family doctor."

"You two seem to have everything under control." Dr. Lancaster waved a cell phone at them. "If you don't mind, I'm going to return a few of my own patient calls. Peabody has been sneezing a lot the last few days and not talking."

"We'll find you if we need anything." Ethan closed the office doors behind Dr. Lancaster.

"What are you doing?"

"Evaluating Peabody." Ethan walked over to the plati-
num bird cage with a dome top that reached above Ethan's
head and peered inside. A blue-and-gold parrot sneezed
quite loudly. "Sorry you're feeling bad, Peabody."

"You don't need me," Grace repeated, both for her and
Ethan's benefit.

"Sure, I do." Ethan opened the door to the Victorian-
style cage and turned toward Grace. He tossed his cell
phone at her. "Can you answer that if it rings, please?"

Grace caught his phone. "Why?"

"I transferred the Blackwell Ranch phones to my cell."
He eyed Peabody. The parrot approached the opening,
peeking his head out, but then retreating. "We don't want
to miss any possible reservation calls for the guesthouse."

"You could've left your phone with me in the truck."

"But how am I supposed to treat Peabody and search
Dr. Lancaster's office at the same time?" he asked.

"This office isn't part of your treasure hunt." Grace put
her hands on her hips.

"I hadn't considered Big E stashing money with a
friend." Surprise shifted into Ethan's voice and then he
shook his head. "Never mind. Big E doesn't trust anyone
that much."

"I'm not searching this office." Grace forced a hard edge
into her whisper. She knew she should've stayed with the
truck. Or better yet, stayed at Brewster's.

"We need Big E's patient folder." Ethan waved his hand
toward the desk and multiple file drawers in the built-in
floor-to-ceiling shelves. "To check my grandfather's list
of medications."

That he liked her suggestion that Big E might've
changed medications pleased her. However, his method
to discover whether or not it was true doused that pleasure
with a wave of annoyance. "That's illegal."

"So is treating poor Peabody without a license." Ethan

sat on the floor and coaxed the pretty parrot out of its cage. The large bird stepped onto a perch Ethan had placed beside him.

Sweet words and a little cooing wasn't going to coax Grace to search Dr. Lancaster's office. "You're saving a life."

"You might be too, depending on what's in Big E's file." Ethan kept his attention on the bird.

That was so not fair. How was she supposed to debate him now? What if there was something in Big E's file that could give them an idea of what was going on? She crossed her arms over her chest and glared at Ethan. He was making her a lawbreaker. Another ding against him. What was going to happen to the baby with two felonious parents? Heaven help her, Ethan scrambled her thoughts, making her as illogical as him. "One drawer. I will look in one drawer."

"Fine. I'll check one thing on Peabody. Where should I start? His eyes? Feathers?" Ethan shifted his gaze to her. Beside him, Peabody sneezed. "That's one thing right there."

He really didn't play fair. She always played fair. Always followed the rules. Except for once, and look where that had gotten her: pregnant and alone. Her irritation caused her to raise her voice. "Do a full exam. I'll peek around over here."

"Careful, Grace. You might find you enjoy breaking the rules."

The lightness and soft laughter in his voice wound through her, brushing away her annoyance. There, on the floor, was the caring man she'd spent a magical night with. When he was like this, relaxed and unguarded, he threatened more than her common sense. Grace escaped behind the desk. "This is a onetime offense."

His phone vibrated against her palm. Grace answered on the second ring, greeted the caller and added, "No, I'm sorry, Mr. Pierce, Ethan is with a patient right now."

Ethan's gaze narrowed in warning.

Grace wanted to snort and yell, *Payback*. Instead, she let her smile ease into her voice. "Randy was right when he told you to call Ethan about your pregnant mare, Mr. Pierce. He specialized in equestrian medicine in veterinary school. You definitely need to talk to Ethan."

Ethan looked like he wanted to specialize in finding Grace's mute button. But Peabody had finally stepped onto Ethan's arm as if it was a perch.

"Yes, you can count on Ethan calling you. I'll make sure he gets the message." Grace opened the top drawer of Dr. Lancaster's desk and closed it. Pens and a pair of scissors wouldn't offer any patient information. "Say hello to those sweet daughters of yours for me." She ended the call and set Ethan's phone on the desk.

"You owe me for that." Ethan's voice came out in a low rumble.

Grace pulled the handle on another drawer. "That's payback for making me search this office like a criminal."

"I'll get my revenge, Grace."

She didn't doubt it. But for now she was too happy. Ethan had another patient in town and he hadn't refused to return Mr. Pierce's call. That was certainly progress. She closed the bottom drawer and cautioned herself not to read too much into anything.

Soon, Grace sighed and scowled at Ethan. She'd searched Dr. Lancaster's office without his consent and discovered only photo albums and years of tax returns. No patient files or any patient information for that matter. Zip. Zilch. Nothing. She'd broken the rules and hadn't gained a thing. That was Ethan's fault.

Ethan spoke to Dr. Lancaster about the antibiotic prescription he wrote for Peabody and explained the benefits of a humidifier and air filter for the office. He was patient and considerate, answering Dr. Lancaster's questions and offering more advice. No one would've suspected that Ethan hadn't wanted to take the call in the first place. That he hadn't wanted to be there.

Grace almost believed Ethan was a part of the town again. That this was his normal routine—making home visits and giving a little extra to each family under his care.

She jerked her gaze away from Ethan. This wasn't his home anymore. This wasn't their thing.

Peabody walked around the outside of the cage and dragged his toys into a neat pile, comfortable with both Grace and Ethan in his space. Ethan hadn't needed long to earn the parrot's trust—less than five minutes.

She had to admit that she trusted Ethan completely and fully. It made her think of their night together.

That was then. This was now. And now, she couldn't trust her heart around Ethan and the illusion he presented. She'd been trained to look at the facts. Numbers were safe, predictable and difficult to argue with. Her situation with Ethan couldn't be more different. Ethan was going to go wherever his new job would take him, to fix a bank account that was all but depleted, and eventually, he'd meet someone that really suited him. She just hoped he'd try to make room in his life for his child, even if visits and phone calls or texts were sporadic.

Grace needed to move on.

The facts hadn't changed no matter what she had seen of Ethan's temperament and character in Dr. Lancaster's office with the bird, or in Brewster's with Gordy's dogs. Ethan's stay in Falcon Creek was temporary. Even if he called Mr. Pierce back, Ethan had promised no more house calls. No more neighborly visits.

The realization that she and Ethan would never have a future together hurt now. But the pain was nothing compared to a broken heart if they actually tried.

CHAPTER TEN

"ARE YOU HUNGRY?" Ethan stopped his truck in the driveway at the Blackwell Ranch and looked over at Grace.

"I can wait a little while longer. But you were the one starving earlier."

"There's something I want to do before we eat."

"What?" Grace asked.

"Check for something in the old barn." He opened his door, but her hand on his arm stopped him from getting out.

"What's in the old barn?" Her voice tightened along with her grip.

"Besides broken tractors and other farm equipment, we used to put all our favorite toys up in the loft to keep them safe." Thanks to Peabody and his meticulous care with his toys in Dr. Lancaster's office, Ethan had remembered the old barn loft. The brothers had split the large loft into territories and organized the space according to their preferences—ones that changed as the boys grew from playing with toys, to hunting and fishing, to sports and then, finally, to spending time with girls.

Grace squeezed his arm. "Please don't tell me you're going to search the loft for Big E's hidden stash of money."

"It's the perfect place." Ethan jumped out of the truck and strode toward the old barn on the far side of the petting zoo. Grace's muttering behind him tugged his smile free.

"I'm not helping you look." She stepped up beside him and patted the giant tote bag she was hoisting onto her shoulder. "I'm going to get on my laptop and finish preparing the profit-and-loss statement for the ranch. That's what productive people do."

"I'm being productive too." Ethan lengthened his strides. Why hadn't he thought of it before? Big E had always told them that their treasures were much safer up in the loft. Better than in the house where they'd get trampled and broken with all the comings and goings. Ethan suspected Big E simply got tired of stepping barefoot on one too many army men and plastic building blocks. Still, the boys had liked the idea of having an entire barn loft to themselves.

If he did find some money, he could take care of the Notice of Default letter from Billings Bank and Trust without telling Grace. He didn't want to see the disappointment on her face when she read the letter. He didn't want her to tell him it was hopeless. That the ranch couldn't be turned around. That making a profit was impossible.

If the ranch became profitable again and Big E remained AWOL, Ethan wanted to sell for the highest return. That would benefit him and his brothers. If he succeeded, Ben, Tyler and Chance wouldn't need to come home, unless they wanted to. As far as he could tell that was the last thing they were interested in doing.

Katie walked around the steel pen he'd built last week for the goats, Hip at her side.

Ethan wondered why Katie remained at the ranch year after year. True, her father was a staple, has been ever since Ethan and his brothers were kids, but there had to be more to it than that to keep Katie on Blackwell land. Ethan wanted Katie to remain on the ranch for as long as she chose, like he had, until he knew it'd been time to leave.

He had to find that money.

Katie and Hip veered right for him and blocked his path to the old barn. "You need to add more space to the goat pen or I'm driving a certain goat out to the back forty before sunrise tomorrow morning."

A brown-and-white goat sprinted toward Katie. Ethan released his laughter into the night air and grinned at Grace beside him. "Billy has developed a crush on Hip. It's cute and harmless."

"Chasing down that escapee of a goat is time consuming and inconvenient." Katie glared at him. "And would you stop naming every animal in this place? I can't keep up."

"You only need to remember Billy as he's Hip's boyfriend." At Katie's scowl, Ethan tossed her his truck keys. "There's a Crock-Pot full of beef burgundy in my back seat."

Distracted from her goat problem, Katie rubbed her hands together as if she could already taste the delicious meal. "Like with real beef, fresh mushrooms and smoked bacon?"

"All of that and homemade bread." Grace continued the distraction. "It's my great-grandmother's recipe."

"You're lucky I can be bribed with good food." Katie aimed Ethan's truck keys at him and smirked. "I left you an updated fix-it list on the kitchen counter."

"I've been anxious all day to see what you've added to that." Ethan stepped aside to let Katie pass. "I can't wait to get started in the morning."

"I'm sure you can't." Katie shook her head and whistled for Hip.

"Katie," Ethan said. "Don't walk too fast. Billy won't be able to keep up."

Katie muttered something he couldn't hear.

"You're all talk, Katie Montgomery." Ethan laughed as he watched Katie slow until the goat caught up to the pair. He turned and headed toward the barn.

Grace caught up to him. "Can't you re-home that goat?"

"Sure, if I wanted to, but Katie likes Billy." Ethan yanked on the old barn door and paused to look at Grace. At the uncertainty pulling her eyebrows together, he said, "She'll like him, eventually. He's quite entertaining."

There hadn't been an *eventually* required when it came to him liking Grace. He'd liked talking to her in high school when he'd gone into Brewster's and she was working. He'd discovered he'd liked her a lot more at Sarah Ashley's wedding reception and into the evening when he'd learned more about her beyond her quick mind for numbers and love for her family. Now, the more time he spent with her, he worried he could like her too much.

He'd only ever intended to stay in Falcon Creek one month. That was all he'd promised Jon. Surely, real, lasting relationships took longer than that to build. Not that he wanted one of those or even a commitment with Grace. That'd require a part of himself he never intended to give up. They shared a baby together and providing for the baby was his priority.

That meant finding Big E's money in order to bring the credit line current and avoid the bank's seizure of the livestock. Having that happen would ruin their chance of selling the ranch for any kind of profit. If they made money on the sale, Ethan could use his share of the proceeds to pay off his personal debts and restore his credit, and maybe buy into an established veterinary practice. Then he could support his child like a father should.

He flipped on the lights inside the barn, grateful the electric bill had been paid. "I'm heading up to the loft. Make yourself comfortable, unless you want to join me."

"I'm good down here." Grace pulled her tote bag off her shoulder and studied the tractors lined up like an exhibit of farming trends over the decades.

"Just pick one of the new models to sit on," Ethan warned before he climbed up the ladder to the loft.

At the top of the ladder, he glanced back at Grace. She touched the seats on several tractors before climbing onto a newer model, although even that one outdated Ethan by a solid decade. Satisfied rust wasn't holding up the tractor Grace had perched on, Ethan stepped into a time machine.

Here was his childhood. Chance's old guitars with the

strings broken. Tyler's scattered poker chips. And one of Jon's early attempts at creating his own branding iron. Here was his old home preserved up in the loft, far from the reach of Zoe's renovations.

Ethan picked up a deflated football and nudged a baseball with the toe of his boot. It rolled into a stack of well-read comic books—the ones they'd race down to South Corner Drug & Sundries to buy the first day they hit the shelves. Fishing rods leaned against the wall; a tackle box waited under the bench. Dust swirled in the fluorescent light as memories churned through Ethan, one toppling over the other. Ethan touched a deck of playing cards. He'd lost more than once to Tyler at poker and yet he kept agreeing to play whatever card game Tyler challenged him to. Ropes knotted in various styles hung from hooks on the wall, a reminder of Jon's constant roping practice.

Ethan eyed a barrel that they'd all hauled up into the loft with only a rope and determination. It'd served as a jail during cops and robbers. A shield during a pretend shoot-out at the bad guys' corral. And a seat on which to thread bait onto fishing hooks. But was that old barrel a safe for Big E's cash?

He gripped the top of the barrel and worked the warped wood until the cover came off. A pile of cash wasn't resting in the bottom. Disappointment swelled, but stalled as Ethan reached for the item inside. More memories rushed in as Ethan stared at his bow—his favorite Christmas present given to him the year before his parents died. The one he'd carried everywhere from breakfast to dinner to bedtime as if he'd been a real-life Robin Hood, always prepared to defend the weak. He reached for the bow and grabbed the half-dozen arrows next to it. He'd forgotten the endless adventures, and, even more, the endless fun the bow had provided.

He walked to the edge of the loft, notched the arrow

and released it. The arrow flew high over Grace's head and jammed into the far wall. Cheering, he leaned over the railing and grinned down at a frowning Grace. "Amazing. This thing still works."

"Preparing to rob a bank with your bow and arrow?" She shifted her computer on her lap. The vintage tractor seat squeaked as if protesting her lack of enthusiasm.

"Funny." Although robbing a bank was probably faster than scouring the ranch for Big E's money. Unfortunately, the only thing he intended to do at the Billings Bank and Trust was plead for an extension on the payment due date.

He stared at the bow, wondering when exactly life had become so complicated. And wishing he could seize those childhood moments—the ones with the laughter and joy and pure innocence—and live them all over again. If only for a minute. An hour. Just long enough for the panic and the stress to recede. Just long enough to remind himself why it all mattered. "This bow and arrow has proven quite useful on more than one occasion."

"Getting into the other bank account will prove useful." Grace kept her focus on her laptop screen, her fingers tapping the keyboard. "We need to discuss these reports I made. The numbers aren't good."

Just like that, his childhood was rammed right back into the past. Reminiscing wouldn't improve his credit or bulk up his checking account or resuscitate the ranch. He didn't need to look at spreadsheets and profit-and-loss statements, with the emphasis on the *loss* part, to understand the financial trouble the Blackwell Ranch was in. "The numbers will be better when I find Big E's hidden stash of money."

"That money stash is a rumor." Grace glanced at him. Persistence strengthened her voice. "But this second bank account is real and contains actual money, Ethan."

They'd already been over this in his truck earlier. But he

repeated himself anyway. "It's money that I can't access. Jon would've already been in that account if it was possible."

"Well, I've texted Rachel Thompson for advice."

"Rachel Thompson, the owner of the Double T Ranch and Zoe's former best friend." Ethan squeezed the bow and an arrow. Attorneys billed by the hour and at rates often ten times higher than an average ranch hand. He couldn't afford to pay a ranch hand, let alone Rachel, Falcon Creek's resident lawyer. "I'll have better luck with my treasure hunt."

"This isn't high school, and we aren't kids anymore." Grace scowled up at him. "We don't have time to chase after gossip and speculation."

No, it wasn't high school. In high school he hadn't been interested in getting under Grace Gardner's skin. Now, that was all he wanted to do. He liked causing that flare of annoyed determination in her eyes a bit too much, he realized. "I'll leave Rachel to you and continue on my search."

At his exclamation of "No way!" Grace called out, "Tell me you found actual cash."

"No. But I did find Tyler's action figures." Ethan lined the toys on the bench as if readying them for a battle. "And Ben's baseball cards."

"What about money? The green, paper kind?" Grace prodded.

"The only green things up here are the army men." Ethan walked to the railing and tossed one of the soldiers onto Grace's keyboard. "There's also a green fishing rod and tackle box."

"Wait." The snap of her laptop closing bounced up into the loft, along with her excitement. "I know this place." Ethan leaned against the railing and studied her, unsure he'd ever heard Grace shout with such animation. "This barn has been on this land since before Big E was born. You told me about this place."

Grace's gaze moved around the barn as if she was seeing it for the first time.

Something in the way she was speaking made him uneasy. The brothers had never revealed anything that happened in the loft. *Ever.* It was an unspoken rule.

Grace scrambled off the tractor and hurried up the ladder. She popped onto the loft, her boots disturbing the dust. She studied the area as if she'd discovered the map for the treasure hunt. Finally, her gaze settled on the corner bench and she lunged forward, her smile wide. "This is where you used to hide out and read about the mating rituals of domestic and wildlife animals."

Ethan cringed. He'd spilled his own secrets. To Grace. During one unforgettable night. "You remembered that?"

"I remember a lot of things from our night together." Grace knelt and tugged a stack of books from underneath the bench. "I still don't know how you managed to hide these from your brothers."

"Desperate times. Jon told me I was too young and refused to answer my questions. I doubt Jon knew himself. It wasn't a matter of need as much as I wanted to have the information. All the facts, as it were." Ethan reached up, rubbed away the dust from Grace's chin with his thumb. "Clearly, I figured out the mating ritual."

A blush stained her cheeks. Her gaze shifted, yet refused to settle. Ethan curved his hand to cup her face. She sighed. Soft. Quiet. But he knew that sigh. He'd heard it before. Then and now he felt that sigh deep inside his own chest. He tipped her chin up, wanting her focus on him. Wanting to know that she felt something too.

Her green gaze, trapped behind her glasses, locked on his. Her lips parted and he leaned forward, pressed his lips against hers. Let her sigh rattle inside him. Let the feel of her consume him.

He pulled her closer, seeking more. Wanting more.

The books smacked against the floor between them. The moment disrupted.

Grace jumped back, out of his embrace. Her voice came out in a flustered rush. "Sorry."

Not as sorry as he was. Sorry the moment ended too soon. Sorry he'd reached for her in the first place. Sorry for the reminder of how much he liked Grace in his arms. Sorry that the moment would never be repeated. *Could* never be repeated.

Grace knelt on the floor and gathered the books.

"Leave it be." The books were part of his past. Nothing important. And now it seemed he had one more memory he could leave up in the loft: one last kiss with Grace. "It's all old junk up here anyway."

"I'd hardly call these sheets of music old junk." Grace picked up several sheets of paper and thrust them at him. "I doubt Chance would."

Ethan took the papers, glanced at the lyrics and tossed them on the floor.

Grace grabbed the falling sheets of paper as if they were more important than money. "Don't be so careless with your childhood memories."

Careless—he'd been careless when he'd reached for Grace. He blamed the setting and the swirl of childhood memories for making him weak. But nostalgia wasn't part of his DNA and reliving times gone by was a mistake. One he wouldn't make again. "Let's get out of here and eat."

Grace stood, holding Chance's crinkled music sheets in one hand. "I'm sorry Big E's money wasn't up here."

He nodded and stared at the window above her head. The sincerity in her voice was almost too much. That money would help solve one problem, but he wondered how many more problems were lying up ahead. Hiding out in the loft held almost too much appeal. But Big E had always told him that a life lost in the past wasn't a life lived. Yet, now, he wondered what life he wanted to live. Another thing to blame on the loft.

Grace stepped up to him, linked her free hand with his and squeezed. It drew his gaze back to her face. "I'm not going to tell you to stop looking for Big E's money, but I did text you Rachel's number as a backup plan. You never know, maybe she has a suggestion about the second account."

He studied their joined hands, took in the connection as if she'd known he needed to hold on to something. Something real. Something grounding. As if she'd known he'd lost his balance. Feared losing his way.

She tugged on his hand. "Come on. I hear there's beef burgundy and chicken soup waiting."

Ethan climbed down the ladder and waited to make sure Grace made it to the ground safely. He switched off the lights, closed the door on the barn and his past. Silence remained as they crossed the large expanse of lawn and made it onto the back porch of the main house. Each step away from the old barn cleared Ethan's focus.

Grace followed Ethan into the kitchen. "Tell me again why you're living in one of the cabins and not here instead?"

"It's not my home. Hasn't been for a long time." Anything left of his childhood home was back in the barn loft where it belonged.

Ethan heated the chicken soup in the microwave for Grace, and then took out bowls and silverware. He'd have to remember to thank Katie for plugging in the Crock-Pot of beef burgundy and leaving the homemade bread wrapped on the counter.

Grace hung her tote bag on the sleek, modern stool and set her laptop on the island, the chrome paired perfectly with the white marble countertop. Grace fit into the kitchen, the house, more than Ethan.

"It's lovely and professional and updated for a chef. My mom would love it," Grace said.

But it wasn't the kitchen where his mom had baked Christmas cookies. Or where his grandmother had made pumpkin pie. Not that he wanted homemade cookies or pies. He didn't know what he wanted, but it was not this. "It's cold, impersonal and flawless." Ethan yanked open a drawer, grabbed a silver ladle and waved it around the kitchen, pausing on each offending appliance. "There was nothing wrong with how this place used to be. The sink had running water with an occasional drip. You just needed to jimmy the handle. The stove cooked with gas. Everyone knew the left side cooked hotter and faster than the right. If you wanted to burn dinner, you used the left burner on the back. The cabinets stored everything, and no one needed glass fronts to peek inside. We just opened the cabinet door to find the essentials stacked up inside."

"Unfortunately, sometimes change is necessary. Stoves stop working. Faucets break." Grace slid onto a stool at the island as if she'd always sat there. Always been a part of his home.

Worse, he liked her here. With him. But he didn't belong here. And he wasn't staying. He set the bowl of chicken soup in front of her. "Speaking of change, isn't it time you stepped out of your parents' place and into your own?"

She picked up her spoon, but never touched her soup. Instead she opened her laptop, a determined edge in her voice. "We're supposed to be discussing the Blackwell Ranch's financials."

"The Blackwell Ranch needs money. Quickly." He piled several scoops of beef burgundy on his plate, added a piece of bread and handed another slice to Grace. "I'm working on that. You're avoiding my question."

"I need clients first." She tore the bread into sections

and avoided looking at him. "More than the four I currently have, including your brother Jon and this ranch."

"When you have more clients, then what?" He took several bites of his dinner. Yet even the delicious beef failed to temper the gnawing agitation inside him. He wanted her settled into her new office. He wanted her business built. Yet he couldn't explain why. Or perhaps he didn't want to admit the truth. The truth that he wanted to know she could move on from her family and Brewster's like he'd moved on without regret. Without second thoughts. Except...

She stirred her spoon around the bowl. "Then I'll need real office space outside of Brewster's."

He paused, allowed her to eat more of her soup. Allowed his own regret over the past to settle back in the shadows. "What are you doing to build your client list?"

"I'm networking."

"With more high school friends," he said.

"Why do you care?" Her spoon clattered on the countertop, followed by her palm smacking the marble. "It's my business."

"The one you intend to use to support the baby." He pushed his empty plate across the counter. She'd told him that change was necessary as if it was as easy to accept as the arrival of spring. Well, change was certainly coming: in the form of a child. He wasn't prepared. He wasn't ready. For all her confidence and talk of strategies, he wanted to know if she was as panicked as him. He wanted to know he wasn't alone in his worry and angst about becoming a father. "It's easy to write goals on a piece of paper, but really hard to make those goals a reality."

He knew that all too well. His résumé listed his accomplishments and the depth of his knowledge. But that piece of paper alone hadn't been enough to move him beyond phone interviews recently. He was no closer to buying into an established practice today than he was prior to his graduation several years ago. His stomach rolled, cramped. That extra scoop of beef burgundy hadn't been the wisest choice.

"What about your ideas to support the baby?"

"Forgive me if I'm still working out those details. I only learned about the baby less than twenty-four hours ago." Ethan rose, paced around the counter. "You've had several months to make adjustments. To change your life."

Grace stood, grabbed her bag. Ethan intercepted her.

"Grace, I'm sorry." What had gotten into him? She wasn't to blame for his grandfather's disappearance. Or his failure to find Big E's money. Or his lack of a job. Or the simple fact that he was struggling to accept so many changes around him. "There's been a lot to take in the last few days. I just think you should put yourself first for once."

"It's not that simple."

"It can be," he countered.

"For you." Her voice lashed out.

Ethan stepped back, rubbed his chin as if her words had slapped him. "What does that mean?"

"Let's be really clear." She dropped her tote bag on the stool. Her gaze steady, her voice curt. "You want me to have a stable business to support the baby because you have no intention of staying in town."

He'd never wanted to raise a family in Falcon Creek. He'd only ever wanted to move beyond the confines of the small town his grandfather—and Grace it seemed—lived for. She wouldn't make him feel guilty for wanting more. "I have every intention of supporting the baby."

"But not here," she said.

The truth in her words stole his breath. Why couldn't she understand? She knew firsthand the Blackwell Ranch couldn't afford to put him on its payroll. There was nothing the ranch could offer him that would help him support a child. He had to leave.

And when he moved on, he wanted to be sure he'd done something more than leaving her pregnant and alone. "I'm here now. I can help you set up your business."

"Fine." Before he could grin, she lifted her hand. "But only if you help the residents of Falcon Creek and their pets."

The residents of Falcon Creek weren't having his baby. He was only interested in assisting Grace, not making more house calls. "No."

"Afraid you might discover you like it here?" She tossed out her question like a dare issued on the playground.

He already liked that spark in Grace's green gaze and that grit in her voice. He never imagined the most reserved of the Gardner sisters would stand up to him. Challenge him. He was afraid he might discover how much more he could like Grace Gardner if he stayed.

But Grace belonged to Falcon Creek. He didn't. Falcon Creek was as much a part of Grace as her expertise with numbers. He'd lost that part of him when he'd left the pain behind and never looked back. "I'm afraid of the liability. Everything is good until someone loses their beloved pet on my watch."

She hadn't expected that argument. He saw it in the way she opened and closed her mouth. And in the way her eyebrows pulled together.

She tipped her chin up, met his gaze. "You wouldn't let that happen."

Her certainty and faith in his abilities humbled him. But that wasn't enough. "Bad things happen even with the best intentions." Like breaking someone's heart or letting someone down. "You're asking too much."

"Maybe." She folded her arms over her chest and studied him. "But you're holding back too much."

"I didn't come home for some happy reunion."

"Why did you come home?"

"Jon asked me to." She winced at his words. He stuffed his hands into the back pockets of his jeans to keep from reaching for her. She needed the truth now more than she needed his comfort. "And yes, I would've come home if you'd asked."

"Before or after you learned about the baby?" she countered.

"That's not fair." Their discussion about their night together hadn't been resolved. They'd left the conversation in the awkward zone, both seeming content to let it rest. But that night lingered like an open blister, raw and sore. "You left without a goodbye the next morning. Nothing but a note."

"You could've called me," she said.

And risk being rejected twice. Not really his style. Not that he'd admit she'd hurt him. "What if I'd called and said that night had been amazing, unforgettable and one-of-a-kind? Would you have called back or run even farther?"

"I didn't run away."

"You ran." She was still running. He should follow her lead and run in the other direction. He'd spent too many years on his own and relying on himself. He was better alone.

"The champagne, the music, the starlit sky made the entire evening a fantasy. But the sun rose, and the fantasy expired."

"I wasn't drunk that night. You captured my attention with your bold red dress." Her poise and confidence had made her stand out that evening. He'd wanted to feel her joy. He'd wanted to be next to her. To make her smile himself. To hear her laughter. Then they'd danced, and he hadn't wanted to let her go. Then they'd talked, and he couldn't learn enough. Share enough.

"That wasn't me. This is me. Plain, ordinary, reliable me." She motioned toward her bulky sweater and jeans. "Hardly the same fantasy woman from that night."

Ethan straightened, surprised that she didn't see herself like he saw her. Another realization followed, knocking him off balance.

She'd sabotaged the next morning, but not because of anything he did. She'd run, not believing that she had anything to offer. Not believing she could ever be enough.

That settled things. He would help her get her business off the ground and to find the courage to put herself first. In another time and another place, she would've been more than enough for him. But that was before family disagreements, rising debt and when he still had a heart he'd been willing to risk.

"If it matters, I happen to like the reliable you." Ethan stepped around her to pick up her soup bowl and his plate. "And you're anything but ordinary or plain."

"I'm not like my sisters."

That he found refreshing. He rinsed the dishes and loaded the dishwasher. "Why do you need to be like your sisters?"

"It's not important." She tugged her laptop across the counter. "We need to go over these spreadsheets, not talk about me."

He'd much rather talk about Grace. But he'd avoided looking at Grace's accounting reports long enough. It was time he learned just how impossible turning the ranch around was going to be.

An hour later, too many numbers and too many equations bounced around inside Ethan's head. Colors from Grace's spreadsheets flashed before him like spotlights.

He watched Grace's car disappear down the driveway and escaped into the horse barn. The two pregnant mares, Butterscotch and Fancy, offered a much-needed refuge.

Ethan shut the barn doors, blocking the stress outside in the cold night. Here with the horses, Ethan's world finally made sense.

CHAPTER ELEVEN

GRACE HANDED MRS. O'GRADY her bag of bird seed, promised to stop by the older woman's house to see her new collection of feeders and scooted onto the stool behind the checkout counter. The last time she'd sat down had been in her mom's office that morning to explain the updates to the inventory program.

The school bell had just rung to release students for the day, and workers nationwide searched for an afternoon pick-me-up snack of caffeine or sugar to finish the last few hours of work.

The front doors opened, and Grace's pick-me-up stepped inside: *Ethan.* Yesterday he'd told her he liked her reliable self. Didn't find her ordinary or plain. His words were distracting. Flustering. Left her unbalanced. She blamed Sarah Ashley for this.

Her sister had planted the seed, even as she'd warned Grace that Ethan would never love her. But the idea lingered inside Grace nonetheless.

But wasn't their relationship, or friendship, already complicated enough with a baby on the way? She didn't need to add any sticky feelings that he couldn't return. That was a one-way street to heartache.

Grace watched Ethan approach the checkout counter and bit her tongue to stop her laughter. Mud covered him from the top of his head to the tips of his boots. Dirt and grime were smeared on his face. Yet his eyes were clear and sharp. His stare too watchful. Too searching, as his gaze found her and finally softened, as if he'd missed her.

Those pesky flutters started again, this time around her heart.

He paused on the other side of the counter. Beneath his

grimace, his voice was rough and coarse, as if he'd swallowed mud too. "Do not laugh."

Grace was now certain he'd been treasure hunting on the ranch. She nodded and clasped her hands together in front of her. Ethan shifted his weight and tiny bits of dried mud fell like snowflakes and her grin escaped. "Did you find what you were looking for?"

"The time capsule that Ben and I buried underneath the trough in the bull's pasture when we were ten." He straightened the cuffs of his flannel shirtsleeves, as if that would fix his appearance.

Laughter burst from inside her. It was so unlike her. She'd always tended to stray to the more serious side. But she'd found laughing came easier, was freer, with Ethan.

"It's not funny." He crossed his arms over his chest, yet the hint of a smile flashed up into his eyes.

Grace dialed her reaction down to a chuckle, but her smile refused to dim. "It is a little."

He didn't disagree, only asked, "Can you get me that special vitamin supplement for the Pierces' mare? The same one I ordered for Butterscotch."

Grace focused on the computer screen, instead of Ethan. He hadn't forgotten to call Mr. Pierce. He'd even made another house call to evaluate the mare, she assumed. She opened her mouth.

"Don't make more out of this, Grace, than there is." He reached to brush his hand through his hair, but stopped as if realizing he'd shower the counter and Grace with more dirt. "The Pierces are Randy Frye's neighbor. Randy has been good to our family over the years."

Grace nodded. Did he realize his explanation made no sense? She didn't care. He'd treated another animal in town. "What can I do?"

"Take a bottle of beta carotene to Dr. Lancaster when you bring him dinner."

"How did you know?" she asked.

"I talked to a colleague who specializes in avian care about Peabody this morning."

That was certainly going above and beyond for a patient—a patient he never wanted. Not that she was going to point that out. He already seemed to resent making that particular confession. "I meant, how did you know I was going up to Dr. Lancaster's?"

"I stopped to make a few moves on Pops's chessboard on my way in. Your mom asked if I wanted some of the extra buffalo chicken casserole she'd made for Dr. Lancaster." Ethan looked at her, his voice and shoulders finally relaxed. "Your mom should've been a chef."

"She loves to cook and adores nothing more than an empty plate." Grace typed on her keyboard, then printed a receipt for Ethan. "I need to get the Pierce supplement ready."

"Mr. Pierce will be in to pick it up before you close for the day." Ethan tucked the receipt in the back pocket of his jeans. "Thanks, Grace. If you have time tomorrow, we can finish going through the ranch projections you put together."

"Wait." Grace gripped the counter. She wasn't ready for him to leave. Her heart cheered. Her mind chided her weakness. She needed to let him go. "Where are you off to next?"

He eyed her. His jaw tensed as if he debated his answer. "To Rachel Thompson's office."

Surprise jolted through her. He'd called the lawyer after all. Had he given up his treasure hunting and taken her advice? Before she could celebrate, horror pushed her to scramble around the counter and rush over to him. "You can't go to her office like that."

He looked down at his clothes as if seeing the mud for the first time. "Why not?"

"I'll go with you," she said. "You can listen from the porch."

He set his hands on his hips. "You want me to stand outside on the porch like I'm the misbehaving family dog not allowed inside."

That was pretty much it. She set her hands on the least filthy part of his shirt—his shoulder—and pushed. "At least go into the bathroom and wash your hands and arms so you can shake Rachel's hand without getting her dirty too."

"It's just a little mud," he argued. "Nothing Rachel hasn't experienced working on her own family ranch. You do remember that Rachel owns the Double T Ranch, right?"

"I can get you a new flannel from the men's area," Grace suggested, her grin and voice hopeful.

He shook his head. "I'll wash up. You sure you can leave the store?"

"I'll be ready in five minutes." Although she guessed Ethan might need more time to scrub his face clean. She waited until Ethan disappeared into the men's restroom and called for her mom and Sarah Ashley.

Not long after that, Ethan and Grace stood on the sidewalk outside Calder & Associates. Ethan stomped his boots, knocking more mud off. He'd left a trail behind him on their walk from Brewster's.

Grace eyed Rachel's one-hundred-year-old, more-shack-than-office building and hoped their meeting with the lawyer ended before the weathered siding disintegrated in the May breeze.

Ethan brushed his thighs and rubbed his hands together. "That's the best it's going to get."

Grace nodded and stepped onto the porch. Ethan opened the door for her. It was clearly warped. She risked a few splinters from the chipped wooden frame, rather than get any closer to Ethan's dirty clothes.

Grace entered the empty reception area as Rachel approached. The women hugged. Grace motioned to Ethan, who'd been hovering in the doorway. "Ethan had a run-in with the trough in the bull's pasture. He'll listen from the porch."

Rachel offered a small smile. "Thanks for staying out there, Ethan. I just cleaned the office."

Grace didn't doubt Rachel had cleaned her office herself. Grace noted her wrinkled blouse and the stain on her slacks. Even the weariness settling beneath her eyes. Rachel wasn't the woman Ethan would remember from their high school days. Rachel had always been well-dressed and never hesitated to offer her judgment on those around her with her best friend Zoe's encouragement. But the death of Rachel's father had altered her world and Grace doubted the lawyer and new mom had much time these days to judge more than herself.

Grace glanced at Ethan. His contained expression gave nothing away.

He rested his shoulder against the doorway. "I appreciate any help you can give us, Rachel."

Rachel nodded. Her voice was sympathetic. "The bank account is part of the trust, Ethan. That means you'll have to go before Judge Myrna Edwards and plead your case if you want to try to access the funds."

"Not Judge Edwards." Ethan stared into space, a look of dread overtook him and his words slowed to a crawl.

Grace twisted in her chair to better study the shock on Ethan's face. "What? She's a lovely, kind lady."

His frown deepened. "And one of Big E's ex-wives."

Grace had forgotten. The marriage had been so brief. That could be more than awkward. Grace looked at Rachel. "Isn't there someone else?"

"Not in this county." Rachel smoothed her palms on the folders in front of her. "Only Judge Edwards handles trust disputes in this part of the state."

Ethan's muttered curse drifted into the room. Grace asked the lawyer, "What now?"

"Give me a day or so to make an appointment with Judge Edwards," Rachel said.

"Probably best to make the appointment in Jon's name." Ethan's head was pressed against the door frame as if he wanted to start banging it. "Or even better, Grace's name."

"I'll use both last names." Rachel pushed off the desk and walked toward the open door. "Judge Edwards isn't one for surprises."

Grace stood and shook Rachel's hand. "Thanks for your help. If there's anything I can do for you, let me know."

"My part is easy. I won't have to go before Judge Edwards." Rachel grabbed the door handle. "I don't envy either of you."

Grace joined Ethan on the small porch and waited for Rachel to wrangle the door closed. "Maybe you should ask your brother to handle this part?" Ethan's twin, Ben, was a high-powered attorney in New York.

"He's all the way across the country." Ethan paced around the small porch, his movements stiff and tense. "I'll talk to Jon. He's better at this sort of thing. Jon can convince her. I can't believe it's Judge Edwards. I can't believe there isn't someone else. Anyone else."

Grace captured his hand, and his attention, hoping to stall his rambling thoughts. She escorted him down the stairs and to the sidewalk. "How long was Judge Edwards married to Big E exactly?"

"Five days." Ethan shook himself as if shaking off the past. "Five *really long* days."

"That's rather quick though." Grace's shoulder brushed against his. They strolled slowly, almost without any real purpose, as if content to linger together between destinations. "Does Judge Edwards even qualify as an ex? That hardly seems long enough to constitute as a marriage."

"She was the first step-grandmother we had and lasted the shortest duration." His voice softened and the frustration eased from his tone.

His hand in hers felt reassuring. Right. Did he feel it too? She didn't want to take her hand away. She didn't want to let go. "How old were you?"

He squeezed her fingers. "Old enough to know I didn't want a replacement mom, but too young to know what to do with my grief."

Grace ached for Ethan and his brothers. To lose their parents at such young ages was traumatic in and of itself. But then their grandfather brought not one but multiple wives home and probably reopened the boys' wounds again and again. No doubt the boys declared each one lacking and unworthy. No wonder Ethan hadn't seen eye to eye with his grandfather. Grace was struggling to understand Elias Blackwell herself.

Elias was supposed to have protected his grandsons. He was supposed to have put his grandsons first. That's what her family did. That's what she'd do for her child. She was angry on Ethan's behalf. "What will you do when Big E returns?"

The question rolled out before Grace's brain could catch up with her mouth. She wanted to erase her words from the air between them like chalk on a chalkboard.

Ethan dropped her hand and stuffed both of his into his jeans pockets, folding in on himself and away from her. He lengthened his stride. "No one in my family has spoken to Big E since March. He might not ever return."

"You don't believe that," she said.

"No, I don't. My grandfather's loyalty to Blackwell land runs through his veins. He'd never abandon the Blackwell Ranch and his legacy." Ethan kicked a piece of broken sidewalk out of his path. "That means Big E is up to something, but I'm not sticking around to see what his latest scheme is. That could be months from now."

"The same time as the baby's arrival." Grace wrapped her arms around her stomach to block out the late-afternoon chill. And to prove she didn't need Ethan to be warm. She had to focus on her world. That was the baby. That was building her business. It wasn't some fantasy about her and Ethan being together simply because they'd held hands.

"I should know your due date." He grimaced as if she'd mentioned a root canal appointment and not the birth of his child. "When is it?"

Grace tucked her heart back behind its protective wall and walked toward Brewster's. "My due date is the twenty-first of November."

Ethan stopped her before she retreated inside the store and the security it offered her. "We need to talk more about the baby."

"Yes, but I need to drop off Dr. Lancaster's dinner. You need to shower and change." Grace clutched the railing behind her. She wanted to talk about the impossible. She wanted to talk about Ethan being more than a temporary father.

He traced a finger over her cheek, his gaze drifting over her face as if he was cataloging every detail. "I can go with you to Dr. Lancaster's house."

"I can handle it on my own." Grace caught his hand and released it. This time, she didn't hold on to him; instead, she climbed the stairs, shutting him out. As it should be. As she wanted.

Grace glimpsed Ethan from over her shoulder as he strode toward his truck. Opposite directions. Just as she suspected they would always live.

Once again, he'd hesitated to give her anything concrete about his future and that made her unsure about everything.

And yet, being with Ethan the past week had made her want more from him. No, she expected more.

She wanted their child to have the same care and attention that Ethan had shown to others in town. And on a regular basis. Their baby deserved no less.

If he stayed in Falcon Creek, what would he lose? What dream would he forfeit? How long before he resented her? She'd be the one who'd trapped Ethan Blackwell. She refused to be that woman.

It was best for everyone if they each went their separate ways.

CHAPTER TWELVE

ETHAN TOSSED HIS cell phone on the passenger seat of his truck and tapped his head against the steering wheel. The extra-large cup of coffee he'd brewed in Zoe's fancy machine only an hour ago gnawed through his stomach. That extra splash of the flavored cream curdled inside him, leaving behind the dual taste of desperation and frustration. And it was only two hours past sunrise. There was still a full day to go.

He had already had one more veterinarian clinic to check off his list of possible practices. One more denial. One more rejection. Phone interviews were getting him nowhere fast. He needed to meet potential veterinarians in person. Then he might be able to convince someone to take a chance on him. If he could prove his worth, how much of an asset he'd be beyond what was listed on his résumé, he might have an advantage. Heaven knew, he needed an advantage, no matter how small. Falcon Creek offered no chance for in-person interviews. He had to leave and soon. November would be here sooner than expected and he wanted to support his child.

Unfortunately, the Blackwell Ranch hadn't booked any more rooms of the lodge and he hadn't found any money to hire more staff or even discovered the magic key to turn a profit. So far, he'd failed.

That stopped this morning. Right now.

He started his truck and headed toward the JB Bar Ranch. He'd convince Jon to meet with Judge Edwards. Then he'd call the Billings Bank and Trust to request an extension at least until after Jon's meeting with Judge Edwards next week. If they gained access to the account, at least he'd bring the credit line current. One problem solved.

That's how he'd do things; he'd take one problem at a time. Then leave to handle his own personal employment issues. And leave Grace. That thought bothered him like an unseen puncture in a horse's sole, that by the time it was discovered, the horse had developed an abscess that could cause severe damage and even death. Surely, he could leave Falcon Creek and Grace without suffering any serious fallout.

After all, his heart was never an issue. The only strings that were attached to him when he departed would be a child that he'd vowed to help take care of. Ethan turned up the volume on the radio and ignored the groans of his old truck and the slow roll of uncertainty through him.

He had everything under control.

After one too many country songs about love lost or the comfort of family, Ethan finally parked in his brother's driveway.

He walked in on breakfast, not the quiet, staid routine he went through each morning alone in his studio apartment back in Colorado, or the rushed, stuffing a bagel in the mouth while walking that Katie always seemed to prefer. Rather a boisterous, laughter-infused family affair with chocolate-chip-pancake-scented air, perfectly brewed coffee, and Jon and Lydia stealing a kiss behind the open refrigerator door.

Ethan rubbed his forehead, feeling like he'd stumbled into a private moment. He would've sneaked back outside if his nieces hadn't squealed his name and rushed to hug him with syrup-stained fingers and cheeks.

Lydia greeted him with a wide smile and pointed her spatula toward the empty chair at the kitchen table and ordered him to sit and eat.

The girls returned to their seats and exploded into conversation, their questions running into their story retelling. Did he know that two of Gordy's daughters, Rosie and

Francie, were friends with Abby and Gen? They said he'd
saved their dogs. Did he know Lucky was the only baby
left 'cause the other puppies had to go to become angels?

Did he know Gen hurt her elbow when she fell off the
porch swing? There was even a sparkly pink Band-Aid
to prove it.

Did he like chocolate chip pancakes? Because those
were their favorites. And if he asked Lydia real nice, she
might even make his pancakes into barn animals too. That
launched a debate over the best barn animals to choose and
whether a barn owl could be considered a real barn animal.

Too soon, pancake-loaded plates arrived and the girls
only managed a smattering of giggles and chopped sentences between bites. Plates empty, the girls sprinted off
to wash up and get ready for their day.

Ethan finished off his pancakes, declared Lydia's
bunny-shaped chocolate chip pancake the best he'd ever
had and poured himself another cup of coffee. "Sorry to
interrupt the morning, Jon, but we need to talk."

Lydia touched Ethan's shoulder and carried his plate
to the sink. "Family is always welcome and never a dis-
ruption."

"Don't tell him that." Jon yanked the coffeepot away
from Ethan and refilled his mug. "He'll be here every
morning. He can hardly make toast and coffee."

"I've mastered Zoe's expensive coffee machine." And
if he were honest, he was becoming partial to it and the
special bean grinder too. "I haven't tackled the waffle iron
or special hot plate for the stove yet."

"I'm sure there are instruction manuals," Jon offered,
his voice mild and helpful.

He wouldn't be here that long that he'd need to learn.
And any instruction manual he picked up would be about
babies and what not to do. Ethan toasted his brother with

his mug. "I don't like to read manuals. I think I'll just come over here instead."

"Look what you started." Jon frowned at Lydia, but the laughter in his gaze ruined the effect. "Now he'll be here every morning and evening." Jon tried to look put out, but his daughters cheered before racing each other outside. Lydia followed, calling for the girls to put on jackets.

Ethan slapped his brother's shoulder. "Don't worry. I've been pretty lucky with dinners thanks to Alice Gardner, so I'll only stop in every morning."

Jon sipped his coffee and considered Ethan with the same look he'd used when trying to find the weak link between Ethan and his twin, Ben. Ben had always run interference for Ethan, since he'd been a fast-talker even as a child and always stalled Jon long enough for Ethan to attempt their latest stunt. And the twins had an endless stunt list. Ethan should've returned the favor for Ben and blocked Ben from being the first Blackwell to get engaged to Zoe Petit.

Ethan looked away from his brother, but never broke his silence.

Jon said, "Alice Gardner's cooking explains why you haven't been over in the evenings."

That and Ethan had been spending most of his evenings with Grace. Not that his brother needed to know that. "Katie keeps expanding the fix-it list hourly. It's neverending."

"Don't you remember Big E telling us that we lived ranch work. You didn't just do it eight hours a day and then call it quits." Jon looked at Ethan as if he'd forgotten where he'd grown up. As if Ethan had forgotten his roots.

Ethan remembered, but he'd never really listened. He'd been too busy rescuing one animal or another. Or taking care of the horses in the barn. His body was listening now. Each twinge and displaced joint hollered at him every morning when he snapped his spine back into place to get ready for the day. He didn't mind the physical labor. He minded that nothing ever seemed to result in bringing in more money for the ranch. "Even if I worked twenty hours a day, there would be more to do the next morning. We need help."

"You found money to hire people?" Jon leaned forward, looking both relieved and wary.

"Sort of." Ethan cradled his mug and reviewed his strategy. None of the brothers had welcomed Myrna Edwards as their new step-grandma. But Jon was the only one who'd stayed in town and still may have interacted with Judge Edwards. Surely Jon would see Ethan's logic. "If we get signing authority on the second account, we can access the money."

"There's money in this account?" The caution in Jon's voice overtook his earlier relief.

"Possibly enough to cover several weeks of pay for the ranch hands until more bookings come in." And it should bring the credit line payments close to current. Ethan nodded as if that would bolster his brother's confidence.

"Great." Jon sat back and tipped his hat up to better see Ethan. "What's the holdup?"

Ethan looked anywhere but at his brother. "There's a small hitch, but it shouldn't be too big of a deal."

"What is it?" Jon's fingers drummed a slow beat on the kitchen table as if he'd sit there all day waiting for Ethan to explain.

Ethan dropped his elbows on the table and met his brother's stare. His words tumbled out. "You have to go before Judge Edwards to ask for signing authority in Big E's absence."

Jon's head shook, and his voice came out in succinct syllables as if he were teaching a preschooler to read. "Judge Myrna Edwards?"

"Yes." Ethan sat back and tried to smile at his brother, but even his lips refused to pretend a meeting with Judge Edwards was something to grin about.

"Why me?" Jon asked.

"You're the oldest. You're the most responsible." Ethan threw his hands up as if he'd scored a touchdown with his final argument. "You're a full-time resident of Falcon Creek." Unlike Ethan. He had no need to have singing authority on Big E's accounts. That would be like a string attaching him to Big E and the Blackwell Ranch. He'd cut those ties when he'd gone to college without Big E's blessing or assistance.

His brother drummed his fingers faster on the kitchen table and stared at him. "You're essentially running the Blackwell Ranch right now. You should appeal to Judge Edwards."

But Ethan wasn't permanent on the ranch. Or in Falcon Creek. Jon lived and worked, and now raised his family, in Falcon Creek. His brother had so many ties to the town there would be no cutting him loose anytime soon. Jon should have signing authority on their grandfather's account. "You make the most sense."

"I'm not appealing to Judge Edwards for anything." Jon crossed his arms over his chest, his gaze narrowed and his mouth set into a firm line. This was the brother that never bent.

Ethan needed Ben. His twin would've already won this argument. "Why not?"

There were any number of reasons none of the Blackwell brothers wanted to approach Judge Myrna Edwards for anything. But out of the five boys, Jon had the cleanest slate from Myrna's point of view.

"She still refers to me as Day One whenever and wherever I see her." Distaste coated his tone as if Jon had bit into Ethan's first and only attempt at making Shepherd's pie. "I won't go into her courtroom, so she can call me Day One with her usual disdain and disapproval."

"You weren't the one who'd hit her tires." Ethan jumped up from his chair and paced the kitchen. She'd imploded on Ethan as the others had watched from the safety of the hayloft.

Ethan had been polite and had even given her a quick but awkward hug on Day One. Day Two, he'd lost his manners and any hint of affection when Myrna had confiscated his bow and arrows.

He'd aimed at her car tires rather than the hay barrels after Ben had told him he'd never successfully flatten the tire. Ethan was the worst shot in the family according to Ben. Ethan had flattened two tires on Myrna's car before Ben had admitted his brother deserved top billing with a bow and arrow.

Myrna hadn't agreed and grounded Ethan as if she were his mother. As if she'd suddenly earned the right to parent him. As if the Blackwell name on a signature line had given her control.

Then, believing there was no alternative vehicle, she'd climbed onto the tractor and driven off into town. Ethan might've escaped with only a lecture if Myrna hadn't turned around and witnessed him doubled over with laughter. He'd still swear that twin horns had sprouted from her head in that instant.

He'd been known as Day Two ever since. His pancakes flipped over in his stomach like cast iron plates, no longer comforting. "You're not seriously going to make me stand before Judge Edwards alone?"

"Absolutely." Jon nodded and laughed. "Maybe you can sweet-talk her with your special cookies."

He'd tried to put himself into Myrna's good graces and earn back his bow and arrows that same evening. He'd made cookies with nuts and chocolate chips. Myrna Edwards had an as-yet-undiagnosed nut allergy that had sent her back into town on the tractor. "This is serious, Jon."

His brother sobered. "I know. And I won't win anything with Myrna Edwards either. We have a mutual dislike of each other."

"It can't be that bad." Ethan had made Myrna Edwards break out in hives from her face to her shins.

"Judge Edwards presided over my divorce, which might've happened in less time if she hadn't added in several arbitrary delays and extensions."

That wasn't good. Jon's slate was apparently as scratched up as those of the rest of the brothers. Ethan rubbed his hands over his face, grabbed his empty coffee mug from the table and dropped it in the sink.

Jon tapped the table. "You could call in reinforcements. Ben has been trained to handle all sorts of difficult clients and judges."

"Ben won't answer my calls." Ethan stared out the kitchen window at his nieces chasing each other around the yard. Growing up, Ben and Ethan had been like the girls, spending every hour together, building forts, hunting or riding.

Ben was not only his twin but his best friend, until Ethan had stood at the altar beside Ben while Ben's bride-to-be, Zoe Petit, had eloped with their grandfather.

Ethan had known what was happening, but hadn't stopped Big E and Zoe, or told Ben, until after it was too late. "This seems way below Ben's pay grade," he told Jon. "I'm sure he has paralegals to appeal for signing authority on a simple bank account."

"It's worth calling him," Jon said. "It's been over five years. He has to forgive us sometime."

Ethan turned around and looked at his older brother. Jon had handled so much after their parents had died. Ethan could do this now. "I'll deal with Judge Edwards and get signing authority."

Besides, Ethan wasn't as convinced as Jon that Ben would forgive them. He'd saved Ben back then, even if his brother still hadn't realized it yet. Ethan wasn't about to apologize to his twin. Or beg for Ben's forgiveness. He still stood behind his decision all those years ago. "I'm stepping back after we get the ranch stabilized."

"Got a job offer?" Jon asked.

"I have several phone interviews scheduled for next week," Ethan hedged. He hadn't admitted the dire condition of his own finances to anyone, not even Jon. He hadn't admitted that his poor credit prevented him from being accepted into most veterinary clinics.

"You should have offers before the end of the month." Jon rinsed his coffee cup in the sink and smiled at his girls giggling outside.

"That's the goal." Ethan studied his brother, who was suddenly frowning. "What's the problem?"

Jon shrugged. "I won't deny that it's been good to have you back and not just to tackle the extra workload. From what I've heard in town, there's quite a few people, and their pets, who're happy to have you home."

He didn't want to discuss his moonlighting. Those house calls to treat various pets were for old neighbors and longtime friends. Or visits Grace had coerced him into. He'd always been a sucker for an animal in need, especially in Falcon Creek.

Ethan moved away from the counter and his brother and his growing uncertainty about wanting a local patient list. "You know I've been applying in Kentucky and Colorado. That's where I need to be to build my career."

"So you've told me." Jon turned and leaned against the counter, his focus on Ethan. "But it isn't only about your career, is it?"

Yes, it was very much only about his career. How was Ethan supposed to support a child without a stable job and regular paycheck? "I've been working toward this since I was a kid. It's all I've ever wanted to do."

"Well, just promise me that you won't forget your family in your race to conquer the equestrian world." Jon smiled and shoved away from the counter to squeeze Ethan's shoulder. "Get the signing authority on the account, make the new hires and I'll see to things on this end with Katie until Big E returns, or we sell the place."

"You're freeing me to head off to my future then?" Ethan could set up some of those in-person interviews finally.

"As free as a falcon."

Doubt stuttered through him at Jon's quick promise. Or perhaps those were Ethan's own doubts about leaving. But he shook that off. He had to go. To build his life outside Falcon Creek, where he had more lucrative opportunities.

He now had a child to consider. He wanted to share the news with his big brother, but...

Lydia walked in and kissed Jon's cheek on her way back outside with different coats for the girls. His brother's grin was as wide as the Montana sky. Ethan was very glad Jon and Lydia had found happiness and were building a life together. Ranch life suited them.

Could Ethan build a life with Grace? Asking her to leave Falcon Creek, leave her family and friends, was impossible. If he remained in Falcon Creek, he'd have nothing to offer her but debt, and a barely solvent ranch that he only owned a portion of. No one would want that. Period.

Unlike Lydia and Jon, a future together for Grace and Ethan seemed as improbable as winning over Judge Edwards.

CHAPTER THIRTEEN

ETHAN DROVE ALONG Front Street, spotted Mrs. Hatfield standing outside Maple Bear Bakery and waved. At the single stoplight in town, he rolled down his window and called out to Mr. Jacobson to ask about their puppy—the one he'd treated last week after the German shepherd had overindulged in brownies.

Just as he was about to step on the gas, Randy, the post-man, shouted his name. Randy walked up to Ethan's window and handed him the mail for the Blackwell Ranch. "Sure nice to have you home and around town. Delivering the mail this way lets me get to the boys' baseball practice on time."

"Glad I could help." Ethan tossed the mail on the passenger seat, waited until Randy stepped back onto the sidewalk and headed toward Brewster's.

Ethan pulled into the store's parking lot and stared out the windshield. He'd been sincere with Randy. He liked knowing that he could help. But Ethan hadn't considered the Blackwell Ranch to be home in years. He'd moved on like he'd wanted to. He rolled his shoulders and forced himself to swallow around his tight throat. Surely, he hadn't discovered some misplaced sentiment for the Blackwell Ranch and Falcon Creek.

He'd told his brother not an hour ago that he intended to leave. That hadn't changed on his short drive through town.

After two quick moves on the chessboard to put the black in position to take Pops's queen, Ethan strode around the back of Brewster's. He had a task to complete before he handed in his get-out-of-Falcon-Creek card to his brother.

Sarah Ashley sat cross-legged on the porch, painting supplies scattered all around her. Her canvas: one of the milk can stools from the porch where Pops played his continuous chess game. She'd piled her hair into a messy bun on top of her head, skipped her usual full makeup and wore more practical than fashion-friendly work boots paired with a Brewster's flannel. He preferred her like this. Sarah Ashley would always be beautiful, but now she looked approachable.

He appreciated Sarah Ashley and her classic beauty, but found himself scanning the back for someone else. He had a longing to search the warehouse for the straight-haired blonde with wise green eyes behind wide frames who'd probably be stocking fertilizer and chewing her lip as she calculated the month-end report in her head.

The one that made him smile.

The one that settled him with only a touch of her hand. The one he wanted to tell his secrets to. Although he'd never admit any of that out loud to anyone, especially Sarah Ashley.

"Grace had to run down to the post office to pick up a special delivery." Sarah Ashley dabbed her brush into the brown paint and turned to her milk can, but not before Ethan saw her knowing grin.

"I came to see you, not Grace." His voice came out stiff and sharp as if she'd caught him sneaking into the cookie jar. But he refused to admit to Sarah Ashley that she was right. He had been looking forward to seeing Grace.

"That's new. You haven't come to Brewster's to see me in a long time." Sarah Ashley dabbed the paintbrush against the canvas. "Even in high school. I always suspected you came here because my mother gave you whatever she'd baked that day, not because you really wanted to see me."

"You were never at the store." Ethan jammed his hands into his jeans pockets as if he needed to hide the candy he'd swiped from the jar.

"Yet you spent more time here in high school than with me on our dates," she challenged.

She was right again, of course. But he hadn't come here to hash out their past relationship errors. She'd moved on, married and had a new life. And he…he only thought of Sarah Ashley as a friend. Had thought of her like that for a long time if he was honest.

He ground his boot heels into the pavement to keep his balance. He owed Sarah Ashley an apology, but he wanted to thank her for introducing Grace to his world. He suddenly wished Grace was beside him.

What was happening to him? He'd been content alone. Until recently. "High school boys pretty much only think about girls and food. I had the girl. I needed more food."

Sarah Ashley laughed and looked at him. "I only cared about clothes and boys. I had the boy and spent my time worrying about updating my wardrobe. Do you think it'll ever be that simple again?"

"No." Ethan should know, he had a baby coming and no income to support the child. "The real world isn't simple, but I think we appreciate everything more now that we have to work harder for what we want."

"Do you know what you want?" Sarah Ashley asked him.

He searched her face, wondering what her game was. The Sarah Ashley he knew always had an agenda. Always. But her smile was genuine, her voice sincere as if she'd asked him if he'd figured out his life and would he kindly share his secret with her. As if they were two friends discussing life's journey, nothing more.

What did he want? He wanted a job he loved. To get out of debt. *Grace*. He kicked at the gravel and pebbles flew, but thoughts of Grace stuck. His heart squeezed. He crammed his fists farther into his pockets, refusing to tap his chest, as if to confirm only his heart beat inside there. Love wasn't part of any plan, or any of his thoughts. *Ever*.

He cleared his throat and cleared his head. Time to focus on what mattered. "I'd like you to help me book more rooms at the guest ranch. I'd appreciate it if you would bring it up to your large network of friends. If they're coming to stay this summer, they should consider the ranch."

"That's rather specific." Now she watched him as if she didn't know him.

"You asked what I wanted. That's it."

"I asked if you knew what you wanted."

"And I told you." Ethan stepped closer to the back porch. "Will you help me?"

"This is new." Sarah Ashley set her brush on the tray. "I'm quite sure no one has ever sought out my help before."

He wouldn't beg. He'd find reservations for the guest ranch with or without Sarah Ashley's assistance. But that would take more time. Time he didn't have. A payment on his college loan was due when the Zigler party arrived. Soon his baby arrived.

"I wouldn't ask, but it's important. The ranch won't survive without more bookings."

"I would never have thought the ranch's survival would matter much to you." That shrewd look in her blue eyes hadn't dulled without her makeup. "I lost count at how many times you swore you were never coming home. And here you are."

"This is about family." Family mattered to him. Always had. Always would. "I won't walk away from them."

Sarah Ashley paused, her gaze fixed on him. She seemed to be working something out. He wouldn't ask, fairly certain she was deciding what she'd ask in return for this favor. Sarah Ashley's help would come with conditions. He'd accept her terms if she filled the guesthouse.

Finally, she blinked and nodded as if she'd finished an internal debate. Pulling out her phone, she asked, "When do your next guests arrive?"

"Two weeks from tomorrow."

She swiped a manicured nail across the screen as if that six-inch device revealed the answers to all of his problems. "You need to add more about the amenities on the Blackcreek Guest Ranch website. That will give my friends something to read about when they research the ranch."

He hadn't expected her to say that. Ethan backtracked. He wasn't dealing with technology and websites too. "Are you sure we need to do this?"

"Yes, and you need to follow through on whatever you write down. And add videos and photos." She aimed the phone screen at him, looking more like a marketing executive than the pampered princess she claimed to like being. "You make promises on this web page and you have to deliver if you want to be fully booked through the summer."

The ranch needed to be busy every second of the summer to turn a profit and put it in the best position to sell. The ranch had to be full so that Ethan could leave without worrying and begin his search in person for a veterinary practice. "What do you have in mind?"

Sarah Ashley tucked her phone into her shirt pocket and picked up her brush as if she'd picked up a pointer for her PowerPoint presentation on the top ten best strategies to capture a new market. "My friends will have specific expectations."

"It's a working ranch just like the website promises." That certainly set his expectations. Ethan held out his hands, basically asking what more could they expect.

Sarah Ashley waved her brush in the air as if covering his words. "They'll want that ranch experience along with the amenities of a five-star spa."

"Meaning?" Something like fear coiled through him. The very same sensation when he'd stumbled upon a rattlesnake, disturbed by his rambling in the woods. He'd retreated slowly that day, never breaking eye contact with the snake, poised to strike, until he'd moved far enough away. He wondered how far he'd need to retreat now to escape Sarah Ashley's requirements for a five-star experience. He'd regretted disrupting that rattlesnake. Would he regret seeking out Sarah Ashley's help now?

"They'll expect the usual—extra-plush towels, Egyptian cotton sheets, bubble bath supplies and a detailed agenda for their approval so they don't ruin their shoes." Sarah Ashley swirled her brush in brown paint and looked up at him. "I almost forgot, mani-pedis and in-room massages."

Ethan watched the bristles disappear into the brown paint and wondered if he'd fallen into a vast pit of quicksand himself. "There's a petting zoo."

"That's quite adorable." Sarah Ashley curved the brush around the bottom of the milk can. "And I suppose fitting."

Ethan swallowed against that quicksand now leeching into his mouth. His voice sounded mud-coated and dull. "It's a ranch."

"I'm aware of that." Sarah Ashley dropped her brush in the water jug beside her and frowned at Ethan. "Do you want my friends, or not?"

He had to have her friends book rooms. He forced the gloom out of his voice. "Well, could you make me a list of what I need to add to the guest rooms?"

"I'll do better than that. I'll put some things together and Grace can bring everything up to you tonight." Sarah Ashley stood up and checked her watch. "That's the end of my lunch break. I need to get back to work."

Ethan had to get back to work too. No doubt Katie had more tasks for him as everything on the ranch seemed to shift sideways daily. But he stayed where he was, once again knocked off balance by his own thoughts. The ones about how much he liked the idea of Grace being at the ranch again and not only so that she could explain the ranch accounts. He just wanted to be with Grace.

Ethan rubbed his forehead, wondering if the sweet tea he'd bought at White Buffalo Grocers had been tainted. "Grace? At the ranch tonight?"

"I just assumed. Grace mentioned your project was important and she's been up there the last few nights." Sarah Ashley fixed her flannel shirt as if she wanted to look her best in her Brewster's uniform. "Mom doubled her stew recipe, which I assumed was for everyone at the ranch. You know cooking for a crowd is my mother's real calling."

"Grace and I are working on a big project." His sweet tea had definitely been spiked. He couldn't seem to think straight.

"Then I'll get everything ready." Sarah Ashley held open the door that led into the supply area. "I'll leave it all with Grace along with instructions."

Ethan stopped her before she disappeared inside. "Sarah Ashley?"

She turned around and smiled. There was something different about Sarah Ashley, but he couldn't exactly pinpoint what. Other than she hadn't asked for anything in return for this favor. That was very un-Sarah-Ashley-like. Ethan rubbed his stomach and considered dropping into South Corner to get antacids for his sudden indigestion. Grace's soup diet might be the way to go. The entire Gardner family had him questioning everything he thought he knew about them and had his stomach in knots. "Thanks."

"Sure." Sarah Ashley waved toward the warehouse. "I have to go help Dad sort horse feed."

Pops strolled around the corner, leading Sunshine and Lucky, both wearing bright pink leashes. He smacked Ethan on the shoulder. "Better come out to the front porch and sit down, boy, before you trip on your own surprise."

"Sarah Ashley just told me that she was going to sort horse feed with Frank."

Pops grinned, causing his forehead to wrinkle even more. "I learned never to question a Gardner girl's heart. Once something gets inside there, it gets stuck for good."

Except Ethan had never known Sarah Ashley's heart to be in the family business. He glanced over at the milk can and studied the quaint scene Sarah Ashley had been painting. The vintage farmhouse beside a field of sunflowers reminded him of Grace: bright, cheerful, but grounded. Why that was important, he had no idea. He only knew that everything for him seemed to circle back to Grace, even when he didn't mean it to.

He shook his head and followed Pops and the dogs. One quick game of chess with the old man and he'd be on his way. And if he was fortunate enough to be on the porch when Grace returned from the post office, all the better. He'd confirm the time when he could expect her at the ranch. And he'd insist she sit and relax while she told him.

CHAPTER FOURTEEN

ETHAN HANDED THE first box to Grace and took the second one from her car trunk. "I can't believe your sister put all this together in the last few hours."

"I don't even think it took her that long." Grace adjusted the box in her arms and walked beside him toward the guest lodge.

Katie intercepted them, extending her streak of interrupting Ethan hourly. "I'm now giving out your cell phone number to everyone that calls the ranch—guests and owners of patients alike."

"I'm not practicing." He squeezed the cardboard box. "I don't have a clinic, remember?"

Katie whistled, calling Hip to her side. "That hasn't stopped you from making house calls all over town."

"Those were special circumstances." No big deal. He tried to keep his voice detached.

"Well, special or not, the locals all over town have been talking about their vet's excellent, hands-on care of their pets." Katie peered into Grace's box and frowned. She picked up the lemongrass bodywash, opened it and smelled the gel. "Now, you're in even more demand."

Ethan took the bottle from Katie, snapped the lid closed and stuffed it into the box he held. He wanted to stuff his degree in there too. Perhaps then the locals would stop referring to him as their vet. "I'm not practicing."

"Well, call those people back and tell them that. I'm not your secretary." Katie picked up a bottle of vanilla-lavender lotion from Grace's box, sniffed, then sniffed again before reading the label. "What is all this?"

"Sarah Ashley's contribution to the ranch." Grace moved beside Ethan, cradling the box in her arms. Her smile lengthened as if she was trying to match the forced enthusiasm in her voice.

Katie looked between Grace and Ethan. "We need paying guests, not lotions and shower gels."

"Sarah Ashley has lots of well-connected friends," Ethan said.

Katie stared at him blankly as if he'd spoken in French.

"Friends who'll pay to stay here if we provide certain amenities." Grace lifted her box as if she were offering a toast to Katie.

"This is a working ranch. *W-o-r-k-i-n-g*." Katie stretched out the word, as if Ethan and Grace had both lost their ability to understand. "Not a spa."

"It's a ranch that needs capital if it wants to continue *w-o-r-k-i-n-g*." Katie couldn't challenge that. No one could. The truth stared back at him in the financials Grace had put together.

Grace nodded beside him. He sighed his thanks at the look of resignation on her face that said, *Sorry, but it's true*.

Katie pointed at the bottles and tins. "You're trying to tell me that this stuff is going to fill all the rooms in the guesthouse and the cabins."

"Sarah Ashley thinks so." Positivity lightened Grace's voice.

"She wants the guests coming in to have special and unexpected features that they can mention in their reviews." Ethan plowed ahead, repeating Sarah Ashley's statement with his own surge of confidence. "The guest ranch will offer a balance of the rustic and refined and that will book new guests."

Katie wasn't buying any of it. Doubt filled Ethan too. But he'd started this. He'd see it through. He was more desperate now that vet calls seemed to outpace reservation calls. "Sarah Ashley wants to show her friends the updated website."

"Great idea." Grace bumped Ethan's elbow.

Something bumped inside Ethan too. He liked her support. He liked her a little too much. He should move away from Grace. He'd be on his way out of town soon. He could not get used to Grace standing beside him. But if he convinced her to leave with him... He edged closer to her, keeping up the contact.

He hadn't given the idea merit until now. Would she leave her family and her roots to be with him? To build new roots? Maybe if he had a stable job at a respectable clinic. Maybe if he had something real to offer her.

Katie aimed the shampoo bottle at his chest and pinned him in place. "You're the one collecting these testimonials and putting them up on the website, right?"

"That's the plan." Nothing could be simpler, or so he'd kept telling himself. Though he was beginning to reconsider his use of the word *plan*. Every time he spoke of his plans, they never turned out like the actual plans.

"This one is all on you guys." Katie pointed first at Grace and then at Ethan with the shampoo bottle. "You're Sarah Ashley's sister. And you're her ex. And I have real, honest to goodness ranch work to do." Katie grabbed several bottles of the vanilla-lavender lotion and green tea shampoo. "I'm only testing these. We want to know if this stuff gives you a rash before we put it in a guest's bathroom."

Ethan and Grace looked at each other and busted out laughing. Even Katie grinned on her way toward the barn.

Ethan strode over to the guest lodge and used his boot to prop the door open for Grace.

She walked into the entryway and set her box on the hand-carved side table and frowned at the supplies inside the box. "I hate to say it, but I'm sort of with Katie on this one."

"But you agreed with Sarah Ashley earlier." Ethan kicked the door shut.

"I didn't want to seem disloyal to my sister." Grace said the words easily as if that explained everything.

He wondered where having a baby with your sister's ex-boyfriend landed on the disloyalty scale. Then there was falling for your ex's little sister. Not that he'd fallen for Grace. He didn't allow his heart to fall. The damage could be irreparable.

"You have something against scented lotions and bath salts?" Ethan set his box next to Grace's and pulled out several bottles, opening, sniffing and closing each one like Katie. "Most women are supposed to love this stuff."

"It's overpriced soap." Grace tugged a bottle of mint-infused hand lotion from him and pointed at the price. "The bars you buy in bulk from the big-box stores clean your skin just the same. I also feel the need to add that the bulk soaps are friendlier on the budget."

"But will the bulk soap book more rooms?"

"I'm not sure smelling like cucumber and mint will work either," Grace said.

"Not a fan of cucumbers," Ethan teased.

"I'm more a fan of natural scents and the outdoors." A blush tinged both cheeks as if she'd revealed a deeply guarded secret.

He was becoming a fan of Grace Gardner. If he picked out a scent for Grace, it'd be something less floral and mundane. Something rare and unique like her.

"What kind of soap do you prefer?" she asked.

He shrugged. "Whatever is on sale."

Grace watched him as if expecting him to tell her more about himself.

But Ethan had lived like a nomad on a slim budget in Colorado. He wasn't sure Grace wanted to hear that. He thought Grace belonged in a bedroom with all the frills and fluffy pillows and fancy hand-dipped soaps. She deserved to be pampered for everything she did for everyone else, including him. But on his limited budget he could only offer the bare essentials.

What if their baby was a girl? He knew nothing about little girls. He loved his nieces, sure, but he didn't live with them. His stomach lurched as if he'd swallowed a bottle of the honey and grapefruit shampoo and chased it with the lemongrass bath gel. There was nothing appealing about debt and possible bankruptcy. Nothing that Grace would want to leave Falcon Creek for.

He hadn't been thinking. He had no right to ask her to go with him. He had no right to keep inviting her to the ranch. This would be the last night. The last time he relied on her. Their last night working together. Already, he missed her.

"Well, the sooner we get our pretty on, the faster we can get back to the real work like Katie." Grace picked up her box and headed for the stairs.

The sooner they finished, the sooner he'd be alone. As it should be. He had nothing to offer her.

Grace waited for him to join her on the wide staircase. "We need to discuss your approach with Judge Edwards on Monday."

"Flattening her car tires one at a time with a bow and arrow until she grants me signing authority probably isn't the best idea." Ethan hugged his box of supplies and pretended he didn't want to hug Grace instead.

Grace laughed. "I thought that was only a rumor."

Ethan shook his head. "Afraid not. I'm Day Two."

"Well, we need to seriously revise your approach."

"It's been years." Ethan followed Grace as she headed along the nearest wing. If he kept following her, he'd end up in Falcon Creek without a practice and without any opportunities in the equestrian world. "Maybe Judge Edwards has forgotten the whole thing by now."

"The woman remembers people's middle names and dates of birth. For fun." Grace walked into the first bedroom. "I doubt she's forgotten the boy who murdered her tires. If anything, she remembers that day in minute-by-minute detail."

"You're not helping." He dropped his box on the king bed, wanting to bury himself under the thick blankets until his grandfather returned and rescued the ranch himself.

Grace squeezed his arm. "We'll get through it."

Her words wrapped around him like a long hug and he relaxed. Forget the bath salts, he only required Grace's reassurance to calm down. That was not good. Not good at all. He'd just told himself this was their last evening working together. He couldn't start counting on her for more than financial reports and advice.

"But first, does the lavender-vanilla scent or rosewater belong in a room like this?" Grace held up two bottles as if she was a game show hostess highlighting the next prizes.

Both wings properly stocked with all things spa-like, Ethan and Grace finished in one of the larger suites. Grace folded a towel with a pocket and hung her creation next to the oversize bathtub.

Ethan leaned against the doorjamb and watched her fuss with the counter to make it perfect. He realized she did that with everything—made things better. She gave whatever she worked on her full attention. And when she offered her help, she never complained, only made the person she assisted feel special. She had a gift. She was a gift.

Ethan paced into the bedroom. He'd obviously sniffed too many sweet soaps that had perfumed his thoughts, making him careless. "I have to head into Billings tomorrow. Between my meeting and Sarah Ashley's supply list, I'll be gone all day." And have no extra time to spend with Grace.

"That's perfect." Grace switched off the bathroom light and turned her attention to the pillows on the four-poster king bed. "We can carpool together."

Yes. No. He seriously needed to step outside, inhale the crisp night air and focus. "What?"

"I have a business meeting in Billings with a potential new client tomorrow." Ethan appreciated her excitement. He liked that glimpse of confidence in her. He wanted to see that more from her. Confidence suited her. Building something of her own suited her.

He knew about her potential new client. He'd called the wholesale supplier himself. He hadn't known Ken Ware had already contacted Grace or that they'd scheduled a meeting. "You're going to be gone from Brewster's the entire day if you ride with me."

"That's fine. I told my parents I needed to head into the city to have a colleague of mine review Big E's accounts before you talk to Judge Edwards."

"Do we need to do that?" A jolt of panic stole his smile and dumped him back in the real world. He didn't want anyone else to see the poor state of the ranch's books.

"No. I'm confident in my work." Grace, satisfied with the arrangement of the pillows, turned to face him. "Judge Edwards can contact me directly for questions."

"You won't be at the court appearance?" He wanted her there, not a phone call away.

"Did you want me there?"

He'd just decided this would be their last working night together. But the meeting with Judge Edwards related to the Blackwell Ranch and it was during the day. "Definitely."

"Then we have an even trade. You'll let me ride along to the city and I'll go to your court appearance with you." She smiled and held out her hand. "Do we have a deal?"

He wanted to seal the deal with a kiss, rather than shake her hand. This was a bad idea. He didn't need to be alone for an hour and a half in the truck with Grace. No one to interrupt them or walk in. Tonight had been challenging enough. Ethan wrapped her fingers inside his and resisted the urge to pull her into his arms. "Deal."

Ethan studied her. "Still haven't mentioned your business to your folks?"

"Not yet." Grace pulled her hand away and walked out into the hallway. "I want to have a solid client base first."

There was a lot the Gardners hadn't been told. He'd promised Grace in the Clearwater Café that he wouldn't run away. He wanted to be an involved father. But to accomplish that, Grace and the baby would need to come with him to wherever he got a job. That wouldn't be Falcon Creek.

Meanwhile, she'd need years to build her business and he needed years to pay off his debt. A conversation now would hardly be productive. He had to have something to offer her—something worthy—before he talked to her.

"What time is your meeting tomorrow?" Grace picked up one of the empty boxes and stacked it inside the one he held.

Ethan blinked. He didn't have an actual meeting. He just wanted to talk to more than the electronic voice on the automated phone lines at the Billings Bank and Trust. He wanted to make his plea for an extension to an actual employee at the Billings Bank and Trust, preferably a kind-hearted and sympathetic customer service rep. "What time did you say you're seeing Ken?"

"Eleven a.m. at Farmhouse Burgers."

"I'll drop you off, head to my meeting and we can shop after that." He pulled out his cell phone with his free hand. "Your sister already texted a list of more items for the guest lodge and cabins. And helpfully explained which stores in the city carry which items."

"What's on the list?" Grace moved next to him to peer at his phone.

He was beginning to really like her being next to him.

Too much really. "What isn't on it." Ethan shifted closer to her and tipped the screen in her direction. "I don't ever remember Sarah Ashley being this detailed about anything of importance."

"She's…different." Grace's voice sounded surprised, yet doubtful. She added, "In a good way, I think."

"If her friends from the city book rooms at the lodge, all this shopping will have been worth it," Ethan said.

On some level it was already worth it to Ethan, given he'd get to spend more time with Grace. Since she was carrying his child, he should know more about the mother of his baby other than she was dependable and financially astute, right?

Of course, during their one night together he'd discovered a lot about the middle Gardner sister and what made her tick. He'd liked it all. It was funny to think that had Sarah Ashley not gotten married, Ethan might've missed his night with Grace.

"So tomorrow it's the city." Grace went to her car, Ethan beside her, and opened the trunk for him to put the empty boxes inside. They'd been given strict instructions to return the boxes. Sarah Ashley intended to refill the boxes with new supplies.

"It'll be you and me all day." He leaned toward her, brushed his lips across her cheek. The barest of a touch, but enough to slingshot through his nerves. He didn't linger, just reached past her and opened her car door. "Text me when you get home. Otherwise, I'll be driving to your parents to make sure you arrived safely."

She brushed her fingers across her cheek as if checking to see if he'd left a mark. Her voice was breathless and surprised. "You wouldn't."

He would. "Try me."

CHAPTER FIFTEEN

GRACE SHOOK HANDS enthusiastically with Ken Ware, her new client, and strolled out of Farmhouse Burgers in Billings. Two more names like the wholesale supplier's, and she'd have a legitimate business. What she had now was a start, a launching pad.

He'd encouraged her from the first time she'd told him about her business idea. He'd never suggested that she reconsider her dream or that she'd be leaving her parents and the store. She wasn't abandoning Brewster's completely, anyway. She was reaching for more.

Soon she'd have more than just herself to take care of.

One text to Ethan and she changed directions, away from the main street toward the small park they'd passed on the way to Farmhouse Burgers. She found Ethan sitting on a wrought iron bench, a paper bag next to him, his face tipped up toward the sun. He looked relaxed and she wanted to curl up against him and laze away the afternoon.

Would he open his arms to her or keep his distance? Grace stepped up to the bench. "That bag is too small to be Egyptian cotton towels for thirty guests."

"This is your lunch." Ethan pointed at the sack.

"I just came from a lunch meeting." Grace sat on the bench, leaving the bag between them.

"Where you didn't eat." Ethan let his gaze drift over her slowly. "You haven't touched a burger since I've been home. The closest you've come to meat was my bacon at Clearwater Café. And that was a rare occurrence from what I've seen."

He'd certainly been paying attention. Had he noticed her small but growing bump? Or that she had trouble not looking at him for longer than appropriate for two friends?

Grace opened the bag, hoping the crinkling of the paper would hide the rumble in her stomach and his effect on her. He was right. She hadn't eaten. "What's this?"

"Cream of broccoli soup from Buttercup Bistro and a warm baguette." Ethan tugged on the bag. "But if you've already eaten, I'll take it."

"Let me try a sample first." Grace dug inside for the spoon and took the lid off on the still-hot to-go container and inhaled. The steam from the soup covered her face, but couldn't warm her as much as Ethan's consideration. "I thought we needed to shop."

"We will." Ethan stretched out his legs, crossed one ankle over the other as if he was settling in to spend the afternoon in the park now that she'd joined him. "I checked in with Katie. Everything is quiet at the ranch. Figured we don't have to rush back."

She'd only ever seen Ethan in motion, moving from one task on his list to the next. Would he be content to sit with an infant sleeping on his shoulder? Or would he hand the baby off, impatient to get back to fixing a fence or an injured animal? Not that it mattered to Grace. She hadn't envisioned him being around full-time. Yet she could imagine them being at a park like this: a paper bag lunch, baby stroller and no desire to be anyplace else.

She concentrated on her soup. The faster she finished, the sooner they'd escape the park and her fantasyland.

Several silent minutes later, she dipped a piece of bread into the last bite of soup and savored the combination. She leaned back, unable to stop her smile of satisfaction from spreading across her face.

Ethan tapped her shoulder. "I thought you only wanted to try a sample."

Her smile widened at the tease in his voice and she closed her eyes, content for the first time in a long while. "Don't talk just yet. I'm enjoying this."

"Of finally not being hungry?" Ethan asked.

"That and the fact that I landed another client." Grace pumped her arm overhead and smiled at the blue sky above her. "It's a very good day."

"Congratulations." Happiness bolstered his voice.

Grace laughed with relief and joy. "I'm going to have my own business. It's becoming real."

"A few more clients and you'll be ready to move out of Brewster's and into your own office space." Ethan took her hand and squeezed her fingers.

Grace set her other hand on her stomach as the soup and excitement listed sideways.

"The soup didn't agree with you? I debated if I should've just stuck with chicken noodle, but decided to change things up for your taste buds." Ethan studied her with the critical gaze of a doctor assessing an ill patient.

"It's not the soup." This wasn't a pregnancy-induced nausea. This was life steam-rolling through her. She was about to step out of her comfort zone—the only zone she'd ever lived in. "I've only ever been at Brewster's, aside from college. Even then I came home in the summers to be at the store. It's as much home as our family house."

"I'm sure your parents would let you stay in your current office." Ethan rubbed his thumb across her palm, his voice as soothing as his caress.

He had to think she was ridiculous. He'd moved all the way out of state. She was talking about moving down the block. She was ridiculous. There was nothing absurd about his caress though. "Wasn't it hard to leave Falcon Creek and your home?"

"Not especially." Ethan shrugged. "I had goals and I knew I wasn't going to get there staying in the same place. Doing the same thing."

A shadow dimmed his gaze and she knew it was from more than the cloud passing over their heads. Even his hold on her hand tensed, less soothing and more rigid. His past still hurt.

Rather than poke at his sore spots, she opted for the easy and light. "You're telling me I need to man up and move out?"

"Your clients would probably appreciate meeting with you in an office that's bigger than a hall closet. Not that your current one isn't quaint."

"I prefer the term *compact*," she said. "I don't want my parents to think I'm abandoning them."

"Your parents want you to live your own life, not theirs. You also have two sisters to share the burden of Brewster's with."

The family store wasn't a burden. Had never been that. Was that how he saw the Blackwell land? "You never told me your strategy for the ranch?"

"Book the lodge with guests through the summer. Turn a profit." Ethan looked away from her, out into the park. That shadow dimmed his voice. "If Big E doesn't return, we'll sell."

He didn't want the homestead. Wasn't here to save the ranch to preserve their family legacy. The place meant nothing to him.

She couldn't ask him to stay for the baby. She'd never ask him to stay for her. To do so, she would have to admit to feelings she had yet to admit to herself. She wouldn't want herself or the baby to become another one of Ethan's worries. Park benches, baby strollers and lazy family afternoons with him wouldn't be a part of her world. "We should get shopping. I'm ready if you are."

Ethan stood up and held his hand out to her. Helping her up, he pulled her closer to him. "Would you like to shop for Egyptian cotton towels or horseshoe shower curtain hooks first?"

Grace laughed. She'd concentrate on the moment while

her hand was still tucked inside Ethan's and he wasn't making any move to let her go. She'd have to let go soon enough. For now, she'd leave the future for the future. "Shower curtain hooks. They're smaller and easier to carry around. Let's save the towels for last."

"Practical *and* efficient." He tapped his shoulder against hers. "I like that about you."

She wondered what else he liked about her. But she put that question into the think-about-later category and went back to the moment. This moment, where they walked hand-in-hand, comfortable and easy through the park as if they'd always been together. As if they'd always walked together like this.

A couple pushed a baby stroller ahead of them. That'd be Grace soon enough, except without Ethan. He had goals beyond Falcon Creek. She refused to hold him back. But if Big E returned, the Blackwell Ranch wouldn't be sold. Ethan would still have a home to return to, if he wanted. "Any news on Big E's whereabouts?"

Ethan shook his head. "Have you heard anything at the store?"

"Only more about how Cynthia Turner flew to Las Vegas to stop Trudy and Walt Sim's elopement." Grace shook her head. Gossip certainly was the pulse of a small town. She could only imagine the rumors that would begin when the locals discovered her pregnancy. Business at Brewster's was sure to pick up. Maybe that would soften the blow from Grace moving out on her own.

"The locals haven't whispered a word about Big E. It's strange."

"All the latest gossip came from Ms. Beverly and she can hardly hear when you shout into her good ear. I really doubt Big E would've confided in her. She also has a habit of mixing up family trees so she might've been talking about anyone."

"I think the town is in the dark as much as we are." Ethan guided her around a city grate in the sidewalk. "But Big E's life is that ranch. He has to come back eventually."

But Ethan wouldn't. She could hear that in the silence that dropped between them. "Surely Big E wouldn't abandon his grandsons. You and your brothers are his family."

"He'll come back for the Blackwell Ranch." Ethan's voice was tight as if he held his breath against some deep pain. "He always told us that if we tended the land, it would give back more than we could imagine. The land is and will always be more reliable than people."

"Do you believe that?"

"I believe the land always comes first with my grandfather. Always."

But Ethan wanted to sell the Blackwell Ranch. Sell the land. Did he believe his grandfather loved the land more than his family? He was wrong, of course. She'd seen the pride and love in Big E when he'd talked about his grandsons at the store. "Do you think Big E will go along with the changes at the guesthouse? He never struck me as a fancy soap, high-thread-count kind of guy."

"Big E is a dive-in-the-river-and-bathe kind of guy." Ethan and Grace followed the family with the stroller into the bed-and-bath store. The family moved into the children's section, while Ethan veered off into the bathroom aisle, pulling Grace with him. "If there's profit from the changes, Big E won't complain."

"He won't thank you for helping out and making improvements?" Grace asked.

"That's never been Big E's style." Ethan examined various shower curtains. "He's never been big on hugs, or showing a lot of public affection. That stuff makes a person weak, he said."

Grace touched her stomach. Little boys needed hugs and cuddles as much as little girls. All children needed praise, especially children who'd lost both parents unexpectedly and had their world turned upside down.

Ethan tossed a beach-themed washcloth at her. "Stop with the pity. Big E raised us as he was raised. We're better prepared for whatever life throws our way."

Perhaps, but she doubted an arm around a shoulder here, or a word of encouragement there, would've made the boys any less prepared for life. How prepared was Ethan to be a father? She wasn't sure. Maybe he didn't want to talk about the baby because he feared he wouldn't be a good dad. She'd have to assure him otherwise.

They'd put off the discussion far too long.

CHAPTER SIXTEEN

GRACE OPENED HER EYES, ready to apologize for sleeping during the entire drive back to Falcon Creek. But the large animal, which looked like it had gotten stuck in a cotton factory, racing between the barns and then out in front of Ethan's truck disrupted her making amends. "Was that a llama?"

Ethan took off his sunglasses and scanned the pastures. "Looked like it."

"When did you get a llama?" Grace caught sight of the giant fluff ball and shouted, "There it goes!"

"I had no idea we were getting a llama." Ethan slowed the truck on the long driveway. "It wasn't here when I left this morning."

"There it is again, but it wasn't that brown. That's definitely a llama too, but not the same one." Grace pointed at the little girl with braids, bright rain boots and an even brighter smile, running and laughing after Katie. "And that looks like one of Jon's girls."

Ethan jammed his truck into Park and opened the door. "That is Gen, and there's Abby, carrying the piglet."

Grace scrambled out of the truck after Ethan.

Katie rounded a corner, holding a goat. "Nice to see you came back finally." Katie handed Ethan the goat. "Now you can catch the llamas and find someplace to put the pair."

Ethan set the goat down. It bleated and scrambled after Katie's dog. "What happened?"

Katie scowled. "That goat won't leave Hip's side. But that's the least of our problems."

Matching squeals pierced the air as Gen and Abby raced to reach their uncle first. Ethan lifted both girls in his arms and squeezed until more laughter erupted.

Grace's mouth dropped open. Big E may have withheld

the cuddles, but not Ethan. He seemed more alive with the twins in his arms.

"The llamas arrived and spooked the pigs and donkeys." Katie threw her hands up and chased after Hip and Billy. "The goats raced around the pen while Billy smashed through every fence he could find."

Ethan bounced the twins, pretended to drop them and earned more laughter. Along with a chorus of *do that again*. "The pens weren't finished."

"I know that now." Katie tried to shoo the goat away from Hip.

Ethan set his nieces down and strode after Katie. "No one mentioned llamas. They need non-climbing fencing over five feet."

Katie gave up on the goat and confronted Ethan. "While you were shopping, I accepted delivery of the llama pair. Surprise."

"We're running out of suitable places to house the zoo," Ethan said.

"That's why you need to work, not shop," Katie shot back.

"Let's get the animals calmed and then we can decide what to do about the pens. Uh, Katie…" Grace stepped forward, but resisted putting her hand on Katie's arm. There was a green goo oozing down from her shoulder. "What is all over you?"

Ethan smiled. "Llama guts." He teased Katie like the sibling she almost was. "What did you do to the llama? They don't usually spit on people."

"Nothing." Katie grimaced at her shirt. "I just tried to guide the stubborn beast into the pen."

"You touched its neck, didn't you?" Ethan shook his head as if he was a mentor disappointed in his apprentice. "Touching its neck can make a llama want to fight. You need to let a llama smell you and your breath first."

Next to Ethan, Abby copied Ethan's stance with her

arms crossed over her chest and her head shaking in time
with her uncle's.

Grace grimaced, vowing to herself to never get that
close to a llama. Ethan and little Abby could befriend the
llamas together all they liked.

"Yes, well, I'm not a llama whisperer." Katie shook her
shirt, trying to flick the green goo onto the ground. "I prefer one-thousand-pound thoroughbreds."

A hammering like a mallet against metal echoed into
the evening air. Grace searched the fields. "Is that another escapee?"

"That's Jon." Katie called Hip to her side and waited
while Billy caught up to them. "I put out an SOS to Jon
before the entire zoo escaped."

Abby tugged on Grace's hand. "I caught one piglet, but
let it go when you guys got here."

"You did very well," Grace said. "Should we see how
we can help now?"

Abby nodded. "Maybe we can catch more piglets."

The group walked toward the petting zoo, Billy and
Hip in the lead. Trout barked a welcome. Lydia released
the fence pole she'd been holding for Jon and came over
to greet them. "Didn't expect our dinnertime to be this
exhausting. It's good to have more hands."

Katie glanced at Grace. "Speaking of dinner, Grace,
your mom dropped off a pot roast with a bag of potatoes,
carrots and detailed directions."

Grace's stomach dropped. She wasn't the best cook
when she wasn't pregnant. She looked at Ethan, longing
for an exit strategy.

"Lydia, would you mind handling the pot roast?" Ethan
touched Grace's shoulder. "I need Grace's help with Butterscotch."

Lydia glanced between them, her gaze jumping back

and forth as if she wanted to ask more. "That depends. Do we get to join you for dinner?"

"There's enough in there to feed the whole guest lodge, if it was full." Katie pinched her dirty flannel shirt away from her body.

"My mom doesn't know how to cook for less than a dozen," Grace offered.

Jon walked up and set his arm around Lydia's waist and grinned. "Then it's dinner at the Blackwell Ranch tonight. Seems fair for the inconvenience of chasing down petting zoo runaways."

Lydia clapped her hands together. "Give me an hour to get everything prepared."

Katie pinched another section of her wet shirt away from her body. "That gives me time to shower, change and burn this top."

"Jon and I will work on the pens," Ethan said. "Grace, can you handle Butterscotch?"

She wouldn't let the concern in his voice soften her. "With my assistants, I can." Grace grabbed Gen's hand and then Abby's. "How about it, ladies? Can you help with Butterscotch?"

Gen nodded, clearly excited to be with the horse.

Abby looked at Ethan. "Uncle, can I help you?"

Ethan lowered on one knee to be face-to-face with his niece. "I have a special favor to ask you. There are two friends in my cabin who are a little scared to be here. Can you check on them for me? Coconut is the rabbit and Pixie is the hedgehog. They might need some water and food. Pixie likes to walk in her wheel at night. Can you make sure the wheel is working for her?"

Abby nodded and clutched her uncle's shoulders, leaning in close. Her expression was serious, her voice matter-of-fact. "Uncle, they also need love. Coconut and Pixie need to know they're loved, then they won't be scared anymore."

"They definitely need love." Ethan set his forehead against Abby's before wrapping the little girl up into another bear hug. He reached for Gen next. His gaze was grateful when he looked up at Grace.

Grace led the girls away to Butterscotch's stall and swiped at her eye. She'd explain something got stuck in her eye if asked. The truth: the bond between Ethan and his nieces touched her heart. He made Big E out to be cold and distant, yet Ethan was anything but with Abby and Gen. Certainly he'd be the same with his own child, wouldn't he?

After order was restored at the petting zoo and Katie took leftover containers to her cabin, Grace helped Lydia dry dishes and clean up the kitchen. Ethan and Jon had suggested a game of Go Fish while the girls waited for the brownies to come out of the oven.

Dishwasher loaded, and the rest of the pot roast stashed in the refrigerator, Grace dried her hands and watched the lively card game happening in the living room. Lydia stepped up beside Grace and handed her a mug of home-made cocoa. "They're fun to watch together."

Grace smiled and stared at the whipped cream swirl dissolving in her hot chocolate, but the image of Ethan with his nieces failed to dissolve from her mind.

Ethan lifted Gen up with a peal of delighted laughter and plopped her down on the other side of him on the sofa. Gen giggled and rolled across the cushion.

Jon waved Lydia and Grace over. Lydia picked up the tray of hot chocolate mugs and marshmallows. "I think the Blackwell boys have a lot of their parents' goodness imprinted inside them. They just need someone to remind them of it every now and then."

Lydia was that someone for Jon. Finished with handing out the mugs of hot chocolate, Lydia squeezed into the recliner beside Jon. His arm circled her waist, her head settled on his shoulder.

Did Grace want that too? She couldn't watch Ethan adore their child like he adored his nieces and not want some of that same affection for herself. Grace set her mug on the coffee table and touched Ethan's shoulder. "I should get going. I promised Pops that I'd bring him bear claws and pecan muffins from Maple Bear Bakery in the morning."

Ethan grinned at her and shuffled the cards like he was a professional card player. "Are you sure we can't entice you to play one round?"

If she played one round, she might want to stay for another. And another. Then she might simply just want to stay. But this hadn't ever been about staying. This was supposed to be about her building her own life with her own child.

Ethan scooted over on the sofa and patted the cushion. "I'll give you a thermos with hot chocolate to warm you up for the drive home after you lose."

"What if I win?" Did she dare play for more than bragging rights? It was a simple game of Go Fish, it wasn't about relationships. Still, as she stood there, looking at Ethan, something in her chest said she wanted to be Ethan's first choice. His one true love.

This had to be her first and last dinner with the Blackwell family. A few hours with the adorable twins and surrounded by Jon and Lydia's love made Grace wish for the impossible.

Ethan grabbed her hand and tugged her onto the sofa beside him. "I'll pick up pastries for Pops in the morning, if I lose."

Grace sank into the couch beside Ethan. That errand would bring Ethan to the store early in the morning. She wouldn't need to make up a reason to see him. She should leave. Escape now. Before she did something unforgivable like giving Ethan her heart.

Ethan nudged her shoulder but failed to nudge any sense back into her thoughts. She told him, "You have a deal. Who goes first?"

SARAH ASHLEY KNOCKED ONCE, then walked into Grace's bedroom. "How goes Operation Rescue Blackwell?"

"What's your angle, Sarah Ashley?" Grace glanced up from her laptop. "You're helping Ethan save the Blackwell Ranch. What do you want in exchange?"

Sarah Ashley sat on the end of Grace's bed. "Why can't I want my little sister to be happy?"

Her sister believed if she was happy then everyone around her should be happy too. Sarah Ashley's happiness should be enough for everyone. Grace closed her laptop. "Well, I'm happy. So you've gotten what you wanted."

Sarah Ashley circled her palm in front of Grace's face. "This isn't the picture of happiness."

"I'm tired. We spent the entire day scouring the stores for your very specific list of items." Scoured how many stores for the perfect soap dish or shower curtain for each themed room. Passed how many strollers with doting parents. So many that Grace wondered if it was family day in Billings. With every passing stroller, she'd wanted to grab Ethan and yell: *I want that too.* Then add in a softer voice: *But only if you do.*

Grace added, "The Blackwell Ranch doesn't have extra money in its budget for all that stuff by the way." From the little Ethan had admitted, his personal finances didn't have any extra room either.

Sarah Ashley waved her hand. "It won't be a total loss. Everything will get used by the guests."

"The guests that haven't booked at the ranch yet," Grace countered.

"My friends will come through." Sarah Ashley braided her hair like they were kids again and going to stay up all night, whispering secrets to each other. "That's all you did today? Shop for the ranch."

They'd also raced through children's sections. Or avoided the baby departments completely. She wasn't talking about that with her sister. "I added another client to my business."

Sarah Ashley's eyebrows pulled together. "You really only ever think about work, don't you?"

Not recently. Thoughts of Ethan, babies and ever-afters infiltrated her workday quite often. Grace pushed up her glasses as if her lenses reflected her common sense. She should've cleaned the lenses earlier; common sense would have told her to leave the Blackwells a lot sooner.

"There's also nothing wrong with enjoying life." Sarah Ashley scooted closer to her.

"Is that what you're doing?" Grace asked. "Enjoying life?"

Sarah Ashley shrugged. "I'm still learning what I want from my life."

"So am I," Grace said. She feared what she wanted. What she could never have.

"You already have it figured out. You've always been a detailed planner," Sarah Ashley said. "You're just too scared to take what you want."

Grace sat back and looked at her sister. "Not everyone is you."

"That's a blessing." Sarah Ashley laughed. "I like standing out too much."

And Grace never had. But she'd stand out soon enough in town. Then she'd have to stand up against the rumors and gossip. Pregnant and unmarried in Falcon Creek. If only Ethan would stay. "How do you do it?"

"What?" Her sister stopped braiding.

"Take what you want and not care about the consequences?"

"It isn't that I don't care about the fallout." Sarah Ashley finished the braid and coiled her thick hair around her head like a professional hairstylist. "I just care about myself more."

"That's rather selfish," Grace said.

Sarah Ashley grinned, grabbed a heart-shaped throw pillow and tossed it at Grace. "You always were too tenderhearted."

And her sister was always too confident. Grace hugged the pillow. "Kindness isn't a flaw."

"Not to you," Sarah Ashley said. "But we've always been different."

"Is that another flaw of mine?" Grace asked.

"It's fact." Sarah Ashley stretched her legs out across the bed. "Here's the thing. I wouldn't have wasted an entire day alone with Ethan shopping for inconsequential things."

"You gave him that list with instructions."

Sarah Ashley crossed her arms over her chest, disapproval etched in her frown and voice like a censuring teacher's. "I gave you time alone with Ethan."

"Why?" Why would her sister do that? Ethan was her ex-boyfriend. Grace hadn't been truthful with Sarah Ashley.

"Like I said before, I want you to be happy." Sincerity from her sister. A sense of genuine caring. Grace was stunned.

"With your ex-boyfriend?" Grace eyed her sister. "The one who can't love me."

"I never said he can't love you. Only that he won't," she said.

Can't. Won't. What did it matter? The result would be the same. Grace would be left with a broken heart and a one-sided love. Grace hugged the pillow tighter. "I don't want to talk about this."

"That's your problem, little sister," Sarah Ashley said. "You don't talk."

"What are we doing right now?" Grace asked. "Sounds a lot like a conversation."

"This right here won't ever get you what you want." Sarah Ashley waved her hands between them. "This is just a diversion."

"From what?"

"From taking what you want and not caring about the consequences." Sarah Ashley's eyes widened with the challenge.

Grace stuttered. She'd even skipped out on saying goodbye to Ethan the morning after. She was a coward. Even now. So she hedged, "We've established that I'm not you."

"Maybe you should try to be me." Sarah Ashley stood and stared at Grace. "Maybe if you tried, you'd find something better than you imagined."

Or maybe she'd find heartache and pain. "No offense, but you're living at home after three months of marriage. Is this everything you imagined?"

"Not exactly, but it will be." Sarah Ashley smiled, the wide, confident stretch of her lips that dared anyone around her to challenge her, and walked out of the room.

Grace punched the stuffing in the heart-shaped pillow back into place. How many times had she bit her tongue today? Not out of fear that Ethan would say no to staying with her in Falcon Creek. But more from fear that Ethan would say yes out of a deep sense of duty. Obligation. Responsibility. He'd stay in Falcon Creek and pretend for the baby. Because of the baby. When she wanted him to stay for her. Because of her.

Grace wasn't anyone's fairy tale, she reminded herself. But she could be Ethan's friend and financial advisor. Right. That's where she excelled. The friend zone. She'd let her sister keep on taking what she wanted and Grace would continue to be herself.

SARAH ASHLEY CLOSED her sister's bedroom door, checked her parents' empty bedroom and went downstairs. She smiled at her father asleep in his favorite recliner and covered him with one of Grandma Brewster's handmade quilts. She followed the light streaming from beneath the study door and found her mom hunched over the coffee table scattered with puzzle pieces. The dogs were sprawled out around her feet.

Her mom pointed at the puzzle box. "This one has over three thousand pieces. Your father insists it'll take me longer than a week to finish. If you help me, I'll win."

No one in the Gardner family could ever seem to resist a challenge. "Isn't that cheating?"

"Only if you tell." Her mom patted the sofa cushion next to her.

"Grace is better at puzzles," Sarah Ashley said. But she was better at love. "You should ask her to help."

"Where is she?"

"In bed."

Her mom frowned. "Then you didn't find out about her day."

Sarah Ashley tiptoed around the dogs and sat next to her mom on the sofa. "There's nothing to find out. They spent the day shopping for the ranch." She held her sister's confidence about starting her own business. She'd let Grace share that news with their parents when the time was right.

Her mother held up a puzzle piece and stared at Sarah Ashley. "That can't be all."

Sarah Ashley snapped an edge piece into place and grinned. "They're going to need more of a push."

"Or a hard shove." Her mother turned back to the puzzle, but from the way she worried her bottom lip, Sarah Ashley knew her thoughts were centered on how best to help her middle daughter.

Sarah Ashley agreed and settled in to build the puzzle with her mom and her sister's love life.

CHAPTER SEVENTEEN

ETHAN KNOCKED ON the front door to the Gardner family home. He'd already dropped off oven-hot pastries from Maple Bear Bakery and freshly brewed coffee for Pops. While visiting he'd cleared both Lucky and Sunshine to return home with Gordy that afternoon. Pops had told Ethan between bites of pecan cinnamon muffin and chess moves that Alice and Frank always rode to the store together every morning around 8:30 a.m. Ethan had checked his watch, made one more chess move and rushed to the Gardner house.

He should've run his idea by Grace, but there hadn't been time. As it was he'd come up with the idea when he'd searched the stainless steel refrigerator for breakfast that morning and decided leftover pot roast was his best option.

Alice Gardner opened the door and smiled. "Ethan, this is a surprise. Are you here for Grace?"

"No, I came to see you." *But I wouldn't object if Grace happened to be here as well.* He hadn't seen Grace since last night when she'd won three games of Go Fish. He'd sent her home with a thermos of hot chocolate anyway, and another almost-kiss.

"Come on back to the kitchen." Alice opened the door wider and waved him inside. "I'm putting together our lunches while Frank savors his first and only cup of coffee."

Frank Gardner sat at the square kitchen table and greeted Ethan with a lift of his coffee mug. The words *Best Dad Ever* were engraved on the large mug. "Only thing I'm allowed to put sugar in these days is my coffee."

"Don't listen to him, Ethan." Alice tapped her husband's shoulder on her way to the kitchen island. Two Tupperware bowls were already filled with lettuce and a variety of garden vegetables. "It's not that bad. Frank still gets the occasional cookie and ice cream."

"Without real cream and sugar, it's only frozen ice. No matter what you want to call it, that isn't ice cream." Frank shook his head and frowned into his mug as if he couldn't figure out where his taste buds had gone. "Eat now, Ethan, before the doctors take away all your joy."

Alice cut up a carrot and tossed a large chunk on the table in front of Frank. "That's to dip in your coffee."

Frank waved the carrot at Ethan. "This is your future, Ethan. Eat all the good stuff while you can."

"I apologize, Ethan. Frank is feeling rather dramatic this morning." Alice chopped a zucchini with the precision of a seasoned chef. "He's always liked farm vegetables and fruits."

"And apple pie. Raspberry pie. Blueberry cobbler. Haven't seen any of those on the dinner table in so long I've forgotten the taste." Frank crunched down hard on the carrot.

Ethan accepted the coffee Alice handed him in a plain, sturdy white ceramic mug. He was glad because he wasn't certain he'd have been able to drink out of a *Best Dad Ever* mug. He wasn't a father yet and already he felt as if he'd failed his child.

He was certain the Gardners wouldn't consider him the best of anything once he left town to start his new career without Grace. But if Grace left with him, the Gardners would most likely resent him even more. They'd lose a daughter and their first grandchild. He was not venturing into that particular conversation with the Gardners without Grace beside him. "Alice, I don't know which I like more, your homemade desserts or fabulous dinners?"

"We've debated that over the years," Frank said. Alice sat next to him at the kitchen table. Frank leaned over to kiss her cheek. "Never did decide what she's best at. Maybe we should have another cook-off. Dinner versus dessert."

Alice laughed, shaking her head before returning Frank's kiss with one of her own. "Nice try."

If Ethan considered marriage, he'd want to be married like the Gardners, who still shared a special kind of affection. He'd want the same kind of unconditional support that only grew stronger just like the Gardners. Had he not spent so much time around the Gardners, he wouldn't have known long-lasting marriages like theirs existed. Although he liked to imagine his parents' marriage would've lasted. The Gardners trusted each other with their hearts. But Ethan wasn't convinced he could ever do that. He'd seen the deep, emotional pain Jon suffered when he separated from his first wife, and the mockery his grandfather made of marriage. The result was he doubted he'd ever have a happy marriage. Good thing marriage advice wasn't the help he required from Alice right now.

"I have an offer for you, Alice." Ethan bet Alice could make a frozen dinner taste good and he banked on her obvious love of cooking now. "It's not for a cook-off as it'd require lunch, dinner and desserts for a week. The only debate would be the menu, but you'd have full control."

Alice set her elbows on the table and leaned forward. Interest was there in her cheerful gaze. "What are you asking?"

"I'm hoping you'll agree to cook for the Zigler family of thirty that arrives at the Blackwell Ranch at the end of next week."

Alice looked at Frank and then at Ethan. Surprise shifted across her face. "You want me to cook for the guests at the ranch?"

Ethan nodded. "You're one of the best in town."

"Big E and Zoe preferred to cater." Frank rubbed his

chin. "Always saw the trucks from the city heading out to the ranch."

"I'd like to make the experience more personal," Ethan said, using another one of Sarah Ashley's suggestions. Besides, he couldn't afford the highly rated personal chef experience the city promised. He paused and drew a deep breath. These days it seemed everything in his life came back to money and his lack of it. "I'd like to tell you that was my only motive. But the other issue is money. Blackwell can pay for the food, but we can't pay for your time."

Frank nodded and glanced at his wife. "Have to respect his honesty."

Ethan choked on his sip of coffee. If he were truly honest, he'd tell her parents that he was having a baby with Grace. Their own daughter. The one he hoped was upstairs getting ready for work after sleeping in as he'd completed her morning tasks with Pops for her. He'd been glad to lose at Go Fish last night to give Grace the reprieve she'd never take on her own. "But I have a barter in mind."

"Let's hear it." Again Alice leaned forward.

Her smile reminded him of Grace's: welcoming, kind, authentic. "I'll give you free vet exams for all your animals." The Gardners had four rescue cats and three rescue dogs and if his suspicions were correct, Mrs. Gardner would take in more animals if they needed homes.

Alice brightened and smiled. "Ethan, I'm sure you and I can work out something. Now what did you have in mind for the menu?"

Ethan skipped his gaze to Frank, silently pleading for inspiration. He'd lived on chicken noodle soup and takeout for far too many years. "I'm assuming pizza every night wouldn't be acceptable."

Frank laughed and picked out an apple from the hand-carved wooden fruit bowl in the center of the table. "Not if you want future guests at the ranch."

"My culinary skills don't extend beyond cereal, grilled cheese and chicken soup." He could also list which fast-food places delivered the quickest and who had the best deals back in Denver. But none of that helped the guest ranch in Falcon Creek.

Alice propped her chin on her hand and studied him. "What about Katie? Does she have any cooking experience?"

"Katie likes food. That is, she likes to eat all kinds." Ethan and Katie had been fighting over Alice's leftovers every day. Which was why he'd hid the pot roast behind the carton of expired milk and the wilted broccoli this morning. With luck, Katie wouldn't touch the stale milk and the pot roast would be waiting for his lunch. "If Katie can cook gourmet style, I haven't tasted it."

"You want me to create the whole menu then?" Delight lightened Alice's voice and rushed across her face.

"Desperately. I can do the shopping if you make me a list." He'd proven yesterday with Grace that he excelled at checking items off lists. And if Katie ever stopped adding to his fix-it list, he might complete that one too.

"You'll also help with some prep," Alice added.

Ethan leaned away from the table and scratched his chin. He hadn't helped anyone in the kitchen in years. Not since his mother had passed away. When his mom had been alive, he'd often been too busy running outside with his brothers to ask if she needed him. He should've asked more often. "I'm not sure you want me in the kitchen."

"I most certainly do want you there." Alice stood up and grabbed a notepad and pencil from the island.

"Where do you want Ethan?" Grace asked. She stood in the doorway behind him, but made no move to come into the kitchen.

Ethan cataloged Grace from her tilted bun to her slightly pale cheeks, to the way her gaze darted from one person to the other without landing for more than a few seconds on anyone. She looked like she needed a nap, more soup and a long hug. He wasn't sure in which order. Surely, she knew he wouldn't tell her parents about the baby without talking to her first.

Her mother filled a mug with hot water from a teapot on the stove and smiled at Grace. "In the kitchen."

Grace's gaze continued to hop around the room. Ethan cleared his throat, pulling her attention to him. "Your mom has graciously agreed to create the menu and cook for the Zigler family arriving at the ranch next week." Ethan pulled out the chair beside him and motioned for Grace to sit. She looked like she wanted to collapse and that would only raise questions neither of them wanted to answer. "She seems to think I'd be helpful in the kitchen with her."

"He will be." Alice set a mug and peppermint tea bag in front of Grace. "But we can settle those details later. There's something we need to settle right now." Alice paused, looked at Ethan and then Grace, as if to ensure she had their full attention. Seeming satisfied, she continued, her voice mild yet slightly curious, as if she wanted to know what they'd put on their Christmas wish list. "Your father and I would like to know what you two are doing about the baby."

Grace spit her tea back into her mug.

Ethan rubbed Grace's back and blurted out the only answer that came to him. "Grace refused to marry me."

"Rightly so." Frank handed Grace a napkin from the holder and frowned. "I don't recall anyone asking for my blessing. Seems that's the first thing that should've happened."

"There are a lot of things that should've happened first." Alice pushed her chair back and took Frank's hand. "But we can't dwell on all that now. It's not productive."

"How did you know?" Grace whispered.

"I was at your sister's wedding too." Alice glanced at

Ethan before tilting her head at Grace. "I also had three daughters so I know a little something about what pregnancy looks like."

Grace set her elbow on the table and cradled her forehead in her palm. "We were going to tell you."

Ethan nodded as if that would prove he and Grace were a united front on all things baby-related. The truth was much more complicated. Or perhaps they'd made it complicated by avoiding the topic altogether.

"I don't doubt that you would've told us eventually." Alice stretched out the last word as if she didn't quite believe her daughter.

"Your mom isn't the most patient when it's something this important." Frank draped his arm around Alice's shoulders.

They were the united front. The ones forcing Grace and Ethan to confront the situation.

"So what are your plans?" Alice asked.

"I have a doctor's appointment late next week," Grace said, talking into her teacup.

"I'm driving her," Ethan put in. Grace glanced at him. Ethan shrugged, although it was more of a quick tensing of his shoulders. What did she want him to say? Neither one of them were offering up engaging conversation exactly.

Alice looked at Frank, her expression bewildered, as if she struggled to figure out why everyone wasn't on the same page. "It's great you have the next few days planned. What about the rest of the baby's life?"

"We haven't gotten that far yet," Grace said.

"We're taking it one day at a time," Ethan added and then cringed.

"That would be fine if this was a conversation about when to start a diet," Frank said. "But you're both having a child. A child that's going to be totally reliant on the parents to have it together."

Weren't parents supposed to make their kids feel better? Grace looked ill, her skin pale and tinged with green. Ethan swallowed, battling down his own queasiness. "I intend to be there for the baby and Grace."

"You were man enough to start this, I'd expect you'll be man enough to be there through the rest of it." Frank's gaze locked on Ethan. His tone was direct, his voice uncompromising. "Children are a lifetime commitment."

What kind of man did Frank expect Ethan to be? The kind that stayed in town with an empty bank account and nothing to give his child. Or the kind that left town to build a career that would allow him to one day pay for his child's college.

Grace straightened beside Ethan, no longer withering into her chair like a teenager who'd broken curfew again. "I'm starting my own accounting business."

Ethan straightened beside her, absorbing Grace's confidence for himself.

"Do you think now is the best time with the baby coming?" Alice asked.

"I've been building up my client list the last few weeks." Grace smiled at Ethan. "Ethan has been helping me."

"It's just that is a lot to take on with a newborn." Alice clenched her hands together on the table.

Grace reached over and covered her mom's hands. "I won't abandon Brewster's."

"The store will be fine." Alice pulled away and sat back as if offended. "Our concern is you, Grace. Even you can only handle so much. That's not a criticism."

Grace touched his arm; her fingers were cold and stiff, unlike her pleasant tone. "I've been looking at potential office spaces already."

"I appreciate that you've decided on a direction for your professional future." Alice took off her glasses and motioned between Grace and Ethan. "But is there a future between the two of you?"

"We'll always be connected through the baby," Ethan said. That made them sound like nothing more than strangers living in the same apartment complex and connected by a common street address. He was definitely excelling at saying the wrong things today. He should probably shut his mouth now.

"People got married in your day, Mom, because of a baby. But it's not like that anymore." Grace pulled her hand away from him. "We don't need a piece of paper to be committed."

"Then you are committed to each other?" Alice pressed.

Ethan coughed and lifted his coffee mug to his lips. It was empty like his comeback.

"We're committed to doing what is best for the baby," Grace said.

Alice stood up and picked up the lunches she'd prepared for Frank and herself. From her brisk movements, Ethan knew she hadn't liked what she'd heard. She'd wanted more for her daughters. He'd seen her pride and joy at Sarah Ashley's wedding. She wouldn't want Grace raising a baby alone. She wouldn't want Grace alone.

Alice walked to the door and turned. "In our day, love brought us together and love kept us together. Love was the bond."

But love didn't provide for a child. Love didn't buy diapers, pay the mortgage or offer security.

Frank slowly slid his chair back from the table. He crossed to Grace, kissed her cheek and squeezed her shoulder. He whispered he loved her before following Alice down the hallway toward the garage.

Ethan marveled at the tight father-daughter bond between Grace and Frank.

Would he be the same with his own child? Would he

fail when his child needed him the most? He'd never really questioned how Big E had raised them, but he wasn't certain Big E's parenting methods would work for a daughter or even a son not growing up on a ranch. He'd never wanted to raise his children on a ranch. He'd given up that lifestyle when he'd gone to college, determined to be a vet. Or more precisely, he'd given up the Blackwell Ranch life. But would his upbringing shape the father he'd be? How could it not. He wondered what Big E's reaction would've been if his daughter had come home pregnant and unmarried? As it was, Big E disowned his daughter over an argument that Ethan still didn't know the exact details of.

What would Big E say when he learned Ethan got someone and not just anyone, but Grace Gardner, pregnant and didn't step up to do the right thing? His grandfather was an old-school man with old-school values despite his faults. Ethan could add another way he'd disappointed Big E. Now he'd disappointed Frank Gardner too. Ethan shoved out of the chair and paced around the kitchen.

Sarah Ashley strolled in and glanced between Ethan and Grace. "I would've assumed Mom's tears would've been happier than that when she learned about the baby."

Ethan gaped at Sarah Ashley. Grace dunked her tea bag into her mug as if she wanted to dunk herself in the ceramic cup too.

"You did tell them about the baby, right?" Sarah Ashley poured coffee into a silver to-go mug.

"They already knew." Grace's voice held less strength than the steam from her tea. "Sort of like you."

"I never talked to them." Sarah Ashley held up her hands, palms out. "But we all live in this house together. Besides, I warned you that you needed to trust someone if you wanted to keep your secret."

"I'm supposed to believe you would've kept this secret?" Grace asked.

"Believe what you want." Sarah Ashley shrugged and grabbed a pear. "But I would've helped you. You never asked."

"You can't tell me you're happy about this." Grace flicked her finger at Ethan as if her willpower alone could cast him out of the kitchen. "He's your ex-boyfriend. I'm your sister."

"It's not how I would've expected things to go." Sarah Ashley washed the pear and dried it, calm and collected, as if they were discussing nothing more life altering than missed dinner reservations. "But this isn't high school anymore."

Ethan grimaced. He was leaving Falcon Creek, but he would take responsibility. "We should've told you."

"Probably." Sarah Ashley bit into the pear and chewed, all the while considering him.

He'd been waiting for her comeback since their confrontation in Clearwater Café after he'd insulted her. From the way her gaze locked on to him like a target, he knew he wouldn't need to wait much longer.

Finally, Sarah Ashley swallowed and said, "But then I should've told you that you were only ever my backup. So we'll call it even."

Ethan shook his head. Not that he hadn't known. Still, he couldn't deny her words sliced through him, clean and quick yet destructive all the same.

Sarah Ashley wasn't finished. "If you promise my sister the world, everything will be better."

Grace's mug thumped on the table.

"Grace is too practical to ask for that." Ethan dropped a second bag of peppermint tea and fresh mug of hot water next to Grace. "Only you would expect the impossible, Sarah Ashley."

Sarah Ashley met his gaze, and her voice was solemn as if she'd made a pledge. "There's nothing impossible when it comes to love."

"Love itself is impossible," Ethan shot back.

Sarah Ashley shook her head and walked over to Grace. She touched her sister's shoulder as if Grace needed support. "Grace, I'll help Mom with the payroll this morning. You can take your time here."

With that, Sarah Ashley breezed out of the kitchen, taking Ethan's conviction with her. Ethan looked out the window and searched for the right words. Words he hadn't gotten right all day. Silence settled in the kitchen and his throat.

SARAH ASHLEY'S CAR pulled out of the garage. Grace had to pull away too. Ethan claimed love was impossible. Her sister had been right about Ethan not being able to love. Yet hearing the words come out of Ethan was a hit Grace hadn't known would hurt so much. "You don't have to take me to the doctor's appointment."

"I should be there." His voice was flat, his expression contained as if he too had pulled away, deep inside himself.

Did he want to go to the doctor with her? She refused to be a burden. "If you have work at the ranch to deal with, it's no big deal. I've been before without an escort."

"No, it's fine." Ethan walked back to the table and sat down across from her. "I'll sort it out."

But it wasn't fine. None of this was fine. She could see that much from his movements, stiff and tense as if he'd stepped into someone else's life. "We've gone back to awkward again."

Ethan covered his face with his hands. "I'm not sure how I imagined that conversation with your parents would go, but that wasn't it. And then there was Sarah Ashley."

"I'm sorry you had to be here." *I'm sorry you regret our one night together.*

Ethan raised his head and reached for her hand. "Grace,

I'm part of this. We made this baby together and we have to deal with that together."

"What does that mean?"

"Well, you're building a client list for your business to support the baby." Uncertainty still controlled his voice. "I'm figuring out how I can help support the baby too."

"By being there. By being in your child's life and not for a weekend, or one month in the summer either." Grace bit down on her lip. She'd just told him that she wanted him around full-time. When had she adjusted her world to include Ethan in their lives on a daily basis?

"That's not enough," Ethan said.

That was all that mattered. Being an involved father. She'd seen him with his nieces. A parent was more than just a financial provider. She wanted for their baby what he gave so freely to his family. "What exactly are your plans?"

"I'm still working out the details. I haven't confirmed anything specific yet, but I hope to soon."

"That's all you ever say." Grace slammed her mug on the table, the tea and her frustration spilling over. "What does that mean?"

"It means I don't have a job." Ethan jumped up and gripped the chair back. "I don't have money to support a child."

"There are other ways to be there for the baby," Grace said.

"You're not listening. I don't have a proper home. Money. Nothing to help provide for a child."

Nothing, but his love. He could give a child his love. But that wasn't an option. That wasn't enough for him. Love was impossible. His words to her sister.

She'd watched him recoil when they'd been talking to Sarah Ashley. He'd folded in on himself at the mere mention of love. "If you had a home. Money. The means to support a child, what then?" *Would you choose me? Could you love?*

"We need to concentrate on what is, not dwell on what-ifs." He crossed his arms over his chest.

She had her answer. "The reality is that we both need to get to work. Katie is probably already looking for you." Grace transferred her tea into a stainless steel travel mug. "And I can't leave Sarah Ashley alone with the payroll." But she could leave Ethan alone.

Grace grabbed her purse and car keys. "Once you've confirmed your plans with respect to how you're providing for your child, we'll talk more."

"You'll be the first to know."

But not his first choice.

Grace walked to her car, leaving Ethan and her useless wishes behind.

CHAPTER EIGHTEEN

ETHAN OPENED THE passenger door and extended his hand to Grace. "Thanks again for coming with me today."

"We made a deal." She accepted his assistance, but dropped his hand as soon as she was free and clear of his truck. "I keep my word when I give it."

It bothered him that Grace had joined him out of a sense of obligation. Because they'd arranged that he'd take her to Billings, and she'd come to the meeting with Judge Edwards. He would have preferred her to be there simply because she wanted to. Because she wanted to support him.

Truth was, he needed her support. And didn't that make him more selfish than Sarah Ashley had ever been.

He should have released her from their deal. He should've left her at Brewster's.

The county courthouse in Livingston loomed large in front of them. They followed the signs to Judge Edwards's chambers, pretending that they were all right, and ignoring the fact that they hadn't talked since their confrontation with her parents three days ago. Not to mention that he'd disappointed Grace and continued to do so every minute he failed to make things right. He just wished he knew what to do.

A clerk led them into Judge Edwards's corner office with floor-to-ceiling bookshelves and thick red curtains at the windows behind her formidable desk. The American flag and the Montana state flag stood like sentries on either side of her tall leather chair. A round conference table with seating for six waited in the back of the office. A love seat sofa with a plush blanket welcomed visitors to curl up with a book. The clerk guided Ethan and Grace to the pair of stiff red leather chairs facing the desk, aware this wasn't a social call.

A vintage mantel clock with a pendulum chimed the hour and Judge Edwards's arrival. Ethan and Grace rose as if a bailiff had called out, *All rise for the honorable Judge Edwards.*

Myrna Edwards's hair had faded to white and more wrinkles now creased her eyes and mouth. But age hadn't softened her sharp nose or intense gaze. The woman commanded the room despite her short stature. She wasn't the traditional sweet grandmotherly type that children wanted to hug. She was the type who'd made infants cry. Ethan wanted to cry himself.

Judge Edwards sat in her chair and trapped Ethan with her unrelenting stare. "You lost your grandfather."

Ethan fixed his gaze on Myrna Edwards and injected confidence into his voice. "Big E took the RV for an extended trip."

Beside him, Grace shifted. He heard the scratch of her suit pants. Ethan held Myrna's stare. If he risked a look at Grace, Myrna might consider him unsure. She always could spot a weakness and attack like a pit viper.

"Elias never claimed to like that rolling house on wheels." Judge Edwards tapped the manila folder on the desk in front of her. "Claimed he could never spend more than a weekend in its confining space."

Big E had already spent more than half a dozen weekends in the RV as far as Ethan knew. "It seems he changed his mind."

Judge Edwards peered at Ethan over the rim of her glasses. "You can't sit there and tell me you honestly believe that Elias Blackwell has changed."

Ethan swallowed. "It's not unheard of for people to have a change of heart."

Her eyes narrowed. Everything about her stilled as if hardened like steel. She'd even stopped blinking. "Then *you've* had a change of heart?"

What did this have to do with him and his heart? He

needed signing authority on Big E's bank account. He needed access to more money to keep the ranch afloat. It was a simple request. Everything was detailed in the paperwork in that manila folder under her cold hands. And yet Judge Edwards's stony face made everything seem complicated. "I'm sorry I flattened your car tires."

"As sure as arthritis stiffens each one of my joints, I know that's a lie." Judge Edwards twisted in her leather chair, picked up a thick book from the shelf behind her and plunked it on the desk. Her finger traced over the gold embossed lettering on the cover that spelled *Bible* as if she was both judge and juror for lost souls. "I realize we are seated in my chambers and not in a courtroom. But I feel the need to make you swear under oath to tell the truth and nothing but the truth all the same."

Ethan put his hands on his knees to keep his legs from bobbing up and down, giving away his guilt. But he had no idea what he was guilty of. He could've sounded more sincere in his long overdue apology, he supposed, but that would've been a lie. He'd been a twelve-year-old boy still grieving the loss of his parents. He'd have resented the intrusion of any woman Big E had married back then. He'd wanted his parents. He'd wanted to return to his old life. Surely even Myrna Edwards recognized that.

He searched her fingers for a wedding ring. If she'd found her soul mate and long-lasting happiness, maybe she'd be more likely to want to others to share in the joy. But besides several swollen knuckles from the arthritis, nothing else adorned her fingers. Ethan's confidence deflated like one of Myrna's tires with his arrow embedded in it. "I'm good not going through the whole oath procedure."

"Grace, you've always been the most levelheaded and sensible of the Gardner daughters. If my sources are correct, and they usually are, your influence has finally impacted your sister. Therefore, I'm certain you'll intercede if you believe Ethan is straying from the truth." Judge Edwards offered Grace a smile that looked more like an order.

"Y-yes, ma'am," Grace said.

Ethan relaxed hearing Grace's hesitant agreement. Nice to know he wasn't alone in his confusion. He was desperate for Judge Edwards to excuse herself for a moment and then he'd ask Grace who Myrna's sources were and where to find them.

Seemingly satisfied that she had both a witness to Ethan's potential duplicity, and an accomplice, Judge Edwards opened the folder and glanced through the paperwork. "You're requesting signing authority on all Elias Blackwell's financial accounts."

Ethan cleared his throat. "That's correct."

"Elias already granted you signing privileges for the main Blackwell Ranch account." Judge Edwards closed the folder and peered at him. Her glasses only magnified the hostility in her gaze. "I have to assume if Elias had wanted you to have signing privileges on the other account, he'd have arranged that at the same time."

"Perhaps he forgot," Ethan said.

"Elias Thurmond Blackwell has a memory like a well-preserved, centuries-old fossil. Impressive and intact." Judge Edwards glanced at Grace and smiled. "Your grandfather Brewster runs a close second, dear. If you haven't recorded Pops's memories yet, you should get to it rather quickly. Otherwise you may miss out on all the family history to pass down to your children."

Ethan sat still but wanted to object. He wasn't interested in scrapbooking family memories of either the Brewsters or the Blackwells. "I need access to that other money."

Judge Edwards's gaze flicked to Ethan and pinned him in place like a scorpion's tail. "To pay off your college debt?"

Ethan's mouth dropped open.

Judge Edwards made a scooping motion with her hand as if trying to get Ethan to close his mouth. "Obviously, you must have debt. You've always been rash. You refused Elias's offer to pay for your college tuition and set out to conquer the world on your own. It seems fair to say you've been less than victorious."

The only victory he'd like to celebrate now was taking his bow and arrow and shooting out all four tires on Judge Edwards's luxury SUV sitting in the parking lot. Judge Edwards's sources lacked information. She only knew one side of Big E's offer to Ethan all those years ago.

The other side had strings attached that would have forced him into a life sentence on the Blackwell Ranch. The other side kept Big E in control of Ethan indefinitely. That was the side Ethan had refused to accept. And in doing so, Big E had severed ties with Ethan, his own grandson. Ethan had been forced out and on his own, and he was still fighting that battle.

Grace's hand reached for his shoulder. Her steady touch drifted down his arm, easing the anger inside him as if she had only to wave her hand to corral a herd of wild horses. "But, Judge, you're not taking in the full picture." Ethan loosened his tightened jaw, alert and ready to defend Grace if Judge Edwards rebuked her or, even worse, held her in contempt.

"Judge Edwards, perhaps our intent wasn't clear. And I apologize if I missed putting the correct financial documents in the folder." Grace sat forward in her chair. "But the Blackwell Ranch is in serious trouble. The request for signing authority isn't for personal gain, it's to hire staff and cover other legitimate expenses for operating the premises."

"Your attempt to keep the Blackwell Ranch solvent is to spend more money?" Judge Edwards glared at Ethan.

Grace started to speak, but Ethan set his hand on her arm and squeezed. He edged forward in his seat until he was side by side with Grace, making them a united front against the veritable and imposing Myrna Edwards. "I'm quite certain Grace didn't leave any documents out of that folder. As you said before, Grace Gardner is levelheaded and sensible. She's also detailed, professional and excels at her job. Grace has advised me that I need to build revenue for the ranch. I cannot do that if I'm also working on the land and the guest lodge and the petting zoo."

"I had no idea you cared so deeply for the place," Judge Edwards said.

He cared deeply enough to ensure the ranch was profitable before he stuck a For Sale sign on the front gate. He doubted that truth would endear him to Judge Edwards. "I too care about having something to pass down to our child."

Judge Edwards slid the Bible across the desk, closer to him. "Careful, Day Two, you're teetering close to perjury and we both know it."

"You want the truth." Ethan set his left palm on the Bible and raised his right hand. "Jon, or Day One as you know him, can't physically run two ranches. Katie Montgomery can only work so many hours in a day. And no one, I repeat no one, can locate our grandfather. Big E may or may not return. But there are people and animals on Blackwell property that need to be taken care of in the meantime."

"How long do you intend to remain caretaker of the Blackwell Ranch?" Judge Edwards asked.

Ethan kept his hand on the Bible and never flinched. "As long as I have to."

With luck and Judge Edwards's approval that would not be much longer. With signing authority, he could hire new ranch hands and with Sarah Ashley's connections book the lodge through the summer all before the Zigler family unpacked in the guest lodge next week. That left only an official job offer from a practice somewhere and he'd relinquish his role and finally get back to his own life.

He pulled his hand off the Bible and shifted, bumping his knee against Grace's. His personal life was a little more complicated. But he was certain Grace would want what was best for the baby, even if that meant him relocating.

"Very well, Day Two, I'll grant you signing authority." Judge Edwards stopped his smile with her hand. "On the condition that Grace provides me with updated financials on a weekly basis."

Why didn't Judge Edwards trust him? He'd apologized and given her the full truth. Well, almost the full truth. Selling the land was only speculation at this point.

Grace touched his knee and grinned at Judge Edwards. "I'm more than happy to provide you with whatever reports you'd like."

"Day Two, I have one more request," Judge Edwards said.

Ethan waited. From her grave tone and serious expression this wasn't a simple request, but a tall order.

"My Spike hasn't been his usual self and I'd like you to check him out." Judge Edwards tapped her cell phone and held it out so that he and Grace could see the screen.

Ethan rubbed his chin, covering his mouth to hide his surprise. He'd figured Myrna Edwards owned a python or horned toad, not a pair of hairless Chinese crested dogs, one with a Mohawk, the other wearing a polka-dot sweater. "Did you say his name was…"

"Spike," Judge Edwards filled in. "And that is his sister, Bonbon. Aren't they the sweetest things you've ever seen?"

Sure, thought Ethan, if you liked Mohawks and doggy booties and tongues that hung sideways.

Ethan stared at Myrna Edwards, wondering if he'd actually just heard her coo over her seven-pound, hairless dogs. The lines in her forehead had disappeared and her pursed lips softened like butter left too long in the sun. She went from hard-edged judge to gentle older woman in an instant. Ethan didn't trust the transformation. Myrna Edwards had sources and an agenda. She never cooed, and she never thawed. What was her game?

Grace took the phone from Myrna and caught her laughter in a quick throat clearing. "They're adorable."

"Rescued them from a bad breeder near the state line.

You should've seen how pitiful they looked when I went to pick them up." Myrna dabbed at the edge of her eye as if the memory still upset her. "I'll never understand people who mistreat animals."

Ethan would never understand Myrna Edwards. How could a woman as rigid as Judge Edwards harbor a soft spot? He looked at Grace, who was smiling wistfully at the photograph of Myrna's rescues. Was Grace buying into Judge Edwards's charade?

"I'll be home at five o'clock. I'll expect to see you this evening to check Spike." Judge Edwards took her phone from Grace. "Unless you'd like to examine him here, since you've used other offices as temporary exam rooms."

Grace glanced around the room. "You bring your dogs to work?"

Judge Edwards's smile made Ethan want to refer to her as Myrna. *Almost.*

Judge Edwards said, "My assistant and I converted a closet into a modified doggy day care. They tend to get anxious if I leave them alone too long."

More likely the dog owner got too anxious without her four-legged companions beside her, Ethan decided. Myrna, the overprotective dog owner, kept glancing at the clock on the mantle and then looking toward the door. Ethan asked, "Does your assistant walk them?"

"Four times a day." Judge Edwards checked her watch. "They should be returning in the next ten minutes."

"We'll wait," Grace said, offering a smile.

"Judge Edwards, I'm not licensed to practice here." Ethan frowned at Grace. He felt compelled to say it, even though no one seemed inclined to listen, including Myrna Edwards.

"We're practically family." Judge Edwards rolled her chair away from her desk and walked to a side door near the bookshelves. "I'm simply seeking your opinion, the same as I do with my second cousin Barbara who's a cardiologist over in Missoula."

But Ethan doubted her second cousin examined Myrna or prescribed medications. Barbara most likely listened over the phone and offered her advice for the judge to take to her own doctor.

"Do you want me to get your bag from the truck?" Grace asked.

No, he wanted to get in his truck and leave. What was Grace thinking? Was this retaliation for disappointing her? No good could come from examining Spike. Judge Edwards could report him for practicing without a license. Was that her revenge after all these years? Her final payback for a misguided boy, grieving his parents. "I need to get Grace back to Brewster's and Katie needs me at the ranch. I'll come by later."

Judge Edwards took off her glasses and studied him. Her gaze once again sharp and intense. "Grace, you should get Ethan's bag from the truck."

Grace jumped up from her chair and fled from the room as if someone had yelled fire.

"I don't trust you'll come back to check on my precious boy, Day Two."

She was right not to trust him. Ethan had no intention of going to her vampire den. He wouldn't lose his license for Myrna's beloved dogs. "That makes us even, Judge Edwards."

Myrna leaned back, her eyebrows lifted. "You don't trust me, Day Two?"

Ethan never flinched. She could be recording their conversation for all he knew. His feelings toward Judge Edwards wouldn't be put on record.

"So be it," she said. "But I know you, Day Two. When those two dogs enter this chamber, you won't be able to refuse to help them. You've always been better with animals than people."

Grace entered, cradling Spike. His head rested on her

arm and he seemed more than content not to move. Grace's concerned gaze clashed with Ethan's. "He walked right into the assistant's desk and flopped down as if stunned." Grace kissed Spike's Mohawk.

Ethan glanced at Judge Edwards. "Does Spike bump into walls and furniture often?"

Judge Edwards moved to Grace's side. Her voice shook, along with her hand, when she reached out to pet Spike. "It's been happening more frequently. He stopped jumping off the bed at night. And prefers that I carry him down the steps."

Grace's eyes widened into a plea. Judge Edwards had been right. Ethan would've struggled to walk away from Spike. But he could've walked away.

Ethan examined Spike and asked Judge Edwards more questions. He'd moved Judge Edwards and Grace over to the sofa with Spike curled up on the thick blanket between the women. Ethan sat down on the edge of the coffee table and faced Judge Edwards. "I'm going to recommend you take Spike to an ophthalmologist as soon as possible."

"An eye doctor," Grace said.

Ethan nodded. "I'm not certain, but I think Spike might be suffering from a congenital eye disease that causes permanent blindness."

Judge Edwards covered her mouth, but not before a sob escaped. "Can it be cured?"

"I'm afraid it can't." Tears pooled behind Judge Edwards's glasses. Ethan leaned forward and touched her knee. "Myrna, many animals live long and happy lives without their vision. There will be an adjustment period for both you and Spike."

Judge Edwards dabbed a tissue to her eyes. "I'd like you to treat Spike."

"If I was Spike's doctor, I'd send him to a specialist for a diagnosis," Ethan said.

"And?" Judge Edwards persisted.

"And I'd run routine blood work and a urinalysis to

rule out any other underlying conditions we don't know about." Because Myrna looked so lost, he added, "And I'd work with you at home to make sure Spike's environment is safe and that you understand his needs going forward."

"I would like that," Judge Edwards said.

Grace dabbed a tissue at her own eyes and blew her nose.

What had happened? He went from wanting to cry in dread when he'd first walked into Judge Edwards's office to sitting with two weeping women on the conversational couch, a patient curled up between them. "I can refer you to several specialists in Billings, if you'd like."

"I'd appreciate your assistance." Judge Edwards picked up Spike and cuddled him close to her. "Spike and Bonbon are my family. I'll do whatever I can for them."

Ethan stood up, helped Judge Edwards stand and went to assist Grace as well. But she was already up, having composed herself. It took another five minutes for Ethan to convince Judge Edwards that Spike would be okay, even without his eyesight. Then he spent five more minutes meeting Bonbon out in the reception area.

Finally, he and Grace climbed into his truck and headed back to Falcon Creek.

"You're really good with the locals and their pets." Grace's voice had too much hope and too much speculation.

Ethan glanced at her. He had to set her straight. "I'm not interested in becoming Falcon Creek's new Dr. Terry."

"There's nothing wrong with Dr. Terry's practice." Grace shifted away from him and looked out the window.

Except that it wasn't focused on high-end thoroughbreds and was located in the wrong town.

CHAPTER NINETEEN

"YOU SHOULD SLOW down to minimize your stress." Ethan took Grace's phone and turned if off before stuffing it in his back pocket. He pointed at the sign in Dr. Wilder's waiting room that read No Cell Phones.

Grace scowled at Ethan, but let him keep her phone. She'd called Ethan that morning when she'd started spotting despite her vow to do things on her own. Despite her vow to leave Ethan alone. She'd kept her promise for two whole days after their meeting with Judge Edwards and Ethan's declaration that he wanted nothing to do with Dr. Terry's practice in Falcon Creek. After that, she'd wanted nothing to do with Ethan.

Until now. She needed his strong shoulders. She needed to share her worry about the baby. She didn't want to face any problems alone just like Myrna hadn't wanted to with little Spike. That might make her weak, but she didn't care.

"How can you keep letting your family take advantage of you?" he asked.

"They aren't taking advantage." She crossed her arms over her chest and stared at the floor.

"Yes, Grace," he said. "Yes, they are."

"There are things at the store only I can do." She had value at the store. She was needed at the store. Was that so wrong?

"Sarah Ashley can manage some things." Ethan set his elbows on his knees and leaned forward. "You trained your sister really well. Trina was promoted to manager and you need to let her manage."

"My parents are less worried when I'm involved." And Grace had a place where she belonged. She knew what was expected of her. Knew where she stood.

"We've been over this. You can't run your business and Brewster's at the same time." He ran his hand through his hair. "Something has to give. It's too much for anyone to cope with."

She'd be able to cope better if she knew what Ethan intended to do. "I don't want to give up either."

"It's not healthy for you or the baby to keep pushing yourself like this." He covered her hands she'd clutched in her lap, pulling her focus to him.

The concern in his voice and his gaze seeped into her, making her want to believe in their future together. But that wasn't real. She couldn't give up on her business or Brewster's. Those were real and would support her when Ethan left. "I'm taking care of myself."

"You only rest when you're up at the Blackwell Ranch."

But she went whenever he'd asked. She'd liked the extra attention and if that made her shallow like Sarah Ashley, so be it. "I sit at Brewster's too."

"For five minutes here and five minutes there."

"What about you?" she challenged. "You've been seeing patients around town and trying to solve every problem on the ranch yourself."

"They're not my patients," he said. "No one else can do what I do."

"Then you know exactly how I feel."

They both sat back and mimicked each other: arms crossed over their chests, stubborn expressions. They'd reached a standstill and neither one wanted to budge.

A nurse opened the door, called Grace's name and led them back into a patient room.

"I know you mentioned you were trying to find a job somewhere else, but you should consider talking to Dr. Terry." Grace lay back on the exam table and watched Ethan. He sat in the chair, then stood, then sat back down.

"He doesn't return phone calls." Ethan jumped back

up and leaned against the counter, his gaze ping-ponging around the exam room.

"Of course not." Grace folded her hands together on her lap. "You have to go to his clinic to see him in person."

"Now that I've made all the new hires at the ranch, I can pursue my job options in person."

"It can't hurt to have a backup plan." She stared at the picture of the beach someone had tacked to the ceiling above the exam table. But even the calm waters failed to relax her.

"What is your backup plan?" he asked. "Is it Brewster's?"

"That's not fair." She tipped her head to look at him. "You know I can't leave my family's store."

"No, I don't know that." He moved to the other side of the room, turned the water on and off in the sink. "Why can't you leave if it's what's best for you?"

"Is it best for you or me if I leave Brewster's?" she asked.

"This isn't about me."

"But it is," she countered. "If I leave Brewster's, you'll think I'll leave Falcon Creek."

"What is wrong with leaving Falcon Creek?"

"What is wrong with staying in Falcon Creek?"

Dr. Wilder stepped into the room, greeted Grace and introduced herself to Ethan. She ran through Grace's cramps and spotting, making notes. Ethan stepped outside for part of the exam, but Dr. Wilder invited him back in for the ultrasound.

He'd held Grace's hand when Dr. Wilder let him hear the baby's heartbeat. He grabbed both her hands when Dr. Wilder pointed out the baby on the screen.

When Dr. Wilder declared the baby healthy and her pregnancy progressing as expected, Ethan kissed her cheek. The same way Grace had seen her father kiss her mother's cheek over the years. With the same tenderness and affection she'd always craved from a partner. In that moment, in that one dangerous moment, Grace fell under the spell and believed they'd be okay.

ETHAN WASN'T SURE whose heartbeat was still echoing in his head: the baby's or his own. In Dr. Wilder's office, everything inside him had raced like wildfire until he'd touched Grace. Until he'd curled his fingers around hers. Then, he'd quieted and absorbed the moment.

He was still in the moment.

He'd stepped outside to give Grace a chance to get dressed and the nurse had given him the ultrasound picture. He'd tucked it in his front shirt pocket, next to his heart. Had his own father felt such awe with each one of his children? What about his mother?

The thought now of leaving Grace and the baby behind made his chest hurt. Yet staying was an impossibility given his predicament. He'd hired the few extra staff at the Blackwell Ranch and Sarah Ashley's friends were booking rooms at a rate that surprised him. He'd brought the credit line at the Billings Bank and Trust current and stopped the seizure of the livestock. He'd solved the problems he'd promised to fix. So, all he had to do was finally start to build his professional career like he'd always wanted. Always envisioned.

All he had to do was leave Grace. That ache behind his ribs expanded. If he didn't know better, he'd have called it a heartache. But he never followed his heart.

He pulled Grace's cell phone from his back pocket and handed it to her. Her fingers brushed over his and his breath stalled. It had been the same in the doctor's office when he'd taken Grace's hand and listened to the baby's heartbeat.

He'd disappointed her in the doctor's reception area. He'd disappoint her again when he left. He struggled to find the right words. Maybe he didn't need words. Maybe she'd hear him if…

Ethan took her hand, lifted it up to his mouth. Kissed her knuckles. Her palm.

Her fingers curved around his cheek. "Ethan?"

He stopped searching for the words. Stopped thinking about apologies, confessions and wishes inside hearts. He simply leaned toward her—she met him halfway. He covered her mouth with his and poured every mixed-up emotion into the kiss.

He'd stopped two more times on the drive home. Pulled over at a rest stop and drew Grace to him. He discovered he hadn't said all he'd wanted with that first kiss. It seemed Grace hadn't either because she'd taken the lead and kissed him at the only stoplight in Falcon Creek. Their kiss extended through three light changes before Ethan drove Grace home.

He'd always considered the phrase *floating on cloud nine* to be nothing more than a whimsical saying. But now he understood the reference. He stopped his truck in the driveway at the Blackwell Ranch and swore his feet never touched the gravel on the walk to his cabin.

A letter had been jammed in the door frame. Ethan opened it, read the contents and knew then that cloud nine existed. He was living in it.

CHAPTER TWENTY

GIDDY WAS THE last word anyone would ever use to describe Grace. But that was the only word she could come up with for whatever boomeranged through her and woke her up with a wide, wide smile that morning.

Yesterday, she'd felt Ethan's tremor and his joy at hearing the baby's heartbeat. She'd watched his eyes get glassy at the ultrasound picture. He'd reached for her in the doctor's office. He hadn't let go.

Then he'd reached for her again inside his truck. That hadn't been baby-induced. He'd kissed Grace. Grace— the woman.

He'd told her sister that love was impossible, though she was sure she'd experienced it in his kiss. In the gentle way he'd cupped her face. In the quiet of the truck when he'd simply held her hand, his thumb caressing her palm.

For now, that was enough. In time she hoped he'd realize what was in his heart. She touched her lips and slipped into her office chair. She might be giddy, but she was still clearheaded enough to work. If she hummed while updating spreadsheets, there was no one to hear her.

Two spreadsheets, monthly P&Ls and one Sarah Ashley crisis later, Ethan strode into her office.

That giddy exploded back through Grace enough to push her out of her office chair. She wanted to be near him. In his arms. Next to him. Grace walked around her desk. "I thought you were busy until lunch."

"This couldn't wait." Ethan tugged her into his embrace and stole her breath. The same as he'd done in Dr. Wilder's parking lot yesterday. And at the rest stop. And the same as she'd done to him at the stoplight.

Grace gave herself over to the moment. To Ethan and

to all the unspoken truths. "I could get used to this kind of greeting."

"Me too." Ethan traced his finger down her cheek and tipped her chin up for another, softer, but no less intense, kiss. "Sorry, I couldn't resist."

"I'm not complaining." She curled her fingers in his hair and stayed pressed against him. "If only this was all we had scheduled for the day."

"What if I told you that I have a place where we could be alone without interruption?" One side of his mouth kicked up.

"I'd tell you to get out your car keys while I grab my purse." She wanted to be that spontaneous. That free. With Ethan, it was possible.

He tucked her hair behind her ear. "It's sort of a long drive."

"We'll be together." Everything was better. Brighter with Ethan beside her.

"That is what we want, right? To be together." His hands settled on her waist. He pulled back to look in her eyes as if he searched for some hidden secret. His voice was earnest, almost a plea. "Tell me I haven't misread this?"

She prayed she hadn't misread this either. Prayed the giddiness would stick around for a while. Hoped Ethan would too. "I want to be with you."

"Me too." He set his forehead against hers and inhaled, his hold relaxing, but sticking. As if he meant to stick too. He asked, "Would you rather drive or fly to Kentucky?"

Grace leaned back to search his face. She'd thought he'd meant a cabin at the Blackwell Ranch. A drive to the Rockies. Or a trip to Billings and their park bench. Not another state. Her giddiness vanished. "Kentucky?"

He held her face in both hands. Joy spun through his gaze and curled into his voice. "I've been asked to join one of the premier equine rehabilitation facilities in the nation." He pulled an envelope out of his back pocket. "Dr. Gaither sent me a personal invitation."

"Kentucky?" Grace repeated. She couldn't seem to move on from that one word. That one place. But she did step away from Ethan.

"The letter arrived last night. I barely slept." He waved the envelope between them. Pride and amazement were splashed across his face. "Invites like these are rare. The odds are worse than winning the super lottery. And for one to be extended to a recent graduate—it is unheard of. It's incredible. Unbelievable."

Reality engulfed Grace like a cold January wind. "Is it genuine?"

"I love your practical side." He laughed. "I thought the same thing too."

She wanted to weep. Their thoughts were not the same. Not even close.

Ethan rattled on. "I spoke to Dr. Gaither on my way here. It's very genuine. It's everything I spent years working for. It's everything I've wanted."

Grace's splintering heart rattled too. But he'd wanted to be with her. Only minutes ago. "That is incredible. Congratulations." How she'd managed that without the tiniest hitch in her voice, she couldn't say.

"I can build my career and our lives in Kentucky." He squeezed her shoulders as if to celebrate.

Grace should have known better than to stray into fantasyland. Coming back always hurt more. "I can't move to Kentucky, Ethan."

"Sure you can." He reached for her. "You told me you wanted to be with me."

She shook her head, holding the tears back inside her. Those were for later. Right now, she had to be brave. This was her heart on the line.

"You meant if it was here. In Falcon Creek." He stuck

his hands in his hair and pulled as if he'd been the stupid one. "On your terms."

"My life is here. My family. My business that I'm building." Grace retreated. "You're asking me to give all that up for what?"

"For us."

"But what are we, Ethan?"

"We're having a baby together."

"That's not enough anymore."

"Anymore." Confusion tinged his words, but a cool distance had already shifted into his gaze. He stepped back, retreating as well. "What does that mean?"

"Two weeks ago, I would've settled for anything you could give me. I would've gone anywhere you asked." She would've taken anything he could give, but then she'd seen him with his nieces and his family. With the animals. With Pops and the locals. So much love, so much affection. She wasn't wrong to want that too. She wanted to love him. She wanted to be loved in return.

"But now?" he asked.

"Now I want it all." Ironic that he'd given her the confidence not to settle for less than she deserved. "I want everything."

"You want the world." His voice dropped to a whisper, but his resentment crashed through the room.

"I want the impossible, Ethan." Grace closed her eyes, unable to watch Ethan pull away. "Can you give me that?"

Silence shuddered into the small office like that eerie moment just before the pristine snow cracked and the avalanche swept down the winter hillside.

Grace opened her eyes, settled her focus on Ethan and her heart. "Do you love me?"

"I want to be with you. Isn't that enough?"

"No." Maybe she was cruel to demand the words. Maybe she'd regret her courage later. But Ethan denied her the best part of himself. The only part she wanted. He'd take her to Kentucky, but he'd never give her his heart. "But you already know it isn't enough. You knew I wouldn't go with you. You don't want me to go."

He crammed his hands into his pockets and watched her, his face blank. He didn't argue. Didn't defend himself. "I have to take this job. It'll launch my career. I can support the baby now. I can finally get out of debt. Finally have something to offer you."

She would've helped him out if he'd asked for finances or support. She would've been his partner if he'd wanted. "The best part is that you can run to Kentucky with your heart still intact, never having opened yourself up completely."

"That's not fair."

It wasn't fair to love alone. It wasn't fair that he wanted her to love enough for both of them. "You've locked yourself away from your family and your home and refused to love. That way you won't get hurt. You won't suffer like you did when you lost your parents."

He rocked back as if she'd shoved him. "This isn't about my parents."

"This is about not living your life to the fullest. It's about always holding yourself back." Grace wasn't holding back now. The mouse had discovered her roar. She should thank him. "But there'll be pain and loss here, in Kentucky or anywhere you run to. The thing is, it's the love shared and the love remembered that cradles any future heartache. We have to love and live for the moments now so that we have memories to carry us through later."

"My moment now is in Kentucky."

"And my life is here." Grace straightened.

"So this is it." He looked away from her, stepped forward, then back.

"This is it."

He nodded, opened the door and turned. "I'll send a check each month for the baby."

Then he was gone. And Grace wept.

SARAH ASHLEY OPENED Grace's door. "Grace, didn't you hear..."

Grace never lifted her head from her desk. Just let her tears continue to leak onto the metal beneath her cheek. The door clicked shut and Grace struggled to find the off button on her emotions.

Ethan had walked out. She'd risked it all. Told him what her heart wanted. And he'd walked away. Left her alone. *Alone.* She was always alone.

She wanted to rage at the world. Yank the file boxes off the shelves. Rip apart the inventory. Lash out and scream. She wanted to vent and yell and curse.

But she ached. She ached so deep inside her that she couldn't move from the pain. The pain of a shattered heart was what finally broke Grace.

Her sister slipped back into her office. She set a large cup of tea on the corner of the desk along with a box of tissues. Then Sarah Ashley wrapped her arm around Grace's shoulders and held her. A one-sided hug that offered comfort and support. That asked nothing in return. That expected nothing in return.

Grace curled into her sister and held on.

CHAPTER TWENTY-ONE

SEVERAL DAYS LATER, Ethan swung an ax against a tree stump. Over and over until the stump split apart. Split apart like his heart.

"I think you killed it," a deep voice said from behind him.

Ethan spun around and glared at Randy Frye. Even hacking a stump in two hadn't dulled the ache inside him. Ethan was beginning to think nothing was going to. "Randy, what can I do for you?"

"I've got a certified delivery." Randy smacked a letter against his meaty palm. "Signature required."

Ethan stilled. The last letter he'd received had been his offer letter to join Dr. Gaither's equine rehabilitation center. That particular letter hadn't worked out anything like he'd expected. "Does it have a return address?"

Randy turned the letter over. "Only initials and a PO box."

Ethan never reached for the envelope. "What happens if I don't accept delivery?"

"Do you mean you don't want to sign?" Randy scratched his fingers through his thick beard.

"That is exactly what I mean." If he hadn't gotten the other letter, he wouldn't have had to make a choice between his career and Grace. He didn't want to be forced to make another choice he might regret.

Randy's fingers stilled. "You'd be the first person not to sign. People like to get mail."

Not everybody. Not Ethan. "Can you write undeliverable and return the letter to the sender?"

"But I'm delivering it to you." Randy set his hands on his hips and stared at Ethan as if Ethan was trying to scam him. "You're right here in front of me."

He knew he should've taken the ATV out to the south

pasture. He'd have been alone with nothing but miles and miles of fencing. "I don't have a pen."

Randy patted his shirt pocket and smiled. "Always carry one with me."

"That's convenient," Ethan said drily.

"You'd be surprised how many people never have a writing instrument on them." Randy shrugged as if he couldn't imagine not walking around with a working writing instrument.

No, Ethan wouldn't be surprised. Because those same people didn't want to accept their certified letters either. Ethan signed for the large envelope and watched Randy amble back to his mail truck. He considered tossing the envelope under the wheels of Randy's mail truck, but he assumed Randy would only stop and rescue the letter for him.

Ethan leaned his ax against the barn and opened the letter. Just the scrolled italic lettering on the top of the white paper convinced him he should've walked away from Randy.

The title of *Falcon County Court Summons* convinced him that he should've stomped Randy's pen into the mud instead of signing the green certified card.

But the paragraph listing Double T versus The Blackwell Ranch in the matter of water rights convinced him that he had to beg Judge Myrna Edwards for mercy.

Double T was Rachel Thompson's family's ranch and the Blackwell Ranch's neighbor. He'd been in Rachel's office last week with Grace. She'd greeted him like a long-time acquaintance and advised him like trusted counsel. He'd even stopped in the following day with coffee and fresh pastries as a thank-you for getting him an appointment with Judge Edwards. Yet she'd never given him a heads-up or a simple "by the way." She'd never even hinted that she'd be seeing him at the Falcon County Courthouse for their court hearing in less than a week. A court hearing to reverse the water rights back to the Double T Ranch for both the river and the aquifer that ran underneath the pasture split by the property line between the two ranches. Water rights that had been given to the Blackwell Ranch years ago after Big E and Ben had argued and won the case.

That was the last time he'd bring Rachel coffee, even if she was struggling as a caretaker of her family's ranch and her mother. He'd save the coffee and the pastries for Judge Edwards.

Surely Judge Edwards would offer some leniency. He'd advised her on Spike's condition and visited her house to help her understand how to care for a blind dog. Showed her how to use carpet runners as guides and helped her dog-proof every room, even the outside porch. He'd brought Spike a fountain water bowl, explaining the bubbling noise would guide Spike to his water. That all had to count for something.

He called the Falcon County Courthouse on his walk back to Cabin Six. His luck seemed to have turned. He had an appointment for nine o'clock the next morning with Judge Edwards. He only had to get through the night.

Unfortunately, his move from Cabin Six to the main house because guests were arriving cut into several hours between searching for the least offensive bedroom (turned out to be Jon's old room), reassuring Pixie and Coconut that their new home was safe and moving his bags. Those he'd tossed in the corner, still zipped as he intended to leave for Kentucky once he worked a deal with Myrna Edwards. He'd spent most of the night staring at the rhinestone-studded ceiling fan blades, listening to Pixie on her wheel and trying not to think about Grace. He'd failed and fallen asleep reliving their afternoon at the park in Billings.

The next morning, Ethan turned the key in his truck ignition and cursed. Thanks to a dead cell phone, his alarm hadn't gone off and now he was running late for his appointment with Judge Edwards. And his truck refused to cooperate.

It was official: luck had abandoned Ethan. Or simply lost track of him. No doubt luck couldn't locate him with all the bling and mirrors covering the walls and furniture in Jon's old childhood room.

He tried the key again. Nothing. Judge Edwards wouldn't abide by tardiness. Jon wouldn't be able to get there in time to loan him a vehicle. That left Katie. He'd owe her for this one. Big time.

After several heated negotiations and Ethan's agreement to deal with the septic tanks, Katie handed over the keys to her truck. Ethan sped down the highway and raced for Livingston and Judge Edwards's chambers.

Judge Edwards glared at him over the tops of her glasses and pointed at the clock on the mantel. "You wasted ten minutes of your thirty-minute audience by arriving late."

"I had truck issues," Ethan said.

"The Blackwell Ranch has several tractors." Judge Edwards frowned at his wrinkled shirt and dust-coated jeans. "You would've taken one of those if you'd been serious about respecting my time."

He would've missed his appointment completely if he'd driven a tractor to Livingston. But he might've won Judge Edwards's admiration. Not that he needed that. He only needed Judge Edwards to agree to a deal. If she refused, he needed her to grant a continuance on the summons. That'd give him time to talk to Jon and even more time to convince Ben to talk to him.

Ben had been the one to work with Big E on the water rights with the Double T Ranch years ago. The case was supposed to be closed. The Blackwell Ranch needed to keep control of the water resources, otherwise Rachel and the Double T could limit their water usage and affect the livestock and the guests staying at the ranch. "I borrowed Katie's truck."

"I'm sure that didn't come without a cost." Judge Edwards's smile was in her gleeful voice.

Only septic maintenance, toilet replacements in two cabins and hen-duty. "She was happy to help out."

Judge Edwards's mouth thinned. "Where's Grace?"

He did not want to talk to Myrna Edwards about Grace. "This isn't about her."

"Everything in your life is about Grace Gardner. The sooner you learn that, the better everyone will be."

He was fine. Well, working on being fine without Grace. It was bad enough he couldn't stop thinking about Grace. He wasn't going to talk about her now. With Myrna Edwards. He'd treated her dogs; she hadn't become his confidante. "I came to request a continuance on the case of the Double T versus the Blackwell Ranch unless we can reach a deal."

"You received your summons," Judge Edwards said. "There will be no deal on that particular court hearing."

"The summons arrived yesterday," Ethan said. "There's only five days before the hearing. That's not enough time to prepare." To get his brother Ben to call him back and come home.

"You'd be surprised how much can happen in five days." Judge Edwards set her hands on her desk and eyed him. "How much one can discover in the course of five days."

Ethan slumped back in the leather chair. Myrna Edwards had been at the Blackwell Ranch for five whole days. In those same five days, he'd learned that he resented anyone who tried to intrude on the memory of his mother. He'd also learned that he had a keen eye for the bow and arrow. A skill he still retained as he'd peppered the old barn with arrows last night. "We need to find representation for the hearing."

"That shouldn't be too difficult." Judge Edwards tapped her pen on her desk. "Day Three is a phone call away in New York, isn't he?"

Ben was only a phone call away if he answered his phone. "Yes, Ben lives in New York."

Judge Edwards consulted her desk calendar. "If you call him this afternoon, he should be able to book a flight this weekend. I'll move the hearing until the following Friday."

"That's not even two weeks," Ethan said.

"But with the holiday weekend, Ben will have plenty of time to get caught up." Judge Myrna smiled as if she'd offered an exceptional bargain. "I added an additional five-day delay. Imagine what you can do in ten days?"

It was going to take that long to convince Ben to come home. "That's the best you can offer?"

"Did you offer your best to Grace Gardner?" Judge Edwards asked.

Why did the woman insist on talking about Grace? Grace wasn't a part of his future. She'd chosen to stay in Falcon Creek. She'd chosen the safety of her home over him. He'd chosen his career over Grace. There was nothing left to talk about. Nothing left to work out, except that gaping void inside him. "Grace wasn't interested in what I had to offer."

Judge Edwards shook her head. "Aren't you tired from so much running, Day Two?"

"Excuse me?" Ethan said. Why did everyone accuse him of being a runner?

"You've been running from the Blackwell Ranch since the day your parents died and you haven't stopped running since." Judge Edwards took off her glasses and sighed as if she was tired for him.

"I'm not sure..." Ethan's voice failed him. Who was she to talk to him about running or his parents? She knew nothing about him. Referred to him as Day Two. He wondered if she even knew his first name. "Is there something I need to sign or paperwork I need to receive for the continuance?"

"Documents will be forwarded to the Blackwell Ranch," Judge Edwards said.

Ethan checked the clock. He had two minutes before his thirty-minute meeting with Judge Edwards expired. He stood up and walked to the door. "Thank you for your time, Judge Edwards, and the continuance."

"Ethan, a word of advice," she said.

The use of his first name stopped him. He turned around, surprised for the second time by Myrna Edwards. First, her love of rescues and now the fact that she really did know his name.

She pointed her glasses at him and said, "If you keep running, you just might miss the best part of your life."

"You ran from the Blackwell Ranch and Big E. Are you telling me that was the best part of your life?" Ethan asked.

Judge Edwards put her glasses back on and shrugged. "Because I ran, I'll never know. But you have the chance to do something I never did."

"What's that?"

"Stop," she said. "Press pause, breathe and look around. Really look around."

He'd be sure to stop and look around at the last stop sign on his way out of Falcon Creek.

"I'LL TAKE IT." Grace turned from the bay window in the living room of the renovated 1925 single-story home on the end of Back Street and smiled at Dana Brantley, her friend and real estate agent.

"It's a one-year lease with an option to purchase at the end of the lease." Dana flipped through a stack of paperwork. "You'd also have the option to lease month to month after the one-year contract expired."

Certainly in one year Grace could turn a profit on her business and discuss something more than a rental. But for now, this home suited her needs with its chopped-up early-century floor plan just like Ethan had told her. She'd convert the living room into her office and keep the front half of the house for her business affairs. The back half of the house would be for living. Both bedrooms could be accessed from the kitchen and the full basement downstairs offered even more living space.

The only downside: she'd drive by Dr. Norman Terry's practice any time she went to Brewster's or anywhere in town for that matter. And she'd be reminded of what she could've had if only Ethan had stayed. But she was having a child. And this would be their home. "When can we complete the paperwork?"

"Give me an hour or so to contact the owners and draw up the contracts." Dana stuffed the folder in her tote bag and checked her watch. "Can you meet me at my office after lunch?"

"Absolutely," Grace said. She took one last look around the living room, already envisioning herself there. She was anxious and eager to begin her journey. She'd reached for Ethan and failed, but she wouldn't fail at this.

Grace climbed into her car and finally checked her phone. She had thirteen missed calls and over twenty new texts. The most recent from Sarah Ashley: Full-on crisis mode at Brewster's.

Grace pulled away from the curb and dialed the private line at the store.

Her mother picked up on the first ring. "Grace, tell me you're on your way."

"I'll be there in five minutes," Grace said. "What happened?"

"Payroll posted wrong," her mother said.

"That's not possible," Grace said. She'd left specific instructions.

"We've been working with the bank," her mother continued. Pages over the intercom for Alice Gardner disrupted their connection.

"The bank?" Grace gunned it toward the store.

"Automatic deposits processed and then this morning reversed." Another page went off for Alice Gardner before her mom said, "Just hurry, Grace."

Reversed meant that the employees' paychecks had been taken out of the employees' personal bank accounts. The phone line went dead. A block away, her cell phone rang. Grace answered, thinking it was her mother calling her back.

But Ken Ware greeted her with a curt and extended, "Grace…"

He'd never given her a chance to ask how he was. He launched into his tirade the second she'd replied. At his accusation that she'd mishandled his quarterly tax payment, Grace clenched the steering wheel and tried to see past the tears blurring her vision.

She could swear she'd sent him the correct forms and the amount. She remembered going to the post office. But she'd picked up several special deliveries from the post office. Maybe she hadn't mailed the forms? She needed to check her office. Grace pulled into the parking lot outside Brewster's. Her mother was pacing the front porch, waiting for her.

She was so stretched, exhausted and forgetful. Maybe she'd posted payroll wrong and never mailed the forms to Ken. What had she been thinking? She couldn't leave her parents—she wasn't stable without them. She was better off at the store in her closet of an office, living inside her safe zone.

What had she been thinking when she'd convinced herself she could be a good single mother? She couldn't even handle the simple needs of her clients correctly. Never mind the needs of a newborn.

And the worst part: all Grace wanted was to break down in Ethan's strong arms.

If that wasn't proof of the mess she'd become, she didn't know what was.

CHAPTER TWENTY-TWO

ETHAN CORNERED HIS brother in one of JB Bar Ranch's new red barns. "Next time, you're meeting with Judge Edwards."

Jon took off his hat and scrubbed his hand over his head. "Didn't go well."

Nothing had been going well for days. *Nothing*. "She gave us another five days and told me to call Day Three."

"Did you tell Myrna Edwards that we have names?" Jon fired back.

Ethan shook his head. He wasn't convinced whether it was good or bad that Myrna Edwards not only knew his first name, but used it. He leaned toward preferring Day Two from Judge Edwards. "She wasn't wrong. We have to call Ben."

"And order him to come home." Jon shook his head. "Like that is going to happen."

"It's going to happen because I need to get to Kentucky," Ethan said.

"You accepted the job then?" Jon locked the barn door and walked beside Ethan toward the house.

"I have to take it." Ethan stopped and faced his brother. "Grace is pregnant. The baby is mine."

"Wow. Okay. I thought there was something between you and Grace Gardner." Jon stopped near Ethan's truck and stared out over the field. "But a baby. That's big."

Ethan waited, letting his brother process the news.

"What now? I'm just supposed to congratulate you and then wish you well as you leave town?" Jon ran the back of his hand over his mouth as if he'd bitten into a rotten apple.

"I'm taking a job that will launch my career, get me out of debt and allow me to send money for diapers and baby clothes." What was so hard for everyone to understand about his choice? Surely no one wanted Ethan in debt and unable to support his child.

"What about being a father?" Jon pushed his hat back and locked his gaze on Ethan. "How does this lucrative, career-building job make you a better dad?"

"You think I should stay and marry Grace." Ethan kicked at the gravel and paced away from his brother like he always did. He'd never been able to stand still and face his brother's judgment. He'd never wanted to see that he'd disappointed his older brother. "You think I should get married because of the baby."

That shocked Ethan. After all, Jon had married Ava when she'd gotten pregnant with the twins. Their marriage had ended in disaster with Ava abandoning Jon and her infant daughters. Jon had still been picking up the pieces from that fallout until Lydia had arrived last month.

"I never said anything about marriage." Jon leaned against the front of Ethan's truck as if content to let Ethan pace around all night in his driveway. As if content to withhold his judgment for the moment.

"Grace refused to come with me to Kentucky." Ethan kicked another stone.

"Did you present her with the same list of reasons you just spouted off to me?" Jon asked with a half smile. "Money and your career."

"They're valid reasons for taking that job."

"Sure, but there are also valid reasons for staying here in Falcon Creek," Jon countered.

"Like what?"

Jon pushed off the truck. "Family for one."

"I can't support a family if I'm in debt," Ethan argued.

"No, but you could open a large-animal clinic in one of the old barns on the Blackwell Ranch. You could actually put yourself on the ranch payroll now that the guest lodge is scheduled to make a profit." Jon studied him. "And Grace has a job and from what I've heard a growing business."

"I don't want to rely on Grace." He'd always relied on himself. *Always.*

"Why not?" Jon asked. "That is what partners who are committed to each other do. One day it'll be your turn to carry her. That's how good relationships work."

"Who said anything about a relationship?" Ethan asked.

"You didn't go to Grace's hotel room that night on a whim. You didn't spend most of your time at Brewster's growing up for the retail experience. And you didn't bring Grace up to the Blackwell Ranch every night to work on the accounts only." Jon punched his shoulder. "Admit it, little brother. There's always been something about Grace Gardner." Jon stuck his finger in Ethan's chest, right over his heart. "There's always been something a little uncomfortable in there at the mention of Grace Gardner."

Ethan knocked his brother's arm away. "I'm admitting nothing."

"And that's why you're going to Kentucky alone." Jon shook his head and started toward the house. "Give your new career my regards and hug your flush checking account. I'm going inside to join my family and have a daddy-daughter game night. I wonder who'll wake up smiling more. Me or you?"

Ethan watched his brother walk back to his house. He heard his nieces' laughter the moment Jon opened the door. He climbed in his truck and headed back to the Blackwell Ranch alone. Just like he wanted to be.

Ethan parked his truck, called his brother Ben and left him another message to call him back ASAP. He added a text to Ben for good measure, then stared at his childhood home. The single light on the back porch wasn't enough to fend off the oppressive darkness. He wasn't in the mood for the happy, sparkly dollhouse world inside the house either.

Ethan headed to the barn, drawn by the soft glow of the light he'd left on in the foaling stall. He'd often sought refuge in the barn as a child. He hoped Butterscotch wouldn't mind the intrusion tonight. He'd checked her that morning and watched the monitor on his phone throughout the day. Katie texted that Butterscotch hadn't eaten dinner, but the mare hadn't been eating well the past few weeks.

Inside the barn, he peered into several stalls and moved on to the foaling stall at the far end of the barn. Butterscotch paced around, seeming as restless as Ethan. He leaned on the gate, checked the time on his phone and watched the mare. He was unsettled about leaving his family; Butterscotch was restless from the impending arrival of hers.

Ethan stepped into the stall, smoothed his palm down Butterscotch's muzzle and assured the mare he'd be there the whole time. He wrapped her tail and stepped outside the stall to grab the birthing supplies he might need.

He'd delivered his first foal with his father when he was seven. In the very same stall. Most likely around the same time of night. His mom had woken him up, handed him a sweatshirt and shooed him out to the barn. His dad had promised Ethan he'd let him assist with the birth. Unfortunately, by the time Ethan had made it to the barn, the foal had arrived. Even his dad had been surprised at how fast the mare had birthed.

The following year, Ethan had slept in the barn in an attempt not to miss the birth. That year, he'd been the one to notice the breach birth and yell for his father. His dad had let him sleep in the barn every year after that, claiming Ethan knew before the mare when the foal was coming. Those nights with the mares and his dad had been some of his favorites. He'd continued sleeping in the barn after his parents' accident, not for the birthings—he'd simply felt the closest to his dad in the barn with the horses.

Ethan stepped back inside the stall. "It's you and me tonight, Butterscotch. Let's keep this simple."

The mare snorted at him.

Despite his years of veterinary school and the dozens of births he'd assisted in during his internships at Colorado clinics, the only voice he heard now was his father's. The only instructor's voice was that of his dad's: calm, patient, helpful. He heard his father now. Calling out the time, instructing him on what to watch for: excessive rolling, too much straining.

Ethan ran through his father's checklist. Butterscotch's water broke and he noted the time. *Not long now.* The mare lowered herself into the thick straw and lay down on her side. Ethan waited inside the stall. *She knows what to do. This is the beauty of Mother Nature, Ethan.*

Ethan checked the time again. The foal's front feet appeared. Ethan sighed for Butterscotch. She wouldn't need to suffer through a breach birth tonight. Yet too much time passed. *You need to see a nose quick, son. Otherwise you gotta help pull the little one out.*

Ethan grabbed the clean towel he'd packed with the birthing supplies and approached Butterscotch. "We're going to do this together, Butterscotch." Like he'd done with his dad. He'd done this many times with his dad, but it hadn't been enough. He always wanted another chance. Another birth. Another night with his dad.

Ethan wrapped the towel around the foal's front feet and tugged. He assisted Butterscotch until the foal's head, shoulders and chest appeared. Then waited and pulled again to bring the foal's hips through the birthing canal. And like that, a new life arrived at the Blackwell Ranch.

Like every birth, Ethan marveled at the new life. Awed

and inspired to be given the chance to be a witness. *Now we step back, son. We let mother and baby bond.*

Ethan edged away from the pair and sat in the far corner of the stall. Again, he watched the time. This time to mark the foal's progress. The foal stirred in less than five minutes, rising to its sternum and struggling to stand. Three collapses and the foal mastered its gangly legs. Butterscotch roused on cue with her baby and started cleaning.

A mother's instincts run deep, son. Never doubt that the moms know what to do.

Ethan watched Butterscotch care for her newborn. Remembered his own mom making birthing areas for the barn cats, rabbits and dogs. One of the barn cats had delivered in an old box on the back porch. Ethan had acted as a bodyguard to keep Tyler and Chance from toppling into the box headfirst. They'd been five and more interested in climbing inside the box than watching the kittens' arrival. Ethan and his mom had eventually relocated the cat and her litter inside the laundry room for safety reasons.

He heard again his mom scolding him for scaling a too-tall tree to peek into a hawk's nest. Weeks later, she'd ordered him to climb back up and tell her if the fledglings had hatched. He'd caught fireflies with his mom, terrorized Chase and Tyler with snakeskins and followed his dad everywhere.

He'd lived every day outside and on the move. Then his world had stopped. But his grandfather had made sure the boys continued to live every day outside. Big E had made sure they lived. They'd learned to drive tractors, herd cattle and take and give a solid punch. He'd discovered a passion for horses and making out behind the barns. He'd broken curfew, broken bones and mended almost everything with his brothers' laughter.

More memories from his childhood collided and toppled over Ethan like a headfirst tumble down the mountainside. He acknowledged the pain of losing his parents, but the vast amount of good memories dulled the edge. And at the heart of every memory was the love. The love of family. The love of home.

Ethan stayed where he was, watched over Butterscotch and her foal longer than necessary. And wished Grace was beside him. She would've helped. She would've soothed Butterscotch. Pulled if necessary. Adjusted the foal if it'd been breach. She would've been beside him like his mother had stood beside his father. Like Alice Gardner stood beside Frank.

And Ethan would've been better for it. He was better with Grace beside him.

But there was more. Sitting inside the foaling stall that had birthed generations of Blackwell thoroughbreds, Ethan realized he wanted to continue the tradition. He wanted his son or daughter to sleep in the barn if they chose. He wanted to teach them about the miracles of Mother Nature inside this barn. Inside this stall where he'd learned himself. Where generations of Blackwells had learned before him.

As he watched the foal with Butterscotch, he realized he wanted to bring new life to the Blackwell Ranch too. To introduce a new generation to his home. He wanted to carry on the traditions and the legacy. And he wanted to do all of that with Grace.

He tipped his head back and laughed. For the first time in years, he'd stopped running and discovered more than he'd imagined. Like Myrna had told him.

He'd tended the land like his grandfather preached and the land returned the favor tenfold.

Now he needed to heed Pops's advice and figure out how to keep Grace with him forever.

CHAPTER TWENTY-THREE

SARAH ASHLEY CARRIED two cups of tea into Grace's room and set them on the bedside table. She pulled two chocolate bars out of the back pocket of her flannel pajama pants. "I raided mom's not-so-secret stash. Twice."

"Did Dad see you?" Grace accepted the candy.

"He might've been with me and he might've taken a candy bar for himself." Sarah Ashley sat on the side of the bed. "I'll deny we had this conversation if Mom asks."

"I wasn't there. I know nothing." Grace held up her hands and then pointed at the chocolate in her lap. "Is this an apology? Did something else break?"

"I haven't been logged in to any Brewster computer system tonight." Sarah Ashley opened her candy bar and snapped off a corner. "If there are problems at Brewster's, it wasn't me."

Grace sighed and leaned back against her headboard, grateful there wasn't an emergency to put out. She wasn't sure she could handle another one tonight. It had taken her most of the afternoon to fix the technical glitch that had reversed payroll. The rest of the time had been occupied searching her office for Ken Ware's tax payment paperwork that hadn't been missing after all.

An hour ago, Ken Ware's wife had called Grace on behalf of her embarrassed husband who'd misplaced the tax filings and payment from Grace in his mess that he called an office. Grace had promised to keep Ken on as a client and his wife had vowed to make him clean his office. Despite the good news, Grace had curled up in her bed after dinner, exhausted yet unable to stop questioning everything about her life. Doubting every decision she'd made recently.

Sarah Ashley finished half her chocolate bar and motioned at Grace. "I stole that for you. You could at least pretend to eat it."

Grace unwrapped the chocolate and wondered how to unwind the last few days. "Do you ever want a do-over, Sarah Ashley?"

"I like to think I'm perfect the first time I do something." Her sister's smile hitched her eyebrows higher, letting her laughter bounce through her gaze.

Grace envied her sister's confidence. Sarah Ashley might be laughing, but there was a hint of seriousness in her voice. Grace toyed with the edge of the wrapper. "So you don't have any regrets?"

Sarah Ashley dropped a piece of candy bar on her lap. Alarm highlighted her words. "Not usually."

Her sister relaxed. "Have you spoken to Ethan?"

"Not since he came to my office." Not since he'd broken her heart. Not since he'd walked out and Grace failed to stop him. "There's nothing more to say. I don't want him to be with me just because of the baby. And his life is in Kentucky."

"But what if he loved you?" Her sister had always been persistent.

Hadn't Sarah Ashley ever listened to Grace before? Grace was the proverbial friend. Why couldn't her sister see that? Ethan was no different than any other guy in her past, other than he was the father of her baby. "Ethan doesn't love me."

Grace had already asked him. He hadn't replied.

"But I think he does love you." Her sister's voice was sincere. "He just can't admit it."

Only in a fairy tale did Ethan love Grace. "He loved you. The vivacious, vibrant Gardner sister. You don't love someone like you and then fall for someone like me."

"He never loved me." Sarah Ashley sobered and edged into Grace's space.

"Sure, he did." Grace touched her forehead, feeling off-kilter. Her hair was a tangled mess and she needed her glasses to see. In an alternate world, she'd have twenty-twenty vision and perfect, shampoo-commercial hair and Ethan's love. "You were the couple most likely to get married. It was written in the high school year book four years straight."

"And also the couple most likely to get divorced." Sarah Ashley finished the last bite of her chocolate bar and eyed Grace's as if she survived on a chocolate-only diet. "He and I have always been better friends than a couple."

"But you stayed together through high school." Grace snapped off part of her candy bar and handed it to her sister.

"It was easy and expected." Sarah Ashley shrugged. "You should know that Ethan went further with you than we ever went."

Grace was still in the present. In the now. In her world, not some alternate one. She set her glasses back on and studied her sister.

Sarah Ashley swallowed the candy Grace had given her and reached for the rest of Grace's chocolate bar as if she hadn't launched a truth grenade into the bedroom.

Grace steadied her breathing, trying to stop her racing heart and the jumble of emotions rolling through her. "You aren't serious?"

"Quite." Her sister crumpled up her candy wrapper and tossed it into the trash like she'd revealed nothing more than her shoe size. "And Ethan isn't a one-night-stand kind of guy."

Grace was suddenly happy she hadn't added chocolate to whatever was churning inside her now. "How would you know?"

"I've met a few guys like that over the years." Sarah Ashley tossed her hair over her shoulder and locked her gaze on Grace. "The truth is that you and Ethan are good together. There's something that's right when I see you with each other."

"Good together like friends are good together. Or like coworkers." Would her sister ever get the point?

"No, there's more." Sarah Ashley covered Grace's hands with hers, pulling Grace's attention to her. "He's different around you. You make him better."

He made Grace better too. She liked who she was with Ethan. She wanted him back.

"Don't leave things between you like this." Sarah Ashley smiled at Grace, her voice encouraging. "You have one more fight in you. I know it."

"Don't you get tired of fighting for what you want?" And being denied. Grace wasn't sure she had it in her. Once again she didn't share her sister's confidence. "But then I suppose everyone always gives you what you want."

"Everyone used to give me what I wanted. All the time." Sarah Ashley bit into her lower lip. "Until Alec came along."

"He loves you. I saw it at the wedding. I hear it in his voice when he calls." Alec hadn't hesitated at the wedding. At the altar. Alec hadn't run from love or her sister. He'd run to Sarah Ashley instead. Unlike Ethan.

"I love him too." Something seemed to glow from inside Sarah Ashley when she talked about Alec and her love for him. It was real and true. Undeniable. Her sister added, "I moved home because I loved him."

"That's backward, you know." If Ethan loved Grace, she wouldn't run from him. She'd be running to him. Every chance she got.

"I had some things I needed to do." Sarah Ashley

squeezed Grace's hands. "The truth is that I came home to become you, little sister."

"M-me?" Grace stuttered, unable to stop herself.

"I've always admired you."

Grace stared at her sister, searching for the punch line, or the "but" or the "just kidding." She saw only her sister's soft smile and open gaze.

"It's true." Sarah Ashley laughed, most likely at Grace's shocked expression. "You're independent and strong. And I swear you can handle any situation with patience." Her sister pointed at her and grinned. "We all know you've needed a lot of patience with me these past few weeks."

"It wasn't that bad," Grace hedged.

"There's that inner kindness. It's like second nature to you. I admire that too," Sarah Ashley said. "And we both know you're lying right now."

Grace grinned, but refused to confirm or deny her sister's claim. She preferred Sarah Ashley like this. More of a confidante than a challenger. More sister than princess. "I still don't get why you wanted to be me."

"I wanted to prove to myself and Alec that I could do things on my own. That I could be dependable."

Her sister just admitted that everyone always gave her whatever she wanted. Why would she want to lose that? "Why?"

"Because I was tired and refused to let people think any less of me any longer." Sarah Ashley raised her hands before Grace could respond. "And I wanted to prove to myself that I could."

Grace wrapped her sister in a tight hug. "You've changed, Sarah Ashley. I'm proud of you."

Sarah Ashley stood up, adjusted the comforter and looked at Grace. "Don't give up on Ethan. Love is always worth fighting for."

Grace hadn't told her sister that she loved Ethan. But

then, she didn't have to. It seemed some things sisters just understood.

Sarah Ashley walked to the door, turned and blew Grace a kiss. "Gracie, I loved you yesterday."

The memory of the sisters' good-night saying from childhood filled Grace's heart. She blew a kiss back to her sister and said the next line. "I loved you today."

Together, they both repeated Nicole Marie's line. "And I'll love you even more tomorrow. Sisters forever."

There wasn't a night through grade school that the three sisters hadn't repeated their saying, even if by text. Why had they stopped? When had they stopped?

Grace supposed it didn't really matter. All that mattered was their bond was still there. Still strong, despite everything.

Grace opened up her laptop, logged on and entered Kentucky office rentals in her internet search bar. She'd always belong to the Gardner family. Always have her sisters no matter where she went.

But now she wanted a family of her own. And she wanted that family with Ethan Blackwell. Her home and her heart would always be wherever he was.

Her sister was right. Grace did have one last fight left in her.

CHAPTER TWENTY-FOUR

"GOOD MORNING, GRACE," an all-too-familiar voice called out.

Grace stumbled on the first step leading to Brewster's front porch. The papers she'd been holding scattered around her. Grace stood speechless and stared at Ethan. He was smiling, standing between her father and Pops.

Her grandfather stepped up to Ethan, squeezed his shoulder and said, "Welcome home, son."

Her father wished him luck and then disappeared inside the store, leaving Grace and Ethan alone with the chess pieces and an awkward silence.

Grace cleared her throat, searched for her voice. "I thought you'd be in Kentucky by now."

"I was headed that way, but I realized I'd left something behind." Ethan bent down and gathered her paperwork. His gaze however fixed on her. "Something rather important."

Grace's heart slammed against her chest, knocking the breath out of her. "What was that?" she whispered.

"My family." He moved down one step toward her. His hand gripped the railing. His words gripped her heart.

She could reach him if she stretched. If she leaned forward far enough. But his words had already knocked her too far off balance. "You told me that everything you ever wanted was in Kentucky."

"But everything I ever needed is right here in Falcon Creek." He stepped down again.

Grace moved up to the step just below him and searched his face, wanting to believe. Fear held her back. "What now?"

His gaze captured hers, steady and certain. "I want to give you the world, but my finances are going to be tight for quite a while."

"I don't need the world, Ethan." Grace joined him and curved her arms around his neck, locking herself to him and him to her. "I only ever needed you in my life."

He pulled her closer. His smile reassured her. An apology lingered in his voice. "You might be supporting us for a while."

"I don't mind." Grace tugged him down and kissed him with all the love inside her. She pulled away and framed his face in her hands, made sure she had his attention. "Our family always takes care of each other."

"I've missed you," he whispered through the soft kiss he placed on her forehead. He lifted up the stack of papers he still held between them. "What is all this?"

"Rental spaces in Kentucky." At his surprised reaction, she shrugged as if it was no big deal. "I want to be with the man I love. Wherever that is. Do you have a problem with that?"

"Not in the least." Ethan wrapped her in a hug and held on as if he wouldn't let her go. "If you really want to move to Kentucky, we can. But I have another idea about staying here in Falcon Creek and starting our own family, surrounded by family."

"I think I like that idea." Grace grabbed the stack of papers and tossed them over the railing. "I like that idea a lot."

Sarah Ashley scurried across the porch and yelled Ethan's name. "I hate to interrupt. And I promise I didn't do it on purpose. I was just trying to consolidate and make room for the summer inventory."

Grace grabbed her sister's arm to get her to focus. "What happened?"

"I moved all the bunnies to the same pen." Sarah Ashley looked at Ethan and lifted her hands as if to plead for his help. "Now I can't tell the girls from the boys."

Their mom peeked out the front door and pointed at

them. "Get in here, all of you, before I have bunny babies. We've got to separate them now."

Grace dropped her head on Ethan's shoulder. "Maybe Kentucky isn't such a bad idea."

"And miss all of this. No way." Ethan laughed, grabbed her hand and tugged her into the store. Once inside, he called out to her sister, "Sarah Ashley, it's time for an anatomy lesson."

ETHAN LEFT GRACE and Sarah Ashley sorting bunnies in Brewster's and headed toward Back Street. He stepped onto the small leaning porch of a shotgun house, smiled at the crooked Open sign in the window and walked inside. Ethan used his boot to ram the door shut.

"Have you come to apologize for stealing my patients?" Dr. Norman Terry stepped out from the compact kitchen of his clinic, a napkin stuffed in the collar of his flannel shirt and a paper plate in his hand.

Ethan opened his mouth. But Dr. Terry pointed his fork at him and shook it until Ethan closed his mouth, having lost the urge to respond.

Nodding, Dr. Terry said, "Come to think of it, son, I don't much like my patients these days."

Ethan watched Dr. Terry shuffle toward the waiting area. He wondered which he should rescue first, the pastry sliding off the paper plate, or Norman. The old doctor would probably stab him with the fork if Ethan offered to help him into a chair. Still, Ethan stepped forward, prepared to intervene if the pastry, or Dr. Terry, listed too far toward the floor.

Dr. Terry dropped into the cushioned chair with only two pops and a small creak. Setting his plate on his lap, he looked up at Ethan. "You're welcome to all my patients."

Ethan rubbed the back of his neck. He'd come to discuss buying into Dr. Terry's practice and a finance contract for the purchase. He hadn't come to take Dr. Terry's patients. "I don't have a license, or practice in the state of Montana."

"You passed the veterinary board exam?" Dr. Terry stabbed his pastry and lifted it up like a massive lollipop.

"Yes, sir, I did."

Dr. Terry took a bite of his pastry and considered Ethan while he chewed. "Then you'll work under my license until you get your Montana one."

Ethan stomped down the jolt of excitement. "You want me in your practice?"

"Heck, I'm giving you my practice." Dr. Terry slapped the pastry on his plate, tossed his fork on the chair beside him and used his hands to pull it apart. "I've lost my patience for all the complaints. You can't imagine what people find to complain about. Last I heard I ate too many apple turnovers, so I switched to bear claws. Although, I'm not sure what my taste in pastries has to do with my skills at treating animals."

Ethan interrupted the doctor's pastry quandary to get him to focus on what mattered. "You can't give me your practice."

"Why not?" Dr. Terry shoved a piece of bear claw into his mouth and studied Ethan as if Ethan could solve the local pastry debate.

Ethan wasn't exactly sure why Dr. Terry couldn't give him his practice. He just knew that the older doctor couldn't.

"I don't have any heirs." Dr. Terry wiped his mouth on his shirtsleeve, seeming to have forgotten his napkin. "But I'll warn you, the clinic could've used an update more than two decades ago."

Ethan wondered if he should step outside and walk in again. Surely, then, this would all make sense. "You're serious?"

"I don't joke about whiskey, or my practice. Ever." Dr. Terry finished his pastry and set the plate on the other chair beside him. He pushed himself up and shuffled into the kitchen, motioning for Ethan to follow. "But I'll be checking in daily. I don't want the folks in town to think I've abandoned them and their pets."

"I have really poor credit." He felt like he had to say something. Anything.

"And I've got arthritis and bone spurs." Dr. Terry glanced at Ethan over his shoulder. "What's your point?"

"I can't buy into your practice." Ethan followed Dr. Terry into what would've been the master bedroom originally, but had been converted into an office.

"I'm not asking you to." Dr. Terry shuffled around the desk and opened several drawers. "I'm asking you to take over the practice once you get your license."

"But you need to get something out of your practice." Ethan crossed his arms over his chest and waited in the doorway. "You've been working in this town for more than fifty years."

"Been a good run. A very good, but a very long run." Dr. Terry moved over to a three-drawer filing cabinet and opened each drawer. "Got very few complaints until recently. Hopefully you can say the same when it comes time to hand off the practice to the next generation."

"Was the clinic given to you?" Ethan asked.

"Nothing is ever free, son."

"What's the catch?" Ethan eyed the older gentleman. He'd always believed in too-good-to-be-true. In his experience, there was always a catch. A but. A however.

"Simple." Dr. Terry pulled an envelope out of the bottom drawer in the filing cabinet and straightened. "You promise not to move your practice out of Falcon Creek."

"I want to open a large-animal clinic out at the Blackwell Ranch." As long as the brothers agreed not to sell the Blackwell Ranch. But he'd deal with his brothers later.

Right now he needed to know the real catch to Dr. Terry's offer. The I-am-giving-you-my-practice-however phrase.

"I can't wait to see that." Dr. Terry's eyes opened behind his thick glasses and something cheerful colored his voice. "The townsfolk will be happy to have those services here finally."

"I have to buy into your practice." Ethan stepped into the office, closer to Dr. Terry. "It doesn't feel right."

"You remind me of myself, son." Dr. Terry smiled as if he enjoyed the memory of the man he used to be. "I might've used those very same words back when I stood in your place."

"Then we can work out a price?" Ethan asked.

"We're going to use the same price that Dr. Vincent Reid gave me over fifty years ago."

Finally, Ethan had a price. Something to work with. He wasn't sure how he'd get a bank loan, but he'd figure that out later. For now, he wanted to make a deal with Dr. Terry. "That seems fair."

Dr. Terry handed him the envelope he'd pulled out of the bottom drawer in the file cabinet. "Inside you'll find the contract and buy-in price. After you've looked over the paperwork, come find me at Misty Whistle." Dr. Terry tapped on the glass of his large round watch. "It's time for my afternoon coffee and bear claw." Never mind that Dr. Terry had already polished off a bear claw not five minutes earlier.

The older gentleman tapped Ethan's shoulder on his way out of the office. "Feel free to look around and take stock. I've not changed much since I moved in. I'm not much for this computer age stuff. I still prefer a firm handshake and looking a person in the eye when you make a deal. But you'll bring some much-needed youth to the place. Building's got good bones. Have to respect that when you update. Honor the past, but build for the future."

Dr. Terry waved and shuffled out to the waiting room. Several minutes later, the front door slammed. If Ethan was buying into this practice and if this was all on the up and up, he'd fix that door first. He didn't want any of his already nervous patients becoming even more jumpy with a slamming front door.

Ethan opened the envelope and pulled out a stack of papers held together with a binder clip.

The top page was a blank contract, listing the buy-in price as twenty-five US dollars.

Ethan dropped back onto the desk and skimmed the contract. Dr. Terry had been right. The catch was that the signee couldn't move the practice out of Falcon Creek. The second stipulation referred to the buy-in price. The buy-in price would be calculated on how long the signee agreed to run said clinic. The buy-in price was set at one dollar per year. The last stipulation required the signee to agree to find a suitable replacement and run said clinic until such time that a suitable replacement could be located. Further, the signee agreed to offer his, or her, replacement the same deal and contract.

Ethan flipped through the rest of the paperwork and discovered Dr. Terry's notarized original contract, as well as Dr. Vincent Reid's. The contracts extended back generations. It was a tradition. One that Ethan was more than happy to continue. He'd just found his own legacy outside of the Blackwell Ranch, yet he didn't have to leave home to build it. And if it all worked out as he'd hoped, he already knew a special little girl that might one day want to step in to run the clinic with her uncle Ethan.

Ethan explored the place, noted some of the changes that needed to have happened yesterday and hurried back to Brewster's.

He found Grace in a rocking chair on the front porch with Pops and Whiskers. Her eyes were closed, but her smile gave her away. She was only pretending to rest, whether to appease her grandfather, or her parents, or Ethan, he wasn't sure and didn't care. As long as she took a break every once in a while.

Ethan strode up the stairs and crossed the porch. "Grace, can I borrow twenty-five dollars?"

She never hesitated. Never opened her eyes. "Sure."

"Don't you want to know why?" Ethan stood in front of her rocking chair, his hands on his hips as he tried to contain the frenzied buzz inside him. How had he won the love of this woman? He didn't deserve her, but he wasn't letting her go either.

She opened her eyes and peered at him. "You're buying me and Pops lunch from Clearwater Café."

Pops chuckled and picked up his water glass. "If you are buying lunch, son, I'll take the burger and sweet potato fries."

"Consider your order placed, Pops." He opened the main door for Pops and returned to Grace. She hadn't moved from the rocking chair. She really was taking her rest seriously. He liked that, but he wanted her attention.

"Can I place an order too?" she asked.

"It'll take another twenty-five dollars."

Grace stopped the rocker and finally looked at him. "What happened to the first twenty-five?"

"I'm using it to buy into our future." He adjusted his baseball cap backward to make sure she saw him. To make sure she understood he was serious. "By way of Dr. Norman Terry's practice."

"You can't be serious." Grace jumped out of the rocking chair. "What happened?"

Ethan handed her the thick envelope Norman had given him. His hand shook. "It's all in there. I'm still a little stunned myself."

Grace opened the envelope and read through the papers. "This actually looks legit."

"We'll need to have Ben check it over, but I think it'll pass." Ethan set the paperwork on her rocking chair and took her hands in his. "So, what do you say? Can I borrow twenty-five dollars?"

"For our future, I'll give you everything," Grace said.

"You already have." He couldn't imagine what more she could give him. "Now it's my turn to give you everything too."

Ethan dropped to one knee and kept his gaze fixed on the woman who'd taught him to believe in the impossible. He'd give thanks to her for that gift every day. "Grace Gardner, you have my heart and all the best parts of me. I can't promise our life will be easy, or lucrative. But I can promise I'll be by your side every moment and every step of the way."

Her big smile disrupted the tears streaming down her cheeks. She didn't let go of Ethan's hands.

He squeezed her hands and said, "I love you, Grace. Will you marry me?"

Grace lunged toward him, tackling him backward onto the porch. Her reply came in between their kisses, broken only by the laughter and cheers from their family and friends looking on from inside Brewster's. Ethan Blackwell was truly happy to be home.

EPILOGUE

Dutch Country, Pennsylvania

ELIAS BLACKWELL PUSHED on the yarn mane of an oak rocking horse and shook his head. He'd run around as a kid with a broomstick for a horse. Until his father had discovered him and dropped him on his first live pony. He'd been four years old. He'd rarely left the saddle since then. He'd rarely left the Blackwell Ranch since then.

Until recently, when his regrets and mistakes had finally overtaken his pride. Ironic that he'd had to leave his home of more than seventy years to right his world.

"Big E, you've got to see this," his wife called. "It's the most adorable thing."

Big E weaved through the collection of handmade furniture. Each piece had been created by an Amish craftsman skilled in the art of woodwork. There wasn't a detail that the craftsman had overlooked.

Big E could've used such a keen eye during his selection of wives over the years. Perhaps if he'd been more adept at the details he'd have chosen differently. For instance, he might've fallen for a woman more thoughtful and less frivolous than his current wife, Zoe.

As it was, he had no trouble locating Zoe in the crowded outdoor furniture market, what with her two-foot-wide, polka-dot floppy hat adorned with purple and orange feathers. The wide brim cast a shadow over her matching polka-dot dress and bright pink heels. She'd adored her Preakness attire so much, she'd worn it again today.

Zoe beamed and ran a manicured nail over the top of an oak bassinet. "Isn't this precious?"

Not that he was well-versed in nursery furniture, but

he could appreciate the quality. And thanks to an early-morning text, he knew exactly who could use such an item. He motioned for assistance and strode off to pay for the bassinet to Zoe's delighted claps.

Zoe continued her browsing, calling out every other minute about a lovely table, or the perfect chair, or the most delightful bed frame. Big E waved her on with a smile and a nod, encouraging her to drift farther and farther down the roadside mart and away from the parking lot.

One of the younger workers loaded the bassinet into the RV and Big E loaded himself into the driver's seat.

He pulled the RV out onto the road, honked the horn and waved goodbye to a shouting and cursing Zoe Petit. He grabbed her yellow tote bag, tossed it out the window and kept on driving.

After all, he wasn't completely heartless.

* * * * *

COMING SOON!

We really hope you enjoyed reading this book. If you're looking for more romance, be sure to head to the shops when new books are available on

Thursday 29th November

To see which titles are coming soon, please visit **millsandboon.co.uk**

MILLS & BOON

Coming next month

BEST MAN FOR THE WEDDING PLANNER
Donna Alward

They were just making their way to the lobby when Holly
gave a squeal and picked up her pace.

'Dan!'

Adele was adjusting her purse strap, but when she finally
looked up, her heart froze and her feet stopped moving.
Holly skipped forward and hugged the man standing in a
tan wool coat with one hand on the handle of his suitcase
and a garment bag over his other arm.

Dan. Just saying his name in her head made her heart
squeeze a little. Daniel Brimicombe. Of all the Dans in
Toronto, he had to be the best man. It was too far-fetched
to be even comical, but here he was, in the flesh, smiling
widely for the bride. The man Adele had once planned to
marry. The one who'd whispered plans in her ear in the
dark.

The man whose heart she'd broken…and in the breaking
of it, broken her own.

Best Man Dan.

Adele Hawthorne, wedding planner extraordinaire,
solver of problems and manager of crises, stood rooted to
the spot with her mouth dropped open and her hands hanging
uselessly at her sides. This was one wrinkle that she hadn't
seen coming.

Adele tried to unscramble the mess that was her brain.
Dan hadn't noticed her yet, thankfully. She was still trying

to recover, and it was difficult because he hadn't changed at all. Oh, sure, there was a slight maturity in his face but really…it was like it had been eight days rather than eight years since they'd seen each other. Dark, perfect hair, just a little stubble on his chin, and the way his coat fit on his shoulders…as if it had been specifically tailored for his build.

He'd always carried himself with that calm confidence. She'd envied it back then. Still did.

And then he adjusted his garment bag, turned around, and saw her.

His face paled. 'Delly?'

Her throat tightened. Damn. He'd used his old nickname for her, and that made it a hundred times worse. She wasn't Delly. Not anymore.

'You know Adele? Oh my God, that is so weird!' Holly seemed totally unaware of the shock rippling between Adele and Dan.

Dan recovered first, and the color came back in his cheeks as he smiled. The smile didn't quite reach his eyes. 'We knew each other in university. I haven't seen her in eight years.'

Eight years, seven months, and a couple of weeks, if they were going to be exact about it.

'Hi, Dan. It's good to see you.' It wasn't a lie. It was a huge mess, but it was good to see him.

Continue reading
MARRYING A MILLIONAIRE
Donna Alward

Available next month
www.millsandboon.co.uk

LET'S TALK

Romance

For exclusive extracts, competitions and special offers, find us online:

📘 facebook.com/millsandboon

🐦 @MillsandBoon

📷 @MillsandBoonUK

Get in touch on 01413 063232

For all the latest titles coming soon, visit millsandboon.co.uk/nextmonth

Want even more
ROMANCE?

Join our bookclub today!